CRIMES OF PASSION

CRIMES OF PASSION

A collection of twenty erotic stories

Edited by Elizabeth Coldwell

Published by Xcite Books Ltd – 2011

ISBN 9781907761805

Printed and bound in the UK

Cover design by Madamadari

Contents

Rough Justice
by Angel Propps

The bike purred under Kelliann's ass and pussy as she headed down the empty highway. Even after two years of owning it, it still turned her on as much as it had the first time she had climbed on board one and asked the woman driving to give her a ride. That had been one hell of a day, and one hell of a ride too, she thought with a nasty grin as the bike throbbed and hummed below her. Late afternoon sunshine glinted through the lacy shadows made by the leaves dangling from the tall trees that stood in unbroken rows alongside the unfurling ribbon of the road, and Kelliann could feel the tension brought about by a week of upheavals in her personal and professional life melting away.

She had needed the escape, she admitted to herself as she walked the bike through a smooth stretch and leant it close and tight around a curve in a move that was confident and totally unselfconscious. Six days before, she had found out that her lover, Jo, had run away to parts unknown with a huge chunk of the funds that belonged to the company they had both worked for, that she had taken a cheap looking cocktail waitress with a head of wildly improbable penny red hair and a nasal drawl with her, and that she herself was under investigation for complicity in those crimes Jo had committed. It had been too much like a bad novel, too incredibly and outrageously painful to be left like that and she had honestly been shocked that her employer had felt the

1

need to fire her "just in case", as he had put it. The whole situation had stripped her to her core and the worst part of it had been that Jo had not been there to help her through it.

Behind her, another bike cruised slowly, its rider watching the woman who was putting the heavy throated Harley through its paces with admiring eyes. The thought that if you wanted to know how someone fucked you should watch how they rode came to mind and so did the thought that the woman ahead rode very, very well.

Kelliann had seen the other rider 20 miles back and still caught occasional flashes of the bike behind her in her mirror, but she was so busy concentrating on riding and not thinking that she forgot she was not the only person out there and began to speed up, slightly at first and then she climbed higher. The wind beat against her and the trees began to flash past, bright, watery sunshine pulsing through the breaks in the tops of those magnificent old pines and oaks.

The rush hit Kelliann dead centre. Her heart thundered and raced, her ass shuddered and quivered as she tightened her thigh muscles against the sides of her fierce machine and her eyes narrowed as she spurted ahead, forgetting about the flashy, trashy waitress, the loss of her job and lover, and just existed in the moment. Behind her, the other rider let a bit of distance widen between the two bikes but kept Kelliann in sight as she finally slowed, turned carefully into a nearly hidden and badly maintained little strip of asphalt, then pulled up in front of a dilapidated cabin that sat snugly in a small clearing.

Kelliann carefully walked the bike across the soft ground and heeled it over on the small concrete walkway that led from the front steps of the cabin down through the shady side yard and to the surprisingly deep lake that lay dreaming under the trees. A smile played across her lips as she thought of the times she had spent in that water. She got off the bike carefully and a frown creased her pale forehead as the sound of a bike came through the treeline and into her small space. She felt fear flash into her chest; the lake was deserted at that time of year. The cabins were all summer cabins and summer had ended officially two weeks before. The tourists and summer families always fled before the first sign of fall could spoil their memories and she had come to her little summerhouse to escape from people, but at that moment she wished there were some about in case the rider approaching was an axe murderer or some other type of psycho.

The rider swung one leg off the bike in one lithe movement and approached. 'Fancy meeting you here.'

Kelliann stared at what she could see of the face looking at her from under a heavy helmet and mirrored sunglasses. The voice was familiar but she could not place it. 'Excuse me?'

The glasses came off and Kelliann's heart sank. It was that damn cop, that hard-faced woman with the broad shoulders and the cocky walk who had drilled holes in her with her eyes during the long hours in the interrogation room, the one who had not believed that she'd had nothing to do with Jo's thievery or leave-taking and who had even gone so far as to suggest that she had been in on the scheme, only to get herself double-crossed and abandoned. To her utter horror she found herself looking at the way the leather jacket rode those shoulders, the way it accented the tucked-in tightness of that waist. Her eyes dropped lower, to the dangerous angle of hip and hard as rock thigh, down to the calves, dropping to those sexy as hell thick heeled black boots and then up again to see a wolfish grin playing along the slightly thin and cruel lips that sat below the aristocratic nose and cold blue eyes.

'So where is she?'

'Who?' Kelliann knew perfectly well who the cop was referring to and anger boiled below her breastbone. 'Do you mean Joanne Lewis? That unfaithful bitch who not only ran off with a waitress but ran off with the pension fund and half my life's savings too? Is that who you are referring to? I cannot believe you followed me out here to question me again!'

Presley Jones was a determined woman who had made detective in a city not known to be good about allowing women to earn that shield, and she was also a firm believer in justice. She had taken one look at the lovely brunette with the pale skin and the long legs and known she had a really big secret, and she was determined to find out just what it was the woman was hiding.

'I think she's here.'

'Then look for her!' Kelliann shouted rudely. 'And if she is here, arrest her ass. Ask her where my money is while you're at it, why don't you?'

'Are you giving me permission to search this house and grounds?'

'Do whatever you want,' Kelliann snapped as she headed toward the front door. She had to force herself not to look back; the truth was that the sexy as hell butch of a cop had turned her on and she was angry and unsettled. She was far too aware that her hips were swaying a little too much, that her back was too straight and that she had thrown her chest back and up in a gesture she knew damn well made her small but firm tits bounce with every step. Halfway up the stairs she remembered why she was there and panic set in, but it was too late to rescind her permission, Presley was so close behind her that she could feel the heat of her body against her hips. She had no choice but to turn the key in the lock and step inside the tiny little cabin.

Presley knew instantly that nobody was there and had not been for a long time. The place smelled musty and felt cold despite the sunshine outside. The windows were heavily covered with blinds and the furniture was all covered with sheets. Every step they took left a track on the dusty hardwood floor.

'Happy?' Kelliann asked sarcastically.

Presley wasn't. Her gut was rarely wrong and she had trusted it enough to follow Kelliann out to the deserted lake. She gave the front room of the cabin a last glance, trying to pinpoint some little clue as to why Kelliann had chosen to come out there, hoping to spot a stray slipper, a sock, but finding only the small feathers of cold air blowing through the cracks around the old wooden frame surrounding the window and the endless dustiness.

Kelliann began to fidget nervously and her gaze kept darting to the closed door that lay off the living room. Presley turned from her inspection and the sight of that furtive gaze triggered her instincts. She strode toward the door and instantly Kelliann moved to block her, a mistake that made Presley's instincts kick in. She knew, without a doubt, that there was something hidden behind that door. Kelliann tried to step in front of her but Presley merely moved her aside. The shock that her warm and very strong hands left on Kelliann's upper arms was disconcerting and somehow exhilarating at the same time.

'I think you have seen all you need to see,' Kelliann stuttered and Presley gave her an icy glare before moving to the door. Kelliann could not help but notice the way Presley moved, how her body cut through the air with a slinky, feline grace. Her heart was thundering with more than fear and a sudden spurt of moisture soaked her panties, startling her and exciting her even more.

No, she told herself, this is not happening, no way do I want her … But she did and she knew it. Her nipples drew tight and her breath became short as she watched Presley try the doorknob of the room only to find it locked. A flush hit Kelliann's face as Presley drew one foot back and kicked the door. A loud crash sounded and the door slammed open with a ripping, tortured squeal. Kelliann remembered what was in there and rushed to stop Presley from entering but it was too late; the cop had disappeared into the room.

An evil grin stretched across Presley's face as she stared

around at the dungeon that had been created inside the bedroom of the cabin. A complicated series of pulleys and ropes hung from one corner, a bed with high wooden posts and a bare mattress sat in the middle of the room and one wall contained a series of hooks from which hung a variety of wicked implements. Presley whistled in appreciation at the sight of the master craftsmanship of the whips and elk hide floggers; their artistry and elegant brutality was obvious from where she stood and she turned her head to look at the manacles hanging from iron loops driven into the opposite wall and the St Andrew's cross. The bright red rolling tool box that stood at chest height interested her greatly and she strode to it, opened a drawer and felt heat fill her lower belly at the sight of needles, cocks in various shapes and sizes, tubes of lube and everything else anyone would need to do a scene.

Humiliation crawled along Kelliann's veins as she stood watching Presley tour the dungeon. She was used to people being afraid or scornful of her proclivities but she had never invited anyone who was not a play partner to the cabin and the sight of an unknown person examining her things and, by extension, her sexual appetites, made her feel ashamed and a little frightened.

'Nice whips, who made these? I have never been able to find a 24 plait this supple.'

'Axel,' Kelliann said and then she really heard the question. Lust bit into her as she watched Presley take the whip from its hook, turning it over and over in her strong capable hands, trying it out by giving it a few practice throws. The cracks that resulted made goose pimples erupt on Kelliann's skin. That Presley was a well versed whip player was obvious and she found herself wanting to kneel, to bow her shoulders and allow that whip to play along the sensitive skin of her back and shoulders.

Presley felt the first surge of endorphins flooding her system as she held the gorgeous and well broken-in whip in her hand. It felt perfect there and she turned to see Kelliann looking at her with an expression of utter longing on her face. That was all it took. The two of them exchanged that one smouldering look and then Presley was in front of Kelliann, her free hand ripping at the soft T-shirt that Kelliann wore, tearing it away. Her silky red bra followed; it fell to the floor and Kelliann shivered as the air stroked her nipples, the sensitive skin of her belly. Kelliann yanked her own jeans down, tangling them into her shoes and then kicking everything off.

The whip stroked the air gently, landing softly on Kelliann's shoulders but not biting, warming her up and turning her on so much that she cried out and pressed one finger to her clit.

'No,' Presley snarled and yanked Kelliann's finger away. Slick, hot liquid bubbled from between her thighs and Kelliann whimpered as she stood still, letting the whip stroke her faster and harder. Her ass cheeks quivered as it landed, leaving behind red lines and making her sob out loud with pain that was being translated into pleasure by her nerves and skin.

Presley put the whip away and dragged Kelliann by her long hair to the bed. She tossed her onto it and asked, 'Are you ready to be fucked?'

'Yes, please fuck me,' Kelliann whispered and Presley grinned, grabbed the rope-laced cuffs at the four points of the bed and restrained her prisoner with her arms stretched overhead and her legs locked up and drawn back until her knees were close to her chest. Kelliann felt her hips jerk involuntarily as she was spread wide and open, as she was caught and held in a position of vulnerability.

'How pretty you are all tied up,' Presley said and went to the tool box. She returned with a blindfold, a small cock and a very large one, a tube of lube and a black leather slapper. Kelliann felt desire override her being; she wanted to be fucked, wanted it so badly she could do nothing but obey the woman who was holding her prisoner.

She cried out again and again as fingers invaded her pussy, opened her and rubbed furiously against her swollen, aching clit. Her thighs were struck with the slapper as her clit was manipulated, causing her to beg for more, and she choked on her words as a large cock was slid between her lips.

'Suck it, pretty, because it is going in your cunt and you want it to be all wet so you can take it all.'

Kelliann looked up at her captor gratefully as she sucked the hard length of the dildo. She arched her back as the insistent finger tormented her clit even further but, to her dismay, that movement made Presley take the finger away.

'Be a good girl and stay still,' Presley warned and then she fucked the wet, willing mouth even harder, her hand moving faster as she worked the cock into the berry red lips, enjoying the sight of Kelliann's face being fucked by it. 'If you move or come without my permission I will stop fucking you. Do you want that?'

'No,' Kelliann drooled out around the cock and then she sighed with pleasure as the cock moved out of her mouth and pressed against the wet outer lips of her pussy before moving away. Her fingers clenched shut and she fought herself desperately to stay still as the slapper moved against the exposed skin of her ass, leaving it a rosy red. Every blow made her want to come, to struggle against her bondage and to beg for more, but she had her orders so she did not.

When she thought she could take no more the slapper was tossed to one side and the cock was pressed into the folds of her cunt. She felt herself opening to accept the wide length of it and shocks of pleasure erupted from her belly and cunt. Presley held the cock inside her, not moving it and not allowing her to move either. The temptation to fuck the cock was proving to be almost impossible to ignore and Kelliann found herself trying to think of anything other than the cock that was possessing her so deeply and fully but her mind was too paralysed by pleasure to think of anything that would help her to calm down.

'Suck this one now, pretty,' Presley ordered and the smaller cock plundered her mouth while the large one lay inside her, unmoving. She slurped and sucked obediently, hoping that if she behaved Presley would let her fuck that cock and let her come. Her mouth was wet and hot, her pussy shook and pulsed around the other cock and Presley added to the mix by leaning her head forward and biting her nipples in a cruel and teasing way; nipping until it just hurt and then rolling her tongue around the tender flesh to soothe it. By the time Presley pulled the cock from her mouth Kelliann was begging in earnest, begging to be fucked, begging to be whipped, begging for everything Presley had to give and she felt her mouth sag open in a shocked O as the smaller cock was lubed and then pressed against the hard pucker of her asshole.

Double penetration took Kelliann over the edge. She sobbed out loud as the cocks beat into her, Presley using them in a rhythm that left her always empty and yet always full. Her legs shook and cries spilled from her. Fluids ran and dripped down her thighs as she trembled on the edge of a violent orgasm and she managed to plead a final time.

'Please,' she got out, 'Please let me come. I will be so good to you. I will do whatever you want. I will suck your pussy or … or your cock … I want it. Please, you do it so fucking good. You are fucking me so hard I can't help it … I have to come. Please …'

'Come then.' Presley said and creamy white come squirted from Kelliann's pussy, ran along the cock and down on to the stained mattress. Kelliann screamed, a long, high-pitched scream that shook her entire frame as the orgasm ripped through her.

'Thank you, thank you so much,' she babbled and Presley grinned and worked the cocks a bit deeper into their holes, watching the flesh suck on them, watching the pussy clenching and opening as her helpless catch did exactly what she was told to do, as she obeyed her orders.

Kelliann collapsed on the mattress and Presley removed the cocks and instantly began to soothe her, to stroke and pet her body as she loosed the bondage and set her free. 'You are a good girl,' she said over and over and Kelliann shivered in the rippling aftershocks that followed a good scene.

'I really don't know where Jo went.'

'I hope you don't mind, but I may have to follow you a few more times just to make sure.'

Kelliann grinned at the teasing and naughty look in Presley's eyes, 'I sure would hate for you to have to put me in cuffs, officer.'

'I would not speed on that bike on the way home if I were you. You might find yourself naked and handcuffed to a tree.'

Kelliann didn't answer that one, but after they were both dressed and her secret little space was shut up and once more silent, she swung one leg across her bike, shot Presley an impish look and said, 'I hope you can ride fairly fast, officer,' before shooting out of the small driveway and heading for the road.

Presley grinned as she took her time mounting her own bike. A little head start would not hurt anything and would certainly make things a bit more interesting. She found herself hoping they never caught Kelliann's embezzling ex; the game that had just begun between them was far too fun to quit. She roared out of the driveway and headed down the road in hot pursuit.

In Brief
by Kate J. Cameron

'Dammit, Jack!'

I stared across the table at the smirking face of Jack Hamilton, my blood pressure rising. My client and I had been working for months to reach a settlement with Jack's client over a breach of contract claim. We had been working for months mainly because opposing counsel, the jackass currently smirking at me, was an arrogant asshole who apparently did not give a damn about the best interests of his client, as evidenced by his rejection of my latest proposal.

Just who the hell did this guy think he was?

Unfortunately, I knew only too well. Jack "The Hammer" Hamilton was one of Houston's top litigation attorneys. Most of the other members of the Houston Bar would concede that he was smart and a top rate attorney, but would be hard pressed to otherwise come up with something nice to say about the man. He was, as mentioned before, an incredibly arrogant, self-centred, egotistical, cut-throat shark of an attorney, with a fat wallet that attracted any number of vapid blondes gunning to be the first Mrs Jack Hamilton. That none had yet succeeded showed maybe he was not as dumb as I had first hoped. The fact that he was six-four, 225 pounds, with blue eyes and dark hair, broad chest, trim waist and a chiselled jaw certainly did not do anything to keep his ego in check. If I had encountered him at a party or in a nightclub, without knowing anything about him, I would be definitely be glad I was wearing some racy lingerie, because

I would be looking for a way for him to admire it later on.

But here in my conference room, oh, I was looking at him all right, to be sure, but not because he was looking as hot as a man in a loosened tie and wrinkled shirt with the sleeves rolled up could look. Which, for Jack, was actually very hot. But I blocked that thought, and instead was trying to figure out the best place to stab him with my ink pen so as to inflict maximum damage.

Rather than go to jail, I dropped the pen and ran my hands through my dishevelled red hair. It was nearly midnight, and we had been working on the language for this settlement agreement all day. My client had prevailed in the mediation, and all that was left was to craft the terms that would allow my client to get paid to finish the work they had started. But Jack was not going to rest until he had nitpicked over every single word I proposed. Meanwhile, I was not going to let him sneak in language that completely changed the intent of the settlement. We had fought the fight, line by tedious line, and were nearly finished. Or so we thought, until we reached an impasse on the warranty provision. After four hours of back and forth, all the associates and paralegals had left, having pretty much given up, leaving only Jack and myself alone in the conference room. From the silence outside the door, we were probably the only two people in the office.

I was exhausted, and stressed to the gills by his intractable position. I wanted nothing more than to tell Jack to go to hell while I went home to my townhouse to pour a glass of Pinot and stretch out in a hot, steamy bubble bath. However, I wasn't about to concede defeat while that smug sonofabitch across the table was still in the game.

Jack leant back in his chair and propped his feet on the conference table. 'I'm sorry, Kara, but I can't accept that wording. The burden would then be on my client to prove the work was defective, and we just won't accept that when your client is the one performing the services. Better that the burden be on your client to prove the work was not defective.'

'Not better,' I snarled. We had been over this a million times, and I was starting to entertain fantasies of picking up my pen again. 'Your client's company man signs off on each and every phase of the work as it is completed. If he doesn't like it, we do it until he is satisfied, but once he signs off on it, it is done! We are not going to remobilise a $150,000 a day barge spread at our cost just because your client thinks there "might" be an issue. However, if your client want to pay us to remobilise the spread, we'll issue a new work order and get to it when our schedule permits. I just don't see any other way to do this.'

Jack laughed again. 'And here I thought you were supposed to be smart. Come on, sugar, you know there is a compromise somewhere in that pretty little head of yours ...' He stood up and walked over to the wet bar and poured himself a glass of mineral water. 'Or maybe you just wear those short skirts and low-cut blouses to distract everyone from the fact that you don't know shit from shinola ...' He tossed the water back and stood there, with that patented crooked grin some women found charming.

I knew he was baiting me (*Sugar*? *Really*?) but I was tired and frustrated. I tried to keep my cool, straining to keep my infamous temper under control.

And then, sure as God makes little green apples, he went there ...

'After all, honey, the "oil bidness" is a man's world. Maybe you should go do family law or something more suitable to your skills.'

In that instant, my professional demeanour that had been out front all damn day took a powder, and every stereotype you can imagine about a hot-tempered Scottish redhead went on display.

I stormed around the conference room table until he and I were within spitting distance. I stuck out my index finger with its perfectly manicured nail and poked him hard in the chest. Even surprised, he stood firm, which pissed me off even more.

I snarled, 'Look, you insufferable bastard. I don't give a rat's ass what you *think*. I kicked your sorry ass the last time we faced off, and I'll do it again now. I came out on top in that mediation, which tells me I have a better than average chance of fucking you up in court again if it comes to that. So don't stand here in *my* conference room, in *my* office, and tell me I can't hang in this boys' club. I know my clients' operations inside and out, and I am telling you what I know to be fact. You need to stop with the personal remarks and instead focus on how you are going to keep me from ripping your balls off and shoving them down your throat in court while your client pays for the privilege of watching!'

Suddenly, his laid back attitude took an abrupt turn of its own. Jack shoved my arm away and stuck his own long finger straight into the space between my breasts, pushing me hard.

'No, you look here, you shrill bitch. Just because the language doesn't read exactly like the great almighty Kara Thomas wants it to does not mean that I don't know my happy ass from a hole in the ground. You think you can hang in this industry, then you need to butch up and learn to take it like a man, or so help me, I will make it my life's mission to school you in that courtroom in front of God and everybody, and let your client pay *me* for the privilege.'

I let out a sharp bark of surprised laughter. 'Schooled? Me? By you? Please. You think you can just waltz into court in your tailored suits and flash your smile and ooze charm like a pig in slop, and the women on the jury will just rush to give you whatever you want. Well, I have news for you, mister. This ain't no fucking charm school and you will have to do better than that if you are going to get past me.' I crossed my arms and gave him a withering look.

He snorted. 'Good grief, woman. I wish you were half the badass you thought you were. Then you might just turn out to be interesting. Right now, you remind me of a Chihuahua. Lots of yapping and snapping and hot air – all bark, no bite. Blah blah blah …'

'Fucking bastard.'

'Cunt.'

That did it. I looked him straight in the eye and said, 'Fuck you – I am going to go call my client and tell him to prepare to file tomorrow. I am done with you. I'll call security to escort your sorry ass out of the building. See you in court, counsellor.' With that, I spun on my heel and started to walk toward the conference room door.

Instead, Jack grabbed my arm and jerked me around to face him. His grip tightened. In a low, menacing voice, he said, 'Just where the fuck do you think you are going, missy? I am not done talking to you.'

I was beyond incensed. Without even a second thought, I jerked my arm free and drew back. The sound the slap made when it hit his cheek was loud and very satisfying. I turned once more to walk out of the room, and actually got two or three steps before he once again stopped me short and whirled me around to face him, his hands tight on my upper arms.

But this time, there was a wicked look in his eye that gave me pause. I started to speak but he interrupted me, growling, 'Shut the fuck up.' Then he grabbed the back of my neck, pulled me close and kissed me.

But it was more than a kiss. It was anger and passion and tension and stress and lust – oh, the lust … His lips and tongue were exploring every crease of my mouth. His hands were digging into my arms, and I knew I would find bruises there tomorrow.

Then he pulled away, his eyes searching mine, almost like a dare. *What are you gonna do about that, hmm?* He gave me a smirk and traced my lips with one finger.

15

Arrogant motherfucker! Thoughts swirled in my head, thoughts of kneeing him in the crotch and then raining the fires of hell down on his head with my pointy toed Via Spigas before the cops arrived. Beating him severely with my new Coach laptop case until every inch of that smirk was wiped off his face.

Instead, I chose a different plan of attack.

I grabbed a handful of his hair and kissed him back.

I dug my nails into his scalp, pulling him closer to me. I bit his lip – hard – and he responded by shoving his tongue even further into my mouth. Then his lips left mine and travelled down the side of my neck. Goosebumps ran the length of my body. I made the astounding discovery that there must be nerves in my neck that were connected directly to my pussy, because I immediately got soaking, dripping wet. And the fun hadn't even started yet.

Determined to maintain at least a semblance of personal control, I needed to know how out of control he was. Know your opponent, right? So I reached one hand down and found an incredibly hard bulge in his trousers. A deeply satisfying purr filled my throat. I ran my nails up and down its length and heard him moan low in his throat. He was ready. And I could not believe how much I wanted to fuck this man, this hot, virile, insufferable asshole of a man. What a fine line between love and hate, anger and lust.

When I touched him, that must have been the signal he was waiting for. Without another word, he backed me up against the conference room table, his lips never leaving my neck. With one long arm, he knocked all the papers out of the way and lifted me up onto the edge of the table. I wrapped my arms around his neck and my legs around his waist and we kissed with all the pent-up emotion of the day rushing through us. Lips and tongue were everywhere in frantic motion.

He reached for the neck of my blouse and without even a pause, he ripped it open, sending buttons flying all over the room. My emerald green lace bra was exposed and he made quick work of it, snapping the front catch with one hand while the fingers of the other entwined themselves in my hair. He dragged his lips down my neck and across my chest to my nipples, licking and sucking each one, using my hair to roughly pull my head backwards and thrust my breasts upwards for his attentions.

While he was busy sucking my rock hard nipples, I yanked his shirt out of his trousers and quickly started to unbutton it. He put a stop to that by simply pulling it off over his head and tossing it across the room. His chest was strong and broad and covered lightly in dark brown hair. His scent – cologne, deodorant, sweat, musk – all combined into an odour that screamed "man".

His hands roamed under my skirt and across to the thong I was wearing. He slipped a finger inside – first inside the thong, then inside me … Suddenly my entire body was on fire, and all I wanted was to fuck this man until I screamed. I reached for his pants, and made quick work of his belt and zipper, leaving only his tight boxer briefs, made even tighter by the huge bulge in front.

Hmmm. So that's why they called him the Hammer …

I grabbed his face in my hands and looked him square in the eye. 'Better enjoy my next proposal while you can, you arrogant prick. I guarantee it's the best deal you will get from me all day.' I slid off the table, and down the length of his body onto my knees in front of him, taking his briefs to his ankles as I went. In one quick motion, I took the entire length of his rock hard cock into my mouth. I felt his knees begin to buckle and he turned so that he was leaning against the table.

He was huge and throbbing in my mouth. I could taste the sweet juices starting to form on the tip of his dick and I licked off every drop. His hands were running through my hair and he was moaning a little as I licked and sucked every inch of him, up and down and back again. I used my nails to

17

trace a line from the head of his penis down the vein on the underside and across his balls, which I then took into my mouth and lightly suckled.

When I thought he was on the verge of coming, I abruptly stopped and stood in front of him, breasts heaving, skirt twisted around my hips. He looked over at me with eyes full of raw, naked passion and stood to his full height. He took a few steps across to where I stood. Towering over me, he said, in a strangled voice, 'Take off your goddamn skirt. Now.'

Two snaps and a zipper later and I was standing defiantly in only my thong and heels. Without another word, Jack smothered me in another one of those brutally painful and incredible erotic kisses as he scooped me up in his strong arms and carried me back over next to the conference table, where he set me down in a rather unceremonious manner.

The kisses stopped only long enough for Jack to strip off my thong. Back onto the table I went. He slid my ass over to the edge, and leaning in, bit my ear as he whispered, 'Time for my counter-offer, Kara.' Before I knew what was happening, he was on *his* knees in front of *me* this time, and his tongue was on my clit. I nearly passed out from the intensity of the sensation, and I grabbed his hair and pressed his face deeper into my pussy. I could not remember the last time I had been this hot and wet. He sucked and licked and fingered me until I moaned 'Fuck me, you sorry bastard.'

With that, Jack stood up and lifted me to my feet. He leant over me and whispered in my ear, 'Bend over and take it if you can, bitch.'

I reared back and slapped his face again, leaving a distinct red mark. I started for a third strike, but he stopped me mid swing, his hand crushing my wrist.

'Do that again, and I will spank your pretty little ass until you beg me to stop,' he said in a hoarse voice.

'Call me a cunt again and it won't be your face that gets slapped,' I snapped back, breasts heaving from the heavy breathing I was doing. 'I'll wear your nuts on a chain around my neck.'

'No woman has ever hit me once, much less twice. Be glad I am a patient man.' He paused, and with a quick flash of his crooked smile, said, 'But I also have to admit that I have never been so fucking turned on in my entire life.' He jerked me close to him and kissed me hard and quick. Then he leant in and growled 'Now bend over so I can fuck you hard like you plainly deserve.'

He spun me around and I dropped my arms to the table to keep from falling. The three-inch heels I was wearing jacked my ass in the air, and my pussy was hot and dripping. Jack stood there for a moment, admiring the view, I suppose. He also took the opportunity to make good on his earlier promise. He drew back and slapped my ass cheeks until they were burning. I jerked up and started for him again, but in one smooth motion, Jack pressed me back down on the table and proceeded to impale me on his rock hard cock. He pumped and thrust into me so deeply that I could feel every inch of him. With every hammered stroke, he leant down and whispered in my ear.

'Oh fuck, I have wanted you all goddamn day. You and your hot body and your teasing smile. You are such a fucking tease. I am going to ride your sweet little pussy until you can't take it any more ... Oh fuck, you feel so good ... You may win in court, but by goddamn, I am gonna win this fight, right here, right now. You are going to come before I do ...'

He reached around and his thumb found my swollen clit. He fucked me hard while his thumb stroked me closer and closer to the edge. My only retaliation move at this point was to clamp the muscles in my pussy down on his cock in a vice grip.

'Fuck me harder, you sorry excuse for a man. Is that all you got?' I gasped. I felt rather than heard his reaction, and the thrusts got harder and faster.

'I am more than you can handle and then some, you ball-busting wench.' The movements of his thumb on my clit got harder and faster too. I could feel the muscles in my legs and thighs getting tighter – I was on the edge of coming but I was not going to give him the satisfaction of getting off first. So I pushed backwards with my hands and stood up. He stumbled, and withdrew.

'What the fuck!' He stood there, incredulous, his throbbing dick still at full attention

I smiled and leant against the table, legs spread. 'I want to see your face when I make you come, you arrogant prick. If you want the rest of this -' and I reached down and stroked my neat bush and the slick, hot wetness between my legs '- you get it my way. Now come here, little man.'

He took two steps, lifted me in his arms, and once again impaled me on his cock. My ass rested on the edge of the table, and I wrapped my legs around his waist, my arms behind me so I was better able to meet his thrusts with my own. I could feel his cock grow even tighter inside me, and I could tell he was about to come.

'Don't hold back on my account,' I purred. 'Feel free to come if you can't hold it any longer …'

He threw his head back and gasped 'Oh Kara, fuck …,' and I knew then that I had won. He inhaled deeply, and as the first spasm made his body shudder, he fingered my clit, and I went off like a sky rocket, just as he cried out and exploded into me. Wave after wave of pleasure rolled through my body and I wrapped my legs even tighter around his waist. He and I held each other close as our bodies shook with simultaneous pleasure, his semen flooding into me while I climaxed over and over.

Finally, he sank to his knees, bringing me down to the floor with him. We literally collapsed on the floor, which was covered with papers and buttons and clothing. For several moments, the only sound was that of tortured breathing.

Jack spoke first. 'Holy shit. That was, to say the least, intense.' He leant over and nuzzled my throat. 'So you ready to concede the point yet or what?' His hands started moving suggestively up my thigh.

I stopped his hand from going any further. 'No, I am not conceding jack shit to the likes of you. But I have a possibility that will resolve our impasse.' I made a suggestion that would allocate remob costs to both parties equally in the event of rework due to warranty claims. Jack's eyebrows raised, and I could see he was looking for a downside, and not finding one.

'I think I could sell that to my client,' he said begrudgingly. 'Fine. Now where was I ...?' And his hand began moving again.

I stopped him a second time. 'Oh no, counsellor. There's more. One final caveat.' He started to protest but I leant over and bit his lip again, effectively shutting him up.

'The caveat is not for your client – it is for you. Within the next ten days, you will buy me dinner at Café Annie and provide a suite at the St Regis – and not bill it back to the client. I want Champagne and dark chocolates and a bubble bath in the room. And you must agree to spend at least the first hour in the suite on your knees between my legs, doing anything I tell you to do. Under those conditions, I think I can guarantee that my client will accept the compromise warranty language.'

'That's extortion ...,' he said, but he said it with a slow grin.

'No, it isn't ...,' I told him as I shoved him on his back and straddled his waist. 'I am just a zealous advocate for my client.' I rose up and back down again, sliding my wet pussy onto his suddenly rock hard dick. 'And as I am so ably demonstrating right now,' I purred as I began to move even faster, 'I always come out on top ...'

Taking Down Her Particulars
by Courtney James

'I'm telling you, Mr Byron, someone is stealing my panties.'

The brunette stared up at Don from beneath her lashes, defying him not to believe her.

How had his career had come to this? When circumstances had forced him to go into the private detective business, he assumed he'd be spending his days tracking down missing persons, maybe getting involved in a juicy divorce case or two. Instead, here he was, standing in the dressing room of The Velvet Slipper Lounge, while a fan dancer made an official complaint to him about her missing lingerie.

Strike that. Honey Deluxe wasn't just any old fan dancer. She was the Lounge's star act, the playbills outside the venue proclaiming her to be "the queen of burlesque". Men queued round the block to watch her strip out of some sequinned little number or other. They said once you'd seen her ride a carousel horse in nothing but her underwear you could die happy.

He had to admit he could see the attraction. She had curves in all the right places, legs that didn't know when to quit and a face that would make a priest burn down the orphans' home. Everything about her screamed sin, temptation and all the good things in life. Maybe he should be taking her predicament a little more seriously.

'OK, Miz Deluxe. Talk me through it again.' He pulled a pen and notepad from the breast pocket of his jacket, ready to take notes.

'Well, it all started about a month ago. I got changed in here, like I always do, stowed my clothes in my locker, and when I came off stage after my routine, I discovered my panties had gone missing.'

'So let me get this straight. You go on stage in different underwear to the stuff you wear to come here?'

'Of course, silly.' She looked at him as if to say, Geez, what kind of rube are you?

He didn't want to admit to her that in all his 36 years he'd never set foot in any kind of strip joint, not in the course of his police work and certainly not when he'd been off duty. Even after Marian had died, and the guys had suggested he ought to get out, have a little fun, it had never crossed his mind to come somewhere like this. It would have been an insult to his late wife's memory to watch another woman undress.

'And do you have any ideas as to who might be doing this?' When she shook her head, he continued, 'Have you seen anyone lurking round the dressing rooms in the last few weeks? Anyone suspicious?'

Honey shuddered. 'Oh, there are always guys trying to get backstage, real creeps, you know? But Lou – that's Mr Ruby – he takes good care of us. He never lets them get anywhere near us.'

Lou Ruby was the club's owner, a greasy, overly avuncular man who'd clapped a big paw of a hand round Don's shoulders, ushering him inside anxiously. 'Sort this one out for me quickly, would you, Donny boy?' he'd asked. 'I don't want any of this leaking out. Bad publicity for the club, you know?' He'd implied Honey Deluxe was a little high-strung, but she was his big star and he needed to keep her happy.

'You dancers must have husbands, boyfriends,' Don said. 'Any of them ever come backstage?'

'Sometimes,' Honey admitted, 'but what would they

want with my panties? What would they want with me?'

Was she really so naïve? Don had seen pictures of the other dancers, pasted up alongside Honey's. They were all pretty enough girls, but none of them quite had the allure of the woman before him, and he was damn sure they didn't earn a fraction of what Honey did. He could see why a man staying in a cheap hotel room might want to spend a night in the penthouse suite every now and again.

'So do you think you'll find whoever's doing this, Mr Byron? There's only so much underwear a girl can stand to lose, you know.'

Privately, Don thought the whole thing was a monumental waste of his time. But Honey Deluxe was paying him a hundred bucks a day, with expenses on top. He owed it to her to put his efforts into solving this little mystery.

'OK, what I'll do is I'll come down to the show tonight, see what I can discover. You never know, maybe I can catch the perp in the act.'

'Oh, I do hope so.'

As Don left the dressing room, he glanced over his shoulder to see Honey blowing him a kiss. An image filled his mind: those plush red lips of hers wrapped round his cock, sucking for all they were worth. His dick stiffened in his pants, the strongest reaction he'd had to any woman since Marian had passed on. He hurried out of the club, past the lurking Ruby, not wanting anyone to see the effect Honey had on him. Don Byron had never mixed business with pleasure, however enticing a package that business came wrapped in, and he had no intention of starting now.

The Friday night crowd in the Velvet Slipper Lounge was raucous but good-natured. Men with a week's pay burning a hole in their pocket and a desire to spend a goodly proportion of it on cheap bourbon and dames with expensive tastes. On stage, a bottle-blonde in a shimmering gold dress was crooning a seductive ballad, its lyrics dripping with innuendo. Her accompanying bump-and-grind movements were designed to warm the audience up for the next act, the star of the show, Miss Honey Deluxe.

The blonde brought her microphone down into the front row, picked out an overweight man in a suit a size too small for him, and settled on his knee. Continuing to sing, she deftly unfastened his tie with her free hand, ruffled his hair and generally made a fuss of him. From the way she wriggled, and the mocking reactions of his buddies on either side of him, it was clear she was causing quite a commotion in his pants. Just when it looked like the guy might actually come from all the stimulation, she hopped off his lap, brought the number to an end, and departed to riotous applause.

From somewhere in the wings, Lou Ruby's voice announced, 'And now, gentlemen, the moment you've all been waiting for. Performing her world-renowned fan dance, the inimitable Miss Honey Deluxe.'

Music boomed out, brassy and vibrant, as Honey took to the stage, carrying two huge ostrich feather fans. She held one before her and one behind her, and from the glimpses the men had of her body as she moved, it was obvious she had nothing on but her blood-red spike heels. Her movements were perfectly timed as she manoeuvred the fans, pulling one away and replacing it with the other so quickly no one was quite sure how much of her naked flesh they'd seen in the process. Teasing, titillating, she promised everything and revealed almost nothing, and the men in the audience loved it. They went wild, whooping and hollering and begging for just a little flash of titty, a peek at her pussy, even though they knew the dancer had no intention of obliging.

Despite all his intentions to remain a detached observer, Don was totally caught up in Honey's performance. Just watching her had him hard in his underwear. So rapt was he, he'd almost forgotten he was supposed to be on the hunt for the elusive panty thief, then he caught sight of a guy sitting in one of the booths close to the stage, cheering Honey on.

He'd know that battered, broken-nosed profile anywhere. Jimmy McGuire, his old partner on the force. He and Jimmy had worked together for the best part of 12 years, until the night they'd been called to a robbery at Mullery's liquor store on Main Street. They'd uncovered evidence suggesting Jimmy's nephew was part of the gang who'd carried out the heist, and somehow, that evidence had disappeared. Don could never prove his partner had tampered with the case, but he'd gone to the precinct chief with his suspicions. Chief Parsons didn't want to know. As far as he was concerned, cops did whatever it took to look after their own. But when Jimmy found out what Don had done, they had a stand-up fight in the street outside the station house. Don was kicked out of the force the following day. Jimmy kept his job.

He hadn't seen McGuire from that day to this, and he didn't want the man to spot him now. More than likely he was here with a few of his pals from the force, and that spelled trouble. Don took the opportunity to make his way backstage. The chorus girls were waiting in the wings to perform their big number, looking like a flock of exotic birds in their plumed headdresses, and the dressing room was deserted – or so he thought.

A bulky figure was rifling through Honey's locker, his back to Don. Don pressed himself tight up against the wall, concealing himself in the shadows. The man gave a gruff exclamation of triumph, snatching something out of the litter of Honey's personal effects. He turned, giving Don a good view of his face. Not that he needed it; he'd worked out the thief's identity as soon as he'd seen the shabby tuxedo he wore. Lou Ruby.

No wonder he'd done his best to convince Honey she didn't need to worry about anyone being in the dressing room in her absence. He was keeping them away so he had the run of the place himself.

Ruby brought the scrap of peach-coloured fabric in his fist to his nose and inhaled. With his free hand, he pulled down his zip, freeing his dick. Don almost gasped aloud at the size of it. His own cock was nothing to be ashamed of, but this thing was huge, out of proportion even for Ruby's big frame. A few pumps of Ruby's hand up and down its length had it standing up, thick and gnarled as a cudgel.

The club owner wrapped Honey's panties round his thick shaft, closing his eyes at the feel of silk against his skin. Don had seen enough. He wasn't going to let Ruby defile his client's underwear any further. He stepped out of the shadows, hand gripping the handle of the little pearl-handled revolver in his jacket pocket.

'OK, Ruby, that's enough. Put those down.'

'What the …?' Ruby's eyelids fluttered open. Dropping his stolen treasure, he hurled himself at Don, intending to knock him into the middle of next week. Don sidestepped his advance at the last minute, and the club owner slammed hard against the row of metal lockers. Growling, he hauled himself upright, swinging a strong left hook that connected with Don's cheekbone. Ruby wasn't going to go down without a fight, and Don prayed he wouldn't have to use his gun, not with a bunch of cops in the house. Licensed private dick or not, he was sure McGuire and his cronies would take great delight in putting him away for a stretch.

Grappling with Ruby, he didn't realise Honey had walked into the dressing room until her voice rang out. 'Mr Byron, what's happening?'

Doing his best to break free of Ruby's grasp, Don looked over to where the dancer stood, a silky robe wrapped round her curvaceous body. Her eyes were wide with alarm.

'I apprehended the panty thief in the act,' he gasped. 'It was Ruby, all the time.'

'Mr Ruby, is this true?' Honey's tone was appalled, as though she'd been told Santa Claus had been caught taking

28

the presents from under her Christmas tree.

'You don't understand,' Ruby grunted, his choke-hold on Don's neck growing tighter in his agitation. 'I only wanted to –'

He didn't get the chance to explain why he'd been jerking off into Honey's underwear. She picked up a bottle of Champagne from her dressing table, a present from one of her many admirers, and smashed it down on Ruby's head. With a moan, he collapsed to the floor, out cold.

Honey shrieked at the sight of the big man's unmoving form. 'My God, I've killed him!'

Don shook his head. 'I doubt it, Miz Deluxe, but someone's gonna have to call an ambulance for him.'

'All in good time.' She came close to him. 'First I want to thank you for solving the case …'

As she put her arms round his neck, standing on tiptoe to plant a kiss on his lips, Don was all too aware that she wore nothing beneath the thin robe. The hard points of her nipples pressed against his chest, and beneath the perfume she favoured, Chanel No 5, he caught a strong trace of her intimate scent, musky and all woman. Teasing an audience with her naughty burlesque routine clearly turned her on, and to walk into a room thick with the testosterone created by two men fighting had stoked the fire already burning in her belly.

Don fought to remind himself of his rule about never getting involved with a client, but it was a battle he was never going to win. Starved of female company for so long, his body couldn't fail to respond to her caresses. His cock hungered for the feel of her, the scent of her, longing to be buried in her cunt.

They had to be quick; the chorus girls would soon be finishing their number and making their way back to the dressing room. He tugged at the belt of Honey's robe, pulling it open, feasting on the sight of her glorious nakedness the way a starving dog feasts on a bone. Her lush breasts, capped with hard red nipples, wasp waist and flaring hips were, to his eyes, a triumph of femininity. Happy to gaze at her beauty all day, he was distracted by her red-nailed fingers yanking at the zipper of his pants.

'Come on, big boy,' Honey urged, 'show me what you've got.'

Reaching into his crisp cotton shorts, she brought out his dick, cooing over its size. He felt the come surge in his balls, stimulated by the feel of a hand other than his own stroking his length for the first time in longer than he could remember.

'Slow down,' he begged. 'I don't want to come anywhere than in your sweet little puss.'

'Is that so?' Her smile was feline. 'Kinda forward, aren't you, Mister Byron? Well, lucky for you, that's just what I want, too …'

She bent over her dressing table, offering him a breathtaking view of her heart-shaped ass. He ran his hands over the twin globes, glorying in their alabaster smoothness. Glancing back over her shoulder, she licked her lips.

'Stick it in me,' she ordered. 'Fuck me till I can't take it any more.'

When she'd first engaged his services, she'd played the part of the demure, classy broad to perfection. Don suspected this Honey, with insatiable urges and a mouth like a stevedore, was closer to her real personality. This was the side of her that drove him wild, and made all further conversation unnecessary.

Lining his cock up with the entrance to her pussy, he shoved home, thrusting in till his zipper pressed against her pillowy sex lips. She shaved herself there, presumably so no hair peeked out of the crotch of her panties when she was on stage, and the feel of her bare, sensitive flesh clinging to his sturdy shaft almost made him lose his load on the spot.

Pulling almost all the way out, he banged back into her, driving her belly against the edge of the table. She pushed her ass back at him, daring him to go deeper, faster. Marian had always liked him to take it slow and easy. Making love, she called it. This wasn't making love; this was fucking, plain and simple, and Honey couldn't get enough of it.

Don's hands gripped her tits, squeezing and mauling them. The rough treatment had her squealing with passion, so loudly he was glad Ruby wasn't awake to hear it. The thought of the club owner, passed out on the floor, caused him to miss his stroke, his cock slipping out of Honey's clutching channel. Impatiently, she grabbed it and guided him back inside her, humping furiously against him.

He couldn't help but notice her eyes were glued to their reflection in the mirror. The woman came alive in front of an audience, but it seemed if there was no one else around to watch her, she'd watch herself. They made a fine couple, though, he thought, the naked showgirl and the fully-dressed, world-weary detective fucking her. Her dark hair was a wild tangle around her head, her pale skin beaded with sweat. In contrast, he looked cool and in control, even if the way his spunk was rising and his heart thundering in his chest meant he was anything but.

As though sensing he was on the verge of shooting, Honey put a hand down between her spread legs, using it to diddle her clit. Her pussy muscles went into spasm around his cock as she came like a firecracker, the rhythmic motion milking every last drop of spunk from him. Knees weak, feeling as though he wasn't entirely sure where or who he was, Don clung to her.

By the time they heard the clattering of high heels and the excited chatter of the chorus girls coming into the dressing room, they'd recovered themselves. Honey was again wrapped up in her robe, Don was checking Ruby's pulse.

'Somebody call an ambulance,' he instructed, as the girls stood round, wondering about the commotion. 'Mr Ruby's had a little accident.'

'I want to thank you,' Honey said, lowering her voice so only Don could hear her. 'For everything.'

'Any time, Miz Deluxe.' He took a deep breath. 'I know you said I was forward and all, but I was wondering ... Would you like to have dinner with me some time?'

Her tone was genuinely regretful. 'I'd love to, but it won't be possible. After tonight, I'm not exactly sure I'm going to be welcome around this place any more. I think it's best if I move on. They say Las Vegas is the place to be, if you really want to make it as a showgirl.'

'I quite understand.' It was for the best, Don supposed. Women like Honey were a delicious fantasy, a rare foray into the exotic. They weren't the kind you settled down with, and that, he realised was what he really needed. She'd shown him there was life after Marian, and now he could move on, too.

He spotted a scrap of peach-coloured silk on the floor, lying where Ruby had dropped it. 'Uh – your panties, Miz Deluxe.'

'Why don't you keep them? Something to remember me by.'

As Don stuffed her underwear into her pocket, already contemplating how good it might feel to breathe in their secret fragrance the next time he jerked himself off, he knew there was no chance of his ever forgetting her.

Diamonds Aren't For Ever
by Tony Haynes

Eve Cassidy was a bad girl. I knew that from the off. Sometimes, you just can't help yourself, though. After dragging her in for questioning, we drew lots down at the station to see who got to interview her. It was a rigged game. By hook and by crook, I made sure I won. There was no way I was missing out on this opportunity. As I entered the interview room I knew that every other cop in the building had their noses pressed tight to the glass of the two-way mirror that looked in on proceedings – even the girls. I couldn't blame them. Eve Cassidy was a classical beauty who smouldered pure sex appeal. Six foot in stilettos, which she always wore, Eve had a tangle of auburn hair that tumbled enticingly onto her shoulders and a pair of cute cupids that practically begged to be kissed. She was guilty, everyone knew it; the only question was, guilty of what?

Eve glanced up at me as I leant back against the door with my broad, brawny shoulders. I fooled myself into thinking that she was admiring my trim torso. Very slowly, very deliberately, she reached into her jacket pocket and withdrew a packet of cigarettes. She made a great play of the fact that it was empty, before scrunching up the box and tossing it over her left shoulder into the waste bin in the corner of the room. 'I don't suppose you'd have one, would you, Inspector Hart?'

I was across at her side as fast as I could move in order to offer her a cigarette. She accepted it with a murmur of thanks and slid it between those to die for lips. The cigarette hung there enticingly for a moment before she asked, 'And a light?'

'I'm afraid it's against the rules to smoke in the interview rooms.'

She shrugged nonchalantly, withdrew the nicotine stick and tossed that into the bin also, hitting the bullseye without even looking. 'I've been meaning to give up anyway.'

'A wise move.'

'I'm full of them.'

'Such as?'

She grinned deliciously. 'That'd be telling, inspector.'

'Tell away.'

'That's not my style.'

'So what is?'

'Excuse me?'

'Your style.'

'Well if you come around to my apartment one evening I might just show you ...'

The sentence trailed off and hinted at a myriad of possibilities that my over active imagination was only too happy to conjure up. With a supreme effort I tried to drag my concentration back to the matter at hand. 'I wonder what else you could show me?'

'Such as?'

'Well, we could start by taking a look at your diamond collection.'

She shrugged for effect. 'I'm afraid that wouldn't take very long.'

'Really? No recent additions, then?'

'Sadly not.'

'So if I was to come around your apartment later, there is no way I would find the Farchetti diamond?'

'The what?' She played innocent as well as anyone I'd ever met. Heaven alone knows how given her foxy, feline figure.

'The Farchetti diamond. It was being displayed at Tiffany's two nights ago when it went missing.'

'You mean they lost it? How careless.'

'No, Eve. It was stolen.'

'That's terrible.'

'As a matter of interest, where were you two nights ago between the hours of ten and midnight?'

'Why, inspector, I'm surprised at you. I would have thought that you of all people would know a lady never tells.'

I bit back my desire to laugh and let out a long sigh instead. 'OK.'

'OK what?'

'You're free to go.'

'Honestly?'

'Yup.'

She stood up, giving me the opportunity to admire those long, lithe legs of hers. 'I must confess to being somewhat surprised. Your reputation is that you grill your suspects a lot harder than that.'

'You're not a suspect, Mrs Cassidy, you're merely helping with enquiries.'

'It's Miss. And -' she leant in close in order to whisper this last comment in my ear '- I'm more than happy to assist you any time.'

With that, she threw her fake mink wrap around her athletic shoulders and sauntered out of the interview room, leaving me with the feeling that it was going to be a tough case to crack.

I was lying to her, of course. Eve was our number one, two and three top suspect, which was why I ended up playing peeping tom on her that night. I stationed myself in the apartment block directly across the alley from hers and got a prime view of her windows. I only hoped that she wasn't the kind of girl who closed the curtains. I suspected she wasn't.

I didn't have long to wait for the action to start. Around 7.30 she disappeared into the bathroom, the one window I couldn't see through. Curse frosted glass. I strained my eyes as much as I could and just about made out the outline of her fantastic figure. My imagination ran riot as I pictured a bar of the most luxuriant soap working up a foamy lather over every inch of that incredible body and then a jet of water from the shower head washing it off. The bathroom window was pushed slightly ajar and I held my breath. The next thing I knew, Eve Cassidy wandered into her bedroom, a towel wrapped tight around that beautiful body of hers. Picking another towel off the bed, she began to dry the excess water from her hair. It was pure poetry. I would have gladly paid good money to watch.

The doorbell to the apartment must have rung, because the next thing I knew Eve rushed out of the bedroom in order to answer her front door. She opened it to reveal quite a short fellow stood there in a dapper pinstripe. I couldn't make out his face, for his trilby was angled downwards so as to cover his features. Whoever he was, he was one lucky guy, for the next moment Eve leant forwards and locked her lips firmly upon his. The kiss was long and lingering and I savoured every moment of it vicariously. I didn't care who he was, I wanted to kill him. Nothing personal, you understand. Pure jealousy, plain and simple.

Eve made her way across to the cabinet on her sideboard, fixed the fellow a drink and then returned to her bedroom. She undid the knot on the towel. I held my breath. It was as if she knew I was watching, for she turned her back to me. While it wasn't the first prize, it wasn't a bad second as I was able to drink in the view of her bare, statuesque frame from behind. Her skin practically shone with that after-shower glow. Her buttocks bounced enticingly below hips that seemed to wiggle in time to the towel as she dried those divine legs. She wandered across to her wardrobe and I prayed that she would turn around. Not for the first time in my life I found myself disappointed as she denied me my wish. In a sleek, swift move, she withdrew a pair of incredibly naughty black frilly briefs from her bedside cabinet and teased them on. She then reached inside her wardrobe and selected a matching bra. She hooked each arm through the loopholes, but hadn't time to fasten the clasp at the back before her bedroom door opened. For a second I wondered what the hell was going on, for I had completely forgotten about her visitor. Eve's hands instinctively shot up to her chest to prevent the bra from falling. She backed away towards the window. My night had suddenly started to look up. Maybe her guest wasn't so welcome, after all, and I might have the chance to play the knight in shining armour and save her from whoever had begun to threaten her.

The stranger said something. Eve shook her head. He took a step towards her, withdrew a .45 automatic from his jacket pocket and waved it at Eve. My gun leapt into my right hand. I'd taken aim and was about to fire as Eve lowered her hands. I knew it was impossible, but time seemed to freeze as that sensational piece of material fell to the floor. Eve's guest gestured again. Eve hooked her thumbs into her panties and slowly lowered them until they rested around her ankles. With one quick flick, she kicked them off and onto the bed. I began to sweat as duty fought with my desire. My conscience won, damn it, so I took careful aim at Eve's guest and cocked the trigger.

Before I had the chance to fire I was treated to my second surprise of the night. Eve's tormentor tossed the gun onto the bed. Eve rushed across to him and flung herself into his arms. I lowered my gun. They kissed passionately. So it had been a game. I wiped the sweat off my brow and settled back to enjoy the show. The kiss was slow and passionate. Lover boy traced his hands down the curve of Eve's spine until they cupped her buttocks. He then lifted Eve, swivelled her around and threw her on the bed. Eve sprawled there and for the first time I saw her perfect, round breasts and the neatly trimmed dark triangle between her thighs. Lover boy lost no time in going down upon her and I couldn't say I blamed him. His technique was fairly impressive, to be fair. He began by feathering the most delicate kisses around the base of Eve's stomach, nuzzling gently into her soft, tender flesh. He concentrated on the region for some time, until I sensed Eve grow frustrated, for she murmured something, which I suspected was a request for him to go further south. It was as if he had been waiting for her to ask him all along. Eve spread her legs wide apart and Lover boy buried his tongue between her thighs. Eve's head snapped back and I could tell she had begun to moan as her friend lapped at the outer folds of her perfect pink flesh. It seemed his time of teasing was over, for he thrust his tongue deep inside her. Eve gasped delightedly and half sat up. She reached down and flipped Lover boy's hat off in order to run her hands through the cascading locks of blonde hair that the trilby had been hiding. So much for my police training. I hadn't even guessed the correct sex of Eve's visitor, for *she* was a sweet and sexy blonde. As she continued to pleasure Eve Cassidy with her tongue, Blondie began to massage Eve's bottom with her fingers. It was too much for Eve and I sensed the orgasm rip through her as she flung herself backwards on the bed, her mouth open wide in that tell-tale "Oh" of pure pleasure.

Blondie eased off her attentions and kissed her way up Eve's torso until she was lying next to her on the bed. They cuddled gently and remained that way for some minutes, kissing and caressing one another, until Eve took it upon herself to undress her partner in crime. She began by undoing Blondie's tie. Blondie helped by shrugging off her jacket. Eve then set to work on Blondie's shirt buttons, prising each one open with relish as it revealed another inch of her lover's flesh. Once it was fully open, Blondie discarded the shirt and Eve removed Blondie's trousers, to leave Blondie lying on the bed dressed only in a pair of matching white panties and bra. The sight seemed to be too much for Eve and she tore Blondie's panties off, ripping them in the process. Blondie wasn't about to protest. What she did do, however, before Eve got too carried away, was twist around 180 degrees head to toe, so that by the time Eve had gone down on her, Blondie was able to kiss Eve's pussy simultaneously. The pair lapped and licked and toyed and teased to their hearts' content and they came again and again, until they collapsed from pure exhaustion into one another's arms.

It was then that I really started to worry about myself, for rather than sit back and continue to enjoy my amazing view, I suddenly realised that with the two girls apparently having drifted off to sleep, it would be the ideal moment for me to search Eve's apartment. It wasn't easy, but I tore myself away from the window and made my way across to the apartment block on the other side of the street. I rode the lift up to the fifth floor and then crept quietly along the corridor until I found myself outside Eve's front door. It didn't take me very long to pick the lock. Every half-decent cop knew how. I eased the door open and sneaked inside the apartment. As I closed the door behind me, I paused in order to listen. The silence seemed convincing enough and so I set to work. Apart from the kitchen, bathroom and aforementioned bedroom, there was only one other room - the lounge - and that was where I began my search. I peeked into every nook and cranny and tossed every drawer, to no avail. The really frustrating part was that I knew that diamond had to be somewhere. I sat back on the sofa momentarily in order to cudgel my brains. The only thing I could think of was that she had hidden it in the bedroom. Dare I go in and try to search it? I held my breath as I heard what sounded like the hammer of a gun being cocked.

'Can I help you, inspector?' Eve asked. She was standing in the doorway to the lounge dressed in nothing other than the .45 automatic in her left hand.

I did my best to remain cool. 'Where is it, Eve?'

'You disappoint me, Inspector Hart.'

'How so?'

'With your dedication to the job.'

'Once a cop, always a cop.'

She slunk across the room, looking sexier than even I had ever dreamt of. 'And there's nothing that I could possibly do to change your mind?'

There was a pause, for about a nano-second, then I practically launched myself across the room at her. Our arms clasped around one another in a tight embrace and our lips smacked together in a heady mix of passion and desire. Technically, I'm not sure it counted as kissing; it felt more like pure, animal lust. She started to tear at my clothes and when she had ripped every last shred from my body she pushed me back onto the sofa. I fell with little grace and sat there mesmerised as I gazed up at the Goddess in front of me. She licked her lips in a minxy manner and stared down at my raging hard-on. Eve then knelt down and padded her way across to me on all fours. My eyes never left her once. It was the sexiest sight I had ever seen in my life - that is until she leant forward and licked at the tip of my penis with her tantalising tongue. She began to run it up and down the shaft of my cock until the end glistened with precome, then she pulled herself upwards until she was sitting in my lap. I had no idea where she got it from but the next thing I knew she peeled a condom on to me. 'Hey, what's with the raincoat?' I asked.

'I don't trust you,' she replied.

'Thanks a bunch.'

She lowered her head and whispered in my ear, 'Yet.'

The yet sounded promising. I hadn't time to give it much consideration though for Eve raised her hips and gently lowered herself onto me, until every single one of my pulsing six inches was nestled deep inside her. She shuddered ever so slightly in satisfaction and grinned coquettishly. It was all I could do not to come right there and then. Slowly Eve began to ride up and down my shaft, thrilling in the twitches of pleasure that she could clearly feel as my cock danced to her tune. Her breathing became shallower as her rhythm increased. I reached up and began to massage her breasts with my hands, teasing the nipples between my fingers. Eve screamed in delight. Without breaking rhythm I leant forward and took her breasts in my mouth in turn. I kissed and licked her nipples as she bucked up and down. As I felt her excitement build, I decided it was about time I took a bit more control and so, to her surprise, I flipped her off me and then turned her around until I was able to enter her doggy style. Eve groaned loudly as I sank my cock deep inside her. I could tell that she wasn't far from climax. I was nearly there myself. The next moment I felt fingers curl around my balls and begin to massage them. Now that was a neat trick, I thought, especially as I could see both of Eve's hands gripping the arm of the sofa as I plunged my cock into her sensational, moist pussy. I turned my head slightly to my left and found Blondie standing there, beaming naughtily. As she continued to knead my balls in her right hand, Blondie bent her head forward in order to kiss me. Our lips met just as I felt Eve begin to melt. Eve squealed delightedly as she came, thrusting her hips backward so as to enjoy every inch of me. I tried to hold on, but it was no use, and I climaxed myself, shooting hot spunk inside her. The three of us collapsed on the sofa in a tangle of limbs. I took it in turns to kiss the girls and they snuggled into me, one on either side. As I stroked my hands through their hair I tried my best to return to the matter at hand. 'Eve?'

'Yes, inspector?'

'About that diamond.'

She looked up at me with those innocent baby blues and replied, 'What diamond?'

I smiled and rewarded her with a passionate kiss, for her

answer meant that we were in for a long and lascivious night.

Sex Rides the Bus
by Landon Dixon

Stephen Marlowe got on the Number 19 bus in the financial district, walked down the aisle, and slid into his usual seat near the back. It was well past 9 p.m., Stephen putting in extra hours at the insurance company he worked at, as usual. He settled into his seat, leaning his umbrella up against the wall of the bus and opening his newspaper.

He was a small man, with a bland face, brown hair and brown eyes, a pinched nose and mouth. He looked every bit the mid-level accountant he was, fastidiously groomed and conservatively dressed, hair parted to the right, dark blue suit slightly shiny with wear.

But even mild-mannered accountants can dream. And so when the tall, slender brunette got on the bus at the next stop, Stephen hoped and prayed she'd sit down on the seat next to him, knowing she wouldn't. The bus was practically empty, plenty of seats available.

The woman deposited her change and began walking down the aisle. She was smartly dressed in a short blue coat, open, a lighter blue blouse, a black knee-length skirt and black stockings. Her taut breasts bounced in her blouse, her slim legs flashing in their nylon coverings.

Stephen watched her over the top of his newspaper. He'd never seen her on this route before; he would've remembered.

The bus lurched as it started up again on a green light, but the woman easily kept her feet with a dancer-like grace,

43

skipping forward on her black high heels, gripping one pole after another; drawing nearer to where Stephen sat, staring.

His fingers tightened on the newspaper, as she surveyed the available empty seats with her dark eyes, flicked them briefly over him. She was only four rows away, and strolling closer.

Her long, lustrous brown hair was pulled back from her face by twin tortoise-shell barrettes, her face a tanned cameo, lightly dusted with make-up. A large diamond ring shone on her left hand, a thin gold watch on her wrist. Stephen thumbed the plain gold band on his own left hand, holding his breath.

She was obviously out of his league, sophisticated and sexy, elegant and erotic. So he could hardly believe it when his fervent, childish prayers were answered, and she swung down and slid onto the seat next to him.

'Hope you don't mind,' she purred, gazing and smiling at Stephen, 'but it's such a long ride home.'

His face and body flooded with the heat of her supple form so close, his head with the rich, intoxicating scent of her perfume. 'N- no, I don't mind,' he stammered, glancing at her.

Her lips gleamed full and glossy, teeth white and even. 'Another day, another dollar.' She sighed. 'No rest for the wicked, I suppose.'

Her voice was smooth, sensual, like the rest of her. Stephen's newspaper shook in his hands. He didn't know what to do, or say. He really didn't want to talk, anyway, happy to just to bask in the woman's sweet, feminine presence; honoured that she'd enlivened the dull ride home by sitting down next to him.

She folded her hands in her lap and looked straight ahead, as he stared at his newspaper without seeing the words. More passengers got off the bus, until Stephen and the woman had the back half all to themselves, just a few riders left in the front half.

'My name's Claire,' the woman said suddenly, startling Stephen.

He glanced at her again, and got caught in the sparkling gems of her eyes. 'S- Stephen.'

His blue and red striped tie choked him, as Claire slid slightly closer, so that her lean thigh pressed up against his thigh. And then he gulped, and jumped, when Claire slid a hand onto his thigh, rested it there.

'Nice to meet you, Stephen,' she murmured, her hand soft and warm on his quivering leg.

Now Stephen really didn't know what to do. He was trapped, on fire, the woman's slender brown hand rubbing his thigh. She glided her palm up higher, and higher, until the edge of her hand slid down Stephen's inner thigh and came gently to rest against the side of his crotch.

'Just something to pass the time,' she breathed. 'You don't mind, do you?'

The newspaper flapped in his hands, his head spinning. He could hardly believe his good fortune. Such things didn't happen in Stephen's quiet, mundane life – a beautiful woman coming on to him.

Claire's hand jostled against his groin, as the bus shuddered to a stop and two more people got off, leaving just Stephen and Claire, one other passenger and the driver on board the bus. Claire's hand slid fully over Stephen's crotch, onto the beating, blatant erection that had swelled up between his legs.

He gasped, jolted down to his sensible black shoes by the hot-soft impact of the woman's hand on his hard-on. The newspaper dropped out of his hands and into his lap. Claire brushed it aside, to the floor, whispering in his ear, 'They can't see. And even if they could, who cares?'

He flushed from the roots of his hair to the tips of his curled toes, tingling all over, Claire gripping his cock, rubbing. He looked down at her beautiful, bejewelled hand on his throbbing erection, up at the nearly empty bus, over into her gorgeous, smiling face. She was right, the openness of it all only added to the incredible sexual tension that was already off the charts.

Claire released Stephen's prick. She poured her left arm around his neck, her right hand on his hard-on, grasping and stroking more warmly, more firmly. His bus stop flew by and he hardly noticed, suffused with shimmering pleasure.

His addled mind did briefly flash on his wife, Esther, at home, probably watching TV and knitting. He wasn't hurting her, he rationalised; this was simply a brief encounter between two bored people on the bus, no strings attached.

Then all domestic thoughts of any kind were shoved aside as Claire pressed her wet lips against his cheek, filled his ear with her tongue and swirled it around, her hand pumping and pumping his pulsating member. He groaned with pure joy.

She squeezed his cock. Then her gloss-painted fingernails latched on to the zipper of Stephen's pants and pulled down, over the bulging length she'd been stroking. His laboured breath caught in his throat, and he yelped, 'Oh, God!' as she reached inside his suit pants and boxers and grasped his bare cock with her bare hand.

She pulled him out into the open, and they both stared at his turgid pink erection in her clutching hand.

The bus rumbled along like nothing was happening. But everything like nothing before was happening to Stephen, Claire's smooth palm gliding up and down his cock, fingers lightly hugging his straining shaft, twirling over his bloated cap. She nibbled his ear, and he arched up off the seat, his cock spearing higher in her hand.

She pumped faster, tighter, more urgently, kissing his neck. The prickled sweat on his forehead rolled down into his glazed eyes, but he didn't blink it away, his field of vision filled by the sight of the woman's hand openly tugging on his prick. He was full of feeling to bursting, his tightened balls boiling.

'Claire! I'm going to -'

'Not yet!' she hissed, noosing his raging member at the base, bottling his juices. 'I'm not done with you yet.' She looked towards the front of the bus, then dipped her head down and engulfed Stephen's hood with her lips.

'Christ!' he bleated, stung by the heat and moistness of her lips, her mouth on his most sensitive organ.

Her head dropped lower, shining hair falling over her face, as she took more of Stephen's cock into her mouth. He bucked, thrusting his dick up against the back of her throat, fully consumed in the cauldron of her mouth.

He was going to come; come in the woman's mouth right there on the bus.

But she sensed it again, noosed him again. Then she dragged her silky lips and beaded tongue up his shaft and off his hood. She tossed back her hair and looked up at him from his glistening cock. 'I need you to give me all your money, Stephen,' she said, shocking him most of all.

He gaped at her. Then he shook his head in a daze, reacting to the word "money".

'Yes, Stephen.'

He rattled his head from side-to-side.

Her fingernails dug into the base of his purpling pole. 'Think of your wife, Stephen.'

He was thinking of the 627 dollars in his wallet, clearly now. He shook his head a third time.

She bared her teeth over his swollen cap, and bit into it. He jerked. He was well and truly caught in her trap now. She bit down harder, sinking her teeth into his blood-engorged shaft.

He fumbled his billfold out of his suit jacket, and she snatched it from his hand. Then she released Stephen's cockhead, leaving her teeth indentations behind.

And before he could make a move to stop her, she stroked his freed cock one final time, setting him off. He

47

groaned and sprayed, pumping out pent-up jack from his very soul, against his will.

He watched helplessly, surging with cruel bliss, spurting semen into the air and down into his lap, as Claire exited the bus with a wave and a smile.

Stephen left work earlier than usual the next three weeks running, riding the various buses out of the financial district, searching for Claire. She was a professional all right, he now knew, and he figured she'd be working her seductive scheme again before too long.

And, sure enough, on a warm, wet night around ten o'clock, on the Number 21 headed to the West End, he was rewarded for his dogged efforts. Claire came aboard, dressed in a pinstriped suit jacket and red satin blouse, pinstriped black skirt.

Stephen watched her over the top of his *Financial Times*, from the three-person benchseat kitty-corner from the driver. She didn't see him, her dark eyes looking off down the aisle towards the rear of the bus. He followed her progress, her taut buttocks clenching tight against the back of her thigh-high skirt, elevated by her high heels, her slim, silk-sheathed legs whispering together as she strolled.

She found what she was shopping for – a pudgy, florid-faced man in a shiny brown suit and a loud tie, yakking on a cell phone near the back of the bus. A gluttonous grin split the man's wide face and he snapped his cell phone shut, when Claire chose to perch on the tiny space left open on the seat by his bulk.

Twelve stops later, the bus was almost empty. Claire's head had disappeared behind the backrest of the seat in front of her and the fat man. He wore a whimsical expression on his beet-red face, his bright blue eyes out of focus. He didn't even notice Stephen bypass the back door of the bus and drop into the seat directly across the aisle from him and Claire.

But Claire took notice, when Stephen said, 'Another day, another dollar, huh?'

Her head flew up and she twisted around, staring at Stephen. The fat man's cock stuck out from between his thick legs like a glistening pink tongue. He grunted, shaking the steam out of his head.

'Stephen, how nice to see you again,' Claire said, quickly regaining her composure, as her intended victim lost his.

Busted, the fat man stuffed his cock back into his pants and yanked down on the signal cord. He lurched to his feet, his gold wedding band cracking off the backrest. He pushed past Claire and hauled ass to the front of the bus, never looking back.

Stephen slid into the seat across the aisle before Claire could slide out. He jammed the elegant brunette up against the wall of the bus, gritted, 'I want my money back.'

Claire calmly ran her fingers through her hair, smiling at Stephen. 'I'm afraid I don't have it any more,' she stated.

'You stole 627 dollars from me,' he said, his bland face set hard. 'And I want it back.' Money meant a lot to him; all money, but especially his own.

Claire licked her gleaming red lips, her eyes shining. She reached over and placed her left hand on Stephen's thigh, dug her crimson nails into the clenched muscles. 'I do it for more than just the money, you know, Stephen.'

He grunted, glancing around the bus – empty. He picked up Claire's hand and put it on his crotch. 'Well, do it, then. Earn your money.'

She gripped his semi-erect cock and eagerly rubbed, biting her lip.

Stephen stared at the diamond ring on her hand, the gold watch on her wrist, surging with a heat more than anger or greed, his cock boning out full length in Claire's shifting hand. He nodded, and she unzipped him, pulled his hard-on out and stroked the pink, throbbing pipe skin on skin.

Her hand flew up and down his meat, as if anxious to get

him off, get out of the trap he'd set for her. But Stephen gripped the backrest in front of him with one hand, barring any escape, steeling himself to her erotic, tugging rhythm. Claire dipped her head down and took his cap into her sensuous mouth.

Stephen groaned, lacing his fingers into Claire's rich, brown hair and forcing her head further down. She easily accommodated all of his prick in the wet-hot velvety confines of her mouth and throat, locking him down pulsing and swollen inside her.

Until, at last, she pulled her head up, and his cock exploded out of her mouth in a gush of hot air and saliva, and precome. She quickly inhaled his hood and half of his dick again, bobbing her head up and down now, sucking on Stephen's cock. The vacuum pressure was incredible, the depth of her depravity immense. Stephen rode her head with his hands, his nut sack bubbling with immense release.

But he was determined to get his money's worth, and more, this time.

So when the driver rocked the bus to a stop and ran outside to grab a takeout cup of coffee from a corner donut shop, Stephen pulled Claire off his prick and into his lap. She held on to the seat in front of her, staring ahead at the empty bus, as he shoved her skirt up to her waist, revealing her bare, mounded bum. Stephen grasped his slathered cock and probed Claire's wet slit with his hood.

She arched her butt upwards, hissing, 'Stick it in me! Fuck me!' Her reaction made Stephen believe maybe she'd been telling the truth about riding the buses for more than just money.

He pushed his knob in between her slick pussy lips, finding her opening and spearing into her tunnel. She sat down in his lap, butt cheeks spreading against his thighs, his cock embedded in her juicy quim.

He gripped her narrow waist and pumped his hips as best he could, fucking her. She bounced up and down on his pole, pacing his thrusting to frenzy level. He groaned, his cock molten in her burning cunt.

He reached around and grabbed her jumping tits through the slippery satin of her top. She moaned, tilting her head back, rattling the seat in front of her, hair streaming and mouth hanging open.

Stephen shot a glance to his right, saw the bus driver standing at the counter of the donut shop, paying for his coffee. He let go of Claire's tits and grabbed on to her wrists, pulling her arms behind her back, holding them as he rammed his cock into her snatch. Her ass cheeks shivered with his pounding, her pussy sucking on his pistoning dong.

'Yes, fuck me! Fuck me!' she cried, seemingly oblivious to her surroundings now.

Stephen unclasped her gold watch and slipped it off, tugged the diamond ring off the third finger of her left hand, still churning her tunnel with his cock. Claire gasped, twisted her head around. But she was too far gone. Stephen fast-fucked her bouncing bottom and she screamed, shuddering on the end of his pummelling cock.

She was still whimpering and writhing with her own uncontrollable ecstasy when the bus driver climbed aboard; when Stephen pulled out and tucked in, walked down the aisle and off the bus with Claire's watch and ring. She could only look on, helpless in her orgasm to stop him.

The Naughty Rich Girl
by Angela Goldsberry

I am the naughty, spoiled daughter of a very rich man. I always get my way. Nothing is too good for me and I'm too good for everything – and everyone. I'm the apple of my father's eye and as far as he's concerned I can do no wrong. If only he knew the kind of girl I really am. I wonder what he'd think of me then. You see, I *love* to be bad. In fact, I thrive on it. My halo is more than slightly tarnished. Only Daddy can't see it.

I'm enrolled in a small Catholic university; I rarely attend. But Daddy sits on the board of directors. I hardly think that, when the time comes, I'll be denied a degree. Quite the contrary: I'm sure the good sisters will do anything to get rid of me, including granting me an honorary baccalaureate. Their prim and proper establishment hasn't been the same since I arrived on campus. Not that it matters anyway. I'll never work a day in my life. I'm having too much fun playing.

I am a beautiful and commanding young woman and I work hard at staying that way. I go to the gym almost every night of the week, continually sculpting and shaping my figure in addition to fucking my personal trainer every chance I get. I'm almost Amazonian in appearance and I rather like it. I consider this as I glance into the rear-view mirror of my new black BMW. I dress to intimidate – it's my motto in life. It doesn't get me very far with most people but, then again, I can't be bothered with people who can be intimidated.

I carefully back out of my parking space in the college parking lot and shift into drive. The back tyres grab the asphalt tightly as I peel down the driveway at breakneck speed. Some day, I'll get expelled for doing that, the groundskeeper has warned me on more than one occasion. I merely laugh in his face. Let them try. Daddy would never allow it.

I roll down the window and let the crisp autumn air whip my chestnut hair about my face. I feel my best when I am in my element, and my element is shopping. So that is where I'm headed today. I light up a cigarette and tap the steering wheel with a brandy-tinted nail in time to the music blaring from my hopped-up speakers. One of my ex-boyfriends installed them for me last year, taking them from his own car after only a little pleading and one magnificent blowjob. I wriggle in my seat at the memory of it and my pussy starts to sweat. I'm such a naughty girl, aren't I?

I wave tauntingly as I speed by a snoozing state trooper parked on the side of the road. 'What shall it be today?' I ask myself, peering behind me to see if the statie's radar has gone off. Seeing that I am alone in traffic, I race along, not bothering to slow down. 'Valentino, Galliano, or Versace? The choices are so limitless. I may have to buy them all!'

I feel around in my purse and pull out my wallet. I flip it open and a long strand of credit cards streams out. 'Ahhhhh,' I breathe with almost sexual satisfaction. 'Plastic – a girl's best friend! I think I need a new pair of boots and, of course, a matching purse. Maybe a hat too.'

I squint into the sunlight and nod slowly. 'Yes,' I purr, with a wicked grin curling my lip, 'it's going to be a *good* afternoon.'

I make my way to one of the more well-to-do shopping centres in the city where I live, a place where I am considered to be one of the more exclusive patrons. I wind in and out of the grassy islands of the parking lot and pull adeptly into a vacant spot near the front door of the most popular department store. I wonder airily how long it will be before they give me a personalised parking space – and then I cackle at my own wit.

I put on a more sombre expression as I enter the store. Like the dignified lady I know I should be, I haughtily scan the area with an air of authority. Inhaling deeply, I savour the aroma of newness and luxury. I mainly depend on the indulgence of my father to support my shopping habit. An occasional five-fingered discount doesn't hurt either. Not that I *need* to steal – not by any stretch of the imagination. I shoplift for the pure thrill of it. It gets me hot. It makes me wet. It's just another of the perks of being naughty.

My eyes wander lazily over the merchandise as I casually stroll through the display tables and counters. I ponder over what should be the pick of the day – make-up, jewellery ... lingerie! Now, *there's* a place to start. One can never have too much sexy underclothing. You never know when it might be handy, or even necessary. I finger a costly chemise with contemplation. The violet silk matches my eyes and accents the light olive hue of my skin. It's perfect for me and I definitely want it. However, it's just too big to pocket.

'I guess I'll just have to *buy* this one,' I murmur saucily, scooping it up. I can feel the dampness between my legs start as the thrill of danger begins to rise.

I grab a matching silk thong on my way to the counter and deftly slip it into the large pocket of my baggy man's overcoat. My thieving coat, I think fondly, smoothing the puffy material until it lies flat against the pilfered panties.

A portly woman at the cash register takes the chemise from me from me and begins to write up the receipt. While I wait, I add a black lace bra, G-string, and garter belt set to the purchase. Then I lean against the counter, nonchalantly drumming my fingers against the glass, smiling innocently at the saleslady. All the while, the muscles in my pussy are churning as I think of all the naughty things I'm going to be able to do with my purchases – and with my stolen goods. My nipples are hard and scratching at my bra to get out. *In a little while, my pets*, I promise them silently. I might have to stop in the dressing room for a little playtime with myself. It wouldn't be the first time, I reminisce with a delicious shiver.

After my lingerie is wrapped and paid for, I neatly tuck the bag under my arm and stray into the accessories department. I check the area carefully for any signs of store security. Getting all hot and bothered sometimes makes me careless. I don't want to get caught. That would ruin all the fun. And store security is usually more careful in this particular section due to the fact that the expensive costume jewellery is very attractive to would-be thieves, including me, and equally easy to make off with. As soon as the coast is clear, I palm an ornate sterling bracelet designed to resemble a small wreath of grapes on twisted vines.

A fraction of a second after the bracelet hits the bottom of my deep pocket, I feel a strong hand on my shoulder. I whirl about in sudden panic and find myself staring into the iciest blue eyes I have ever seen in my entire life. I don't know whether to faint or cream. In any case, the clit-ometer rises another notch, and I unconsciously wriggle a little in my tight jeans.

'You'll have to come with me, miss,' the man says quietly.

I thank God that this posh establishment is so damned snobby they're extremely hushed about shoplifting incidents. The silent walk back to the security office with the plainly clad store detective escorting me gently by the elbow appears no more out of the ordinary than a gentleman accompanying his woman around the store. It gives me time to try to think of a quick and easy way out of this mess. I *absolutely* have to make sure that I'm not arrested. It would never do. Daddy would have a fit. He'd put punitive restrictions on me. The hindrance of my freedom would be intolerable and a criminal record would ruin any possibility of my marrying into the upper crust of this town.

I compose myself as much as possible as Mr Security Man leads me to the back of the store and through the double swinging doors that open into the warehouse. He quickly manoeuvres me around forklifts and between high stacks of empty wooden pallets until we reach a locked wooden door marked *Eric Lexington, Director of Security*. As he draws out a large ring of keys and fits one into the lock, I survey him more closely. He's *very* attractive, about six-four with thick brown hair that keeps wanting to fall on to his forehead despite the fact that he's slicked it back with some sort of product. He's sporting a nice 5 o'clock shadow – the kind that Hollywood has made acceptable to wear even when dressed to the nines. His bottom lip is full and generous and his chin is square and rigidly set. His charcoal suit coat fits snugly across his shoulders and I am able to catch a glimpse of his muscular thighs rippling beneath his trousers as he uses his knee to nudge open the door when it sticks in the jamb. A lusty spark goes off in my mind. It appears that this predicament might not be so hard to extract myself from after all – hard being the operative word.

'In here,' he instructs with a curt nod of the head.

I precede him into the dark room and almost stumble over a chair by the desk. He quickly flips on the fluorescent light and apologises for the close proximity of the quarters, explaining that his regular office is being renovated and he's temporarily being holed up here. I sit quietly in the chair to which he directs me, trying to seem a little more vulnerable than I actually feel. It will be necessary to first appeal to his sense of pity and, then, to his sense of desire if I am to carefully escape prosecution. I fold my hands on my lap and softly clear my throat as he turns to close the door.

'Now,' he says, finally spinning about to face me, 'would you like to tell me what you were doing back there?' He leans back against the closed door, a sardonic smile touching his face as he waits for what he knows will be a lame answer.

'Well,' I begin hesitantly, 'I'm not quite sure I know what you mean, Mr –'

'Oh, I think you do,' he interjects, nipping my first little plan in the bud. I decide to finish up this pathetic little scenario and quickly move ahead to Plan B.

'I was shopping. See for yourself.' I hold up the bag for his inspection.

He gingerly takes it from me and peers inside. With a barely suppressed grin, he removes the undergarments and places them in a neat pile on his desk. Checking the receipt, he notices the obvious absence of the bracelet and looks up at me with a wry smile. 'I was talking about the jewellery.'

'Oh – *oh*! You mean the *bracelet*!' My hand flutters up to my throat and then quickly into my pocket, drawing out the heavy silver bauble. I fail to notice, however, that the clasp of the bracelet has caught the strap of the purple thong, and it is now left peeking over the rim of the coat pocket.

'This?' I ask innocently. 'I'm *buying* this.' I realise that he's not buying my story any more than I'm buying jewellery. 'Really, I am. I'm just so forgetful and in such a rush, I must have accidentally slipped it into my pocket. Here,' I offer, pulling my wallet from my purse, 'I have the money to pay for it.'

His eyes mock me, I think to myself. The bastard is actually enjoying this. If he weren't so gorgeous, I'd be offended.

'I'm not interested in your money, miss. It's a bit late for that now. I'm a little more interested in *this*.' He leans over me, his breath dangerously heavy on the hollow of my throat. I gasp and draw back as his arm brushes my already tingling breasts. His hand slips deftly past my purse to retrieve the thong from my pocket. He stands back up, twirling it around his index finger.

'What about this?' he demands, the laughter hinting in

his voice.

He has me cold now. I know it. It's time to play for keeps. 'Look ... *sir*. I can't afford to get in trouble. My father has a lot of money. I –'

'I'm not interested in your daddy's money either, missy. Do you think my loyalty to this establishment can be bought and sold like ... like a pair of panties?' He accentuates his last quip by tossing the thong back at me.

The purple silk smacks me in the chest and I gather it up in my hand. He's playing with me. OK then, I'd do well to give him a little taste of his own medicine. I lower my lashes coyly, and lightly flick my top lip with the soft tip of my pink tongue, as if debating some desperate decision. I see the tightening of his thighs beneath his trousers and I know I have him hooked.

'I would *never* suggest that you were dishonest,' I protest with feigned shock. 'But,' I continue, greedily eyeing his belt buckle, 'maybe we could still come to a satisfactory arrangement – you know, just between the two of us. No one else needs to become involved.'

I slowly set my purse on the floor next to the chair and run one perfectly manicured hand through my auburn locks, drawing the heavy tresses back to expose my long, creamy neck. I linger in the chair for effect, and then push off my haunches to kneel on the floor in front of him, as if in sacrifice. A small growl of animal want rises in his throat as he feels my hot breath against the increasing tension behind his zipper. Maybe he can't be bought, I think as he reaches behind him to turn the lock on the door, but he's certainly sold on this idea. My hands slide languorously up his sinewy thighs and he leans back against the safely latched door.

His breath begins to come in short, heavy gasps as I run my mouth over his still clothed cock. I nip the bulge with my teeth, teasing him, pressing my lips lightly to his groin, giving him only enough contact to torture him. He pushes his hips forward a little, wanting more from me than I am giving at the moment. I pull away and demurely bat my eyelashes at him.

'Patience,' I purr softly. 'These things take time.'

'Take off your top,' he commands without further ado. Apparently, he wants to direct a little more than I had planned.

'Why?' I ask, more curious than afraid.

'You seem to like sexy underwear. I want to see some.'

It's a simple enough request. I shrug out of my overcoat and lift my heavy sweater over my head. I cross my arms over my breasts, rubbing my shoulders with my hands.

'Is this to your liking?'

'I'd like it better if I could see more of it,' Mr Lexington retorts, sniffing at the blocked view.

I run my hands up my arms and then downward, stopping when my hands come to rest on my hips. I kneel up to give him a closer look at my ample cleavage. 'Better?'

The increased rise and fall of his chest is all the answer I need. Still, he tries to downplay his excitement. 'A little,' he replies dismissively.

I can see that this is going to be a battle for control that will go on until the last orgasm subsides. Well, I'm not about to go down – so to speak – without a fight. I reach between my breasts and flick open the catch on my bra. The burgundy satin pops apart as my tits spring free. I catch them in my hands and start to squeeze them, feeling the firm flesh fill the spaces between my fingers as I roughly massage the globes. I close my eyes and let my head fall back as I pinch my nipples with my long nails. I gyrate my denim-clad hips in a slow grind as I kneel before my captor, my ripe melon breasts turned upward, my nipples hard enough to cut glass, my full lips softly parted, ready to pay him oral homage.

'Better, *much* better,' he murmurs throatily.

I slowly lean forward to release him from his cloth confines. First, the gold buckle of his belt, then the onyx button of his trousers. The zipper slides down easily, humping smoothly as it rides over his sequestered erection. I slide the expensive material over his hips and let it fall in a pile around his ankles. Then I tug at the silk of his boxers. His cock bounces out and I am pleased. Big, but not overbearing; thick, but not bulky. His large balls are held tight against his body and are velvety smooth as a result of some careful manscaping. It's a perfect specimen and I waste no time in getting to it.

I breathe gently on the head and kiss away a drop of the nectar that has leaked out onto the tip. Then I slowly ease him into my mouth, using every bit of cock-sucking skill that I have. After all, he's doing me a special favour. I can at least reciprocate. I suck him up and down, lightly at first, then more insistently. I lick the crease of his groin on either side, where it meets his legs, and then I suck his balls, taking each of them into my mouth, one at a time, for a glorious tongue bath. Eric Lexington is a happy camper, grunting and moaning as he shoves more of his crotch into my face, and I'm glad. I like watching him writhe beneath my mouth as I do very naughty things to him.

'Stand up,' he gruffly orders, just as I think he's about to pack it in. I comply. 'Over there.' He ushers me toward his desk as he removes the rest of his clothes. His hard cock sways back and forth as he meets me on the side of the large mahogany structure. 'Take your pants off, missy. You still haven't paid off that bracelet.'

I slide my jeans off, leaving my panties on.

'Very nice,' he hums approvingly as he comes to stand behind me, admiring my thong. 'But tell me something,' he continues, running an exploratory finger up and down the thin strip of satin between my cheeks, 'why bother to wear anything?'

'Why indeed?' I agree, slipping them off.

'Bend over,' he orders, pushing me forward onto his desk. Then, he's at me. I feel the bristle of his stubble against my tender flesh as he runs his mouth over my ass. He smoothes a cursory hand up and down my thighs before cupping my pussy with his palm. He nuzzles the lips with caressing fingers then starts stroking me, working his fingers into the wet folds. I'm panting hard now and he quickens his clit massage to keep time with my breathing. I try to back up on to his hand so that I can get his fingers inside me, but he pulls away.'

'Not yet, little lady. Payback is a bitch.'

He's going to make me suffer. The prick is still playing alpha dog with me. And I'm beyond caring. I need to be fucked and I need to be fucked *now*.

'Please,' I whimper, '*please* fuck me. I need to feel your big cock inside me.'

'Tsk, tsk,' he chides with a shake of his head, 'such language. Does your daddy know you talk like that?'

Silently, I shake my head. My snatch is throbbing, and I stroke it with a comforting hand.

'Somehow,' Lexington says stroking his own junk expectantly, 'I don't think he'd approve. I think he'd want me to punish you.'

'Oh yes! Please! *Please* punish me!' I grab my ass cheeks and spread them wide for him. My slick pussy is now open for him, just waiting for him to fill it. He presses the head of his cock against my anus and my ass contracts involuntarily as I think that he might try to penetrate me unprepared. He lets out a little chuckle and moves on down the line. He rubs his cock between my wet pussy lips and then poises himself at the opening of my sex.

'You are a *naughty* girl,' he whispers hotly into my ear as he plunges into me.

'Oh *yes*!' I groan, feeling him fill me to the hilt.

'What would your daddy think of you now?'

I shake my head. With him sawing his big hard cock in and out of me, I can't answer.

'I think he'd say you were a whore,' he tells me,

accentuating each word with a thrust of the groin. I nod in agreement. He reaches around and grabs my tits, squeezing them in his big hands.

'Do you like that?'

'Yes, oh *yes*!' I moan breathlessly.

'Your pussy is *so* wet! Do you like having my stiff cock in you, *fucking* you?'

'Yes!'

'Tell me,' he demands, his balls slapping my pussy as he pounds me harder and harder. '*Tell* me how much you like to be fucked.'

'I love it!' I cry out, submitting to him at last. 'I love your big cock fucking my pussy. Fuck me harder!' I moan as I roll my clit beneath my fingers.

'That's it,' he urges as he feels my cunt muscles tightening around his staff. 'Come for me, you naughty girl! Come all over my cock!'

He clamps down on my nipples with his fingertips and it's all over. Wave after wave of pleasure washes over me as the intense heat of orgasm floods my pussy. Lexington gives me his last few good strokes and then tears himself free from my snatch.

'Oh!' he yells loudly, letting his load loose all over my ass. 'You whore! You beautiful fucking *whore*!'

I smile. Who am I to disagree?

Approximately 82 minutes have elapsed, according to my watch, since I was escorted to the security office at my favourite local department store. I emerge quietly, and thoughtfully close the door behind me so that Eric Lexington will not be caught with his pants down. For that is how I left him: naked on the floor, trousers in a heap next to him as he sat smoking a cigarette, totally pleasured and thoroughly drained. I smack my lips with avaricious delight as I make my way to my car, the tingling of my pussy reminiscent of the excellent fucking I just got. I all but skip across the parking lot, the boots and purse that originally brought me here long forgotten. A giddy laugh bubbles up through my lips as I reach into my pocket and feel the mingled textures of silk and silver beneath my fingers. Damn, it feels *so* good to be bad!

Foot-fall
by Lynn Lake

David moaned, rolled his head from side to side, eyeballs jumping under twitching eyelids. The nightmare was on him again, his agonised mind reeling in total blackness, echoing with the clickety-clack of high heels on hard floor – loud and insistent and sexy. But going away; walking away from David.

He woke up screaming.

He'd been attending to another guest at the front desk, when he'd first heard the clickety-clack of her silver-tipped heels on the polished marble floor of the luxury hotel lobby. And to a man like David, steeped in the fetishism of women's legs and feet, every high heel made a distinctive sound, indicating to his sensitive ears and soul the height, point and composition of the heels, the height, weight and leg-length of the woman wearing the erotic footwear.

So, as he stood near the printer with his back to the lobby, waiting for the guest's registration information to print out, the clickety-clack of these particular high heels heralded four inches of reinforced leather with metal tips, a tall, lean woman of lengthy leggage used to flaunting her lower limbs in such heels. David turned, and the delight signalled by his ears became the rapture before his eyes.

Lillian Lancombe stood six feet away from the raised counter, presenting David and the astonished guest with a full view of her and her long, luxurious legs.

She was dressed in a form-fitting dark-blue dress, a gold chain necklace and gold hoop earrings, her jet-black hair pulled back sleek and shiny from her high-cheekboned, imperious face, lips red and full and glossy, eyes dark and gleaming. She had high breasts and narrow hips, and her legs flowed out from beneath the mid-thigh hem of her dress lithe and silky, wrapped in dark-blue stockings, feet platformed in the spike heels, tilted arches and slender ankles clasped by dark leather straps.

'I'm Lillian, the new night manager,' she said.

The printed registration page, when David handed it to the speechless guest, was damp and crumpled.

Two nights later, he was on his knees in Lillian's office, at her stockinged feet.

They were pirouetted on their pointed tips right in front of David, silk-sheathed legs shimmering in their night-shaded coverings. Lillian sat in her leather executive chair with her legs slightly parted, looking down at David. 'You see how it's going to be?' she said, more than asked. And lowered her legs just a little, her toes splaying out before the kneeling man.

David swallowed and clasped his hands tighter together, his small body trembling, his eyes locked on those twin noir waterfalls of limbs, the splash of toes way down at the bottom of the plunging arches. 'Do - do we have to?' he mumbled.

Her right leg lashed out, striking David across the face with her bladed foot. His glasses went flying, and he groaned. Lillian planted the supple stem back on the carpet, then raised her other limb, and pushed its tapered tip against David's mouth, gently at first. Until the toes flowered in the stretchy fabric and she roughly shoved David's head back.

'Any other questions?'

David reeled from the silken touch and perfumed scent of Lillian's ballerina legs, the brief and tantalising rustle and taste of her hose. He scrambled his glasses back on and shook his head. And was rewarded, Lillian lifting and unfolding both of her elegant legs and holding them out at full length, permitting David to clasp her pointed feet in his hands.

He gazed along the stunning lengths of the exquisitely contoured limbs, fingers clutching, probing the dizzying depths of Lillian's curvaceous soles, the sensuous smoothness and roundness of her sky-high arches. His hands moved higher, cradling the delicate bulbs of her heels, then slipping up on to her finely constructed ankles, fingers covetously wrapping around and squeezing.

She pulled her feet away, snapping, 'That's enough. For now.'

The man was a well-heeled businessman, in Toronto for the annual general meeting of his publicly-traded company. He was tall and thin and silver-haired, with a tan that didn't come from the Great White North in March. By early morning, he was at Lillian's feet, sucking on her toes.

She was perched on the edge of the queen-sized bed in the penthouse suite, completely naked except for sheer black stockings. The sexy hosiery sported darker, reinforced toe-tips, and cross-hatched seams down the back, and they hugged Lillian's legs like a second skin, despite the man ardently pulling on them with his lips.

She'd gone up to his room late that night to enquire about his general comfort, and the lonely, handsome stranger in town had invited her in for a drink. One thing had led directly to another, and now one of the most powerful businessmen in Canada was down on all-fours, naked, excitedly sucking on Lillian's slim-stemmed, plump-topped toes, one at a time and all at once.

She wiggled her toes in his mouth and moaned, 'Yes, Foster!' a hand in between her long legs, rubbing.

As David watched the whole thing on his computer in his

cubbyhole of an office in behind the reception desk. His fists were balled in rage, cock rock-hard in his pants.

Foster inhaled all of Lillian's one tapered foot-tip and tugged on it, then the other, his face gone red under his tan, hands clutching Lillian's ankles. And when he pushed both of her feet together and crammed all of her toes into his big, hungry mouth, she lifted her feet, and his head. He rose up on to his knees, biting into the silken stocking and skin.

'Oooh!' Lillian moaned, before wriggling her feet free and placing them on the man's shoulders, on either side of his head, soft and damp and perfectly matched.

He grinned, and she turned her soles inward, fitting her insteps into his neck, toes clutching and feet squeezing. He gasped, grabbing her sharp-edged shins, as she applied more pressure, her heels pressing into his windpipe from either side. Foster's face burned crimson and his bloodshot eyes teared, mouth hanging open.

'Jesus!' David breathed, on the edge of his seat.

The lean muscles of Lillian's half-exposed thighs rippled, feet choking, toes curling almost together at the back of the man's neck. He gurgled, his face purple now, knuckles white on Lillian's legs, his cock stretched out and as hard as the expression on her face.

But then Lillian's locked, vibrating legs suddenly went supple again, and she released Foster's neck.

He gulped with relief, David with disappointment.

She hooked her foot-tips around the back of the man's neck and pulled his head forward, in between her legs. And he dove down to her pussy, anxiously licking, lapping at her slit.

Lillian and David both groaned.

'I hope you enjoyed your stay?'

Foster looked up from his bill and grinned at the desk clerk. 'It was … delightful.'

Another guest drifted away from the general vicinity of

the reception desk, and the pleasant expression on David's face fell flat. 'I'd like to show you something before you leave, sir.'

Foster frowned, glancing at his Rolex, all business again. 'Well, make it snappy.'

Inside his office, David clicked on the icon labelled Gue$t on the computer screen, and Lillian and Foster filled the 21-inch monitor, Foster squeezing Lillian's legs to his chest and licking at her soles, as he banged away at her pussy; Lillian flat on her back, gripping and squeezing her tits. David adjusted the volume, so that the pair's passionate moans and groans filled the small office.

Foster's face had gone pale under his tan, and his mouth gaped open. 'How ... Why?'

'I mounted a camera with a built-in microphone inside the sprinkler head,' David stated proudly. 'I can even rotate it – see.'

The door burst open, and Lillian stormed in. 'What's going on in here?' she demanded to know, over the shrieks of ecstasy coming from the computer.

She stared at David, Foster, then down at the monitor, which David had pivoted her way. 'Oh my God!' she gasped. Her hands fluttered up to her mouth.

Foster slipped an arm around her waist, as it looked like she might faint. 'I - I have a husband and three children,' she sobbed. 'It was all - all a ... mistake.'

'Tycoon Foster here has a wife and four children,' David added. 'Along with all those shareholders to think of.'

'Oh my God,' Lillian breathed, turning to Foster. 'If - if I hadn't had all those drinks you kept offering me, I'm sure none of this ...' She turned to David. 'You want money, is that it? I can get some from the hotel safe. Five thousand dollars, maybe?'

David laughed.

'How much?' Foster growled.

They settled on 50 thousand, Foster gallantly covering

Lillian's share of the blackmail, of course.

She lifted herself out of her chair and strolled around her desk in her shiny black leather stilettos, long legs swishing sweetly together in their black nylon coverings. Music to David's burning ears.

She stood in front of him, smiling contemptuously. Then she kicked her right foot out, striking David's ankles and knocking his legs out from under him. He fell to the carpet, and Lillian stood over him, hands on skirted hips, legs planted and parted.

He stared up the gleaming skyscraper limbs towering above him. Then scrambled onto his knees and grabbed the curved swells of her calves, fingers digging into the bunched muscles under the shifting nylon. His hands slid higher, into and around the soft hollows at the backs of her knees, rubbing and caressing. Then up and up to the taut, lean masses of her thighs, hem-high.

'Sofia Morneau is checking in tomorrow night,' Lillian said. 'The poor little rich girl herself. I think we can get an even hundred thousand out of her.'

David's damp, trembling hands froze on the tight mounds of Lillian's buttocks under her short skirt. 'You mean ... the woman whose husband was just killed in that plane crash in British Columbia a few months ago?'

Lillian looked down. She stepped out of David's arms, and away from him. 'Maybe I'll let you kiss my feet and legs, afterwards. Maybe.'

It was like watching a snake consume a rabbit.

Lillian feigning sympathy, holding Sofia in her arms, as the young woman wept. The lengthy embrace on the edge of the queen-sized bed leading to a soft, lingering kiss on the cheek, then the lips, Lillian gently stroking Sofia's long, blonde hair and gazing into the girl's moist, blue eyes. She pushed one of Sofia's dress straps down off her shoulder and kissed the smooth, rounded flesh; did the same to the girl's other shoulder.

Sofia shivered, twisting her hands around in her lap. As Lillian tugged the dress down, exposing her pale, rising and falling breasts. 'I - I don't know,' she briefly protested, feebly trying to cover up. 'I've never …'

'Don't worry,' Lillian breathed, moving Sofia's arms aside. 'I have.' She cupped the young woman's soft, tender breasts and kissed the hopelessly swollen pink nipples.

David stared at his computer screen, at the blonde's slim, shapely legs wrapped in snow-white stockings, on full display in the pink minidress she was wearing. Sofia had smiled shyly at David admiring her legs when she'd checked in. And he'd glimpsed the mixture of hurt and healing in the young woman's eyes, when he'd looked up.

He'd even considered giving her another room. But then Lillian had walked by, her spike heels tattooing the marble floor, legs flashing under the chandeliers. David had booked Sofia into the penthouse suite.

And now he watched with a mixture of lust and disgust as the hesitant kissing gave way to ardent frenching, to tit-sucking and to fucking. After Lillian licked Sofia's shaven pussy to the very precipice of orgasm, the two gasping and moaning women scissored their legs together, rubbing their pussies against one another's, hips undulating, fingernails digging into firm, naked leg-flesh. David gaped at the awesome display, the tangle of bare, clenching limbs, toes clutching at the bedspread.

But their shared climax wasn't his climax, because something like a conscience niggled at the back of his leg and foot-obsessed brain. He would gladly take abuse from a leggy woman, but this seemed too much like giving it out. And that was something David just had no stomach for, treating a pin-perfect woman so badly.

'Ohmigod!' Sofia shrieked, staring in horror at the computer screen. Then at David. 'So - so that's why she came on to me so strong. So you two could ...'

David turned off the monitor, but the searing image of Lillian finger-fucking Sofia to screaming orgasm lingered on. 'She's - we've done it to other guests,' he said. 'Rich guests.'

'Blackmail! You're going to make me pay?'

David looked down from the girl's anguished face to her legs, where they cascaded long and supple and naked out of the bottom of the green ruffled skirt she was wearing, the bare, creamy-white skin glowing under the single light bulb in his office. Her size nine peds were bare, as well, in pale-green pumps with gold buckles, arches soaring up and out. 'I'm going to turn her in to the police,' David stated, staring at those youthfully innocent limbs. 'I just can't do this any more. And I'm going to fix it so that you're left out of it.'

She grabbed his shoulders, searched his eyes. 'Can you? Will you? My family ...'

David smiled reassuringly at her legs, so smooth and sculpted and unblemished, so close. 'Yes. It's just a matter of permanently deleting a few files. Mind you, it *is* destroying evidence.'

Her grip softened on his shoulders, and her shy smile reflected in his glassy eyes, as he glanced upwards. He quickly shoved his chair out of the way and dropped down on all fours, at her feet. He clutched her polished leather shoes and kissed the soft, tender arches of her peds. She murmured and sat down on the edge of his desk, letting her legs and feet dangle in front of him.

They were all his, and he knew it, to do with as he desired. It thrilled and terrified him. He was used to leggy women ordering him around, walking all over him, allowing him a touch here, a kiss and lick there.

But as he rose to his knees and lifted Sofia's feet and legs with him, gazed along the curvy expanses of gleaming flesh and up into her shining face, he drew strength from the faith

72

she had placed in him by entrusting such delicate and delicious limbs to his keeping.

He slipped off her shoes, fully baring her feet, cradling her balled heels. Then he slid his palms on to her curved soles, gently clasping the sensitive skin, rubbing the breathtakingly contoured bottoms of her feet. She shivered, goose bumps flaring all along the incredible length of her quivering legs.

David kissed her toes, one by one, on the trimmed, blossomed tips, taking his time, seeking to pleasure her as much as himself. Because this leggy woman was so different from the other controlling leggy women who deigned to indulge his fetish. And so he treated her legs and feet differently, not just as objects of lustful worship, but as parts of a female whole.

Placing her peds against his chest, he lightly laced his fingers around Sofia's slender ankles and squeezed. Then brushed his fingertips up her well-turned calves and around her bladed shins, in behind her knees. She gasped, legs shaking. And he burned with the eroticism of it all; a controlled, smouldering fire that heightened every stunning sensation, rather than the usual conflagration that burned hot and fast and out.

And so, after strumming and stroking the taut flesh of Sofia's thighs, when David finally climbed to his feet and lowered his pants, she instantly reached out with her peds and clasped his erection between her warm, bare soles, and began stroking. 'Yes!' he groaned, surging with all-consuming pleasure.

He gripped her ankles and helped her pump her feet, back and forth on his pulsating cock, as she leant back on the desk and stared up at him with glistening eyes. Her soles were baby-smooth, and he gazed into her eyes as they both worked her feet on his cock, making a heartfelt connection with the leggy woman he'd never made with one before, the naked, honest emotion of it all making his head spin and soul sing.

She moved her feet faster, muscles clenching on her lower limbs, toes clutching David's shaft, foot-bottoms rubbing and rubbing his cock. It became too much for him.

'Yes!' he cried, jerking on the end of Sofia's legs. Hot semen leapt out of the tip of his ruptured cock over and over, the girl's precious peds tugging him to an ecstasy of unimagined intensity.

Until Lillian suddenly burst into the room, screaming, 'You fucking cheating bastard!'

She'd been watching the whole thing from her computer at home, having previously wired David's office in anticipation of just such a double cross.

Sofia ran out of the room barefoot. David quickly wilted under the venom of the abuse Lillian spewed out at him until his eyes were cast down on the black diamond-patterned stockings clothing her long legs. And then all the way down to her feet, in their black, high-heeled sandals.

'Get the fuck out! You're fired!' Lillian shrilled at last.

David left, head hanging and spirit broken, once again.

Two hours later, the police arrived at his home to arrest him. He meekly surrendered. The only footage left of the blackmail scheme, thanks to Lillian, was her interlude with Foster, and the subsequent shakedown of the pair, by David.

He moaned, rolled his head from side to side, eyeballs jumping under twitching eyelids. In the agonised black night of his mind, the clickety-clacking of high heels on hard floor echoed and echoed – loud and insistent and sexy. But now, they were coming his way, coming towards him.

His eyes shot open. He was awake.

Heels clicked against hard floor, indeed coming closer – the heavy, blocky heels on the boots of the guard making his rounds of the prison tier.

David screamed. And screamed. And screamed.

The Surveillance Operation
by Gary Philpott

'That is him up ahead, isn't it?' DC Henderson sought some reassurance. The relentless rain meant he had been following a glaring pair of red tail lights for the last six miles. Keeping at least one car between their unmarked car and the target vehicle reduced the risk of them being clocked, but increased the risk of losing it.

'That's our boy, two cars up. My guess is that we are heading for the retail park.'

Although Henderson was cursing the driving conditions, he was also thankful for them. All Johnson would be seeing in his rear-view mirror was one pair of dazzling headlights after another. There was little chance that he would be aware of the colour of the cars behind him, yet alone their make and model.

DS Helen Baxter was proved to be right as the target indicated left and turned into a large parking area. Henderson followed at a distance.

'How romantic,' quipped Baxter, 'he's taking his tart out for dinner.'

'Not exactly splashing out, though, is he?. What's the choice here - burger and chips, pizza, or poor quality Mexican food? This is a place to bring your kids, not a hooker.'

'Just park up here, and then let's see where they go.'

Henderson followed his senior officer's instruction and parked up facing Pizza Hut. They both unfastened their seat belts and pivoted round to look out of the back window.

'He's cruising round full circle. The bastard's making sure he's not being followed,' stated Baxter.

The headlights carried on round and headed back towards them. They then turned down the parking row adjacent to theirs. Henderson and Baxter kept watching as Johnson and the young woman got out of the navy blue BMW.

'Oh shit!' exclaimed Baxter, realising the couple were going to squeeze down the side of their car. 'Quick, kiss me.'

Henderson froze momentarily. Could he really kiss his senior officer? She reached out for him, pulling him over to her side of the car. He was still moving when their lips met. With a mind of its own, his hand went to where it always went in such circumstances. For the first time in his life, he snatched his hand off a woman's breast.

'Put it back,' insisted Baxter.

Once again, Henderson did as he was told. He suddenly became aware of how nicely she kissed, and how good the softness of her breast felt. It was turning him on.

Two shadows passed the side window. Neither Henderson nor Baxter even so much as flicked their eyes towards them. They stayed locked together, playing at being a courting couple lost in an embrace. Temptation got the better of Henderson; he squeezed a little harder.

Baxter pulled away. 'Ease off, stud,' she chuckled.

Henderson manoeuvred himself back into the driver's seat, still not believing what had happened. The semi-hard-on pressing against his jeans subsided as he watched Johnson hold the door open for the young woman. She was wearing a skirt far too short for the weather conditions. It was probably nervous regret that made the next sentence pop out of his mouth.

'I bet she's got a cold pussy.'

'Well, there must be quite a draught blowing up there.' Baxter laughed. 'OK, let's get ourselves into position in the next parking block back. We can't afford to still be here when they come back out.'

'Not unless we moved on to the back seat.'

'In your dreams, DC Henderson, in your dreams.'

Well, at least in my fantasies, he thought.

Once they were in their new parking space, he asked, 'Should I leave the engine running?'

'Yes, we are far enough away, and we need to keep the windows clear. Just don't put the wipers on when they come back out.' She directed her eyes towards the pizza restaurant. 'I thought for a moment you were going to freeze back there.'

'Mmm, I hadn't planned on that. I'm just glad Devonshire couldn't make it tonight.'

'Huh, do I sense a bit of homophobia there?'

'Well, Geoff's a great bloke, but I have no desire to kiss him,' he laughed.

'Not even in the call of duty?'

'Crikey, no. Besides, that certainly would have drawn attention to us. Did you say he's gone to question the victim's boyfriend?'

She hesitated before answering. 'Yes.'

'I'm not sure I understand why Geoff was the best person to do that.'

'It's complicated, Mike.'

He picked up on two things. Baxter seemed to be deliberately keeping him in the dark about why Geoff had been reassigned to other duties at the last minute, and she called him Mike. He looked over and ran his eyes up and down her. Her thick woollen coat covered much of her body, but she was wearing heels and black tights below a figure-hugging purple dress. Not the usual attire for a plain clothes surveillance operation. He then started to wonder if indeed they were tights. His cock stirred again as he thought about the possibility of there being some bare thigh up there. If station information was correct, Baxter had six years on him, but she certainly was an attractive woman. Many a male copper had made remarks like, 'Her husband is a fucking lucky man to screw that whenever he wants', or 'I wouldn't my resting my head on those.' And here he was, alone in a car with her, having already planted his hand on one of those gorgeous tits. If his cock got any harder, he would have to reach down and adjust it.

His amorous thoughts were interrupted. 'As it happens, I always think it is better to have a mixed couple on a job like this. Two blokes sitting in a car on a dark, rainy night might just as well paint "police surveillance team" on the side of it.'

'Well, it certainly worked to our advantage tonight. Though I have to say, I'm sorry about, you know …'

'Don't worry about that, you didn't damage it.'

'And I shan't tell anyone.'

'I wouldn't even flinch if you did. No one back at the station would believe you; they know what you are like.'

She was right; it was a problem he had. Every time he exaggerated a little when recounting stories of his mini-adventures, sexual or otherwise, he always regretted embellishing them, but somehow he could not stop himself. What worried him even more, though, was the fact that Baxter knew about it.

'Wipers off, engine off,' commanded Baxter.

He looked up to see Johnson and the hooker leaving Pizza Hut.

'I wonder how much she's costing him for the evening,' mused Henderson aloud.

'She could be a freebie. We know he has friends in the sex trade.'

Three minutes later they were following the BMW out on to the main road.

'Any guesses where they're going this time, ma'am?'

'I have my suspicions, but let's just wait and see.'

They were led two miles around the ring road. Johnson then turned right at a roundabout and headed out of town.

'Do you think he's taking her to the Rattlesnake?'

'That would be my guess,' replied Baxter.

They followed for a mile and a half until the BMW turned into a lane running up the side of the Rattlesnake Club, and towards the small car park at the back. Henderson hit the left indicator.

'Drive on past.'

'But …'

'Do as I say.'

He carried on by.

'OK, do a U-turn and get us back to your place.'

Henderson became terribly confused.

'We need to get you into some clubwear.'

'Ma'am, you do know what goes on inside that club, don't you?'

'This could be our one and only chance. If you think I am going to fuck up just because you're a prude, you are very much mistaken.'

'I am not a prude, ma'am, in fact I'm …'

'Well, what are you waiting for? Get this car turned around. And by the way, put on your best boxers - unless you have some sexy underpants, that is.'

A few butterflies fluttered in his stomach as they approached the entrance. A large man in a long, black coat stepped out and held the door open for them.

'Good evening, madam.'

'Good evening, John. Put my friend's entrance fee on my husband's account, would you?'

'I think we can waive that tonight, madam. Have an enjoyable evening.'

'Thank you, I am sure we will.'

Henderson was still in semi-shock as Baxter directed him towards the male locker room. 'Just lose your coat for now;

79

the night is still young.'

When he emerged back into the lobby, Baxter was waiting for him. If she had looked good in the car, she looked stunning without the coat to obscure his view.

'OK,' said Baxter. 'I can see you are a bit nervous, so let's start with a drink at the bar.'

'I can't drink and drive, ma'am.'

'You will not be driving home from here tonight, and neither will I. If we are going to blend in, you need to loosen up. Oh, and by the way, I turned into Charlotte the moment we crossed the threshold.'

'Right then, Charlotte, let's go and get a drink.'

'OK then. Put your hand on my arse as we approach the bar.'

'My pleasure.' He could not believe his luck.

After ordering a second round of drinks on her husband's account, Baxter guided Henderson on to the dance floor. The digital clock behind the bar indicated that it was getting close to midnight.

She put her arm around his waist, and her mouth to his ear. 'Can I give you some friendly advice? When the time comes, lose your shoes and socks first.'

Baxter then let go and started to gyrate in front of him. She moved exceptionally well. His eyes went over her body like a rash. He considered himself to be quite a good dancer, but soon realised his boss was in a different league. Her moves were not dramatic, but they were incredibly seductive and, at times, incredibly suggestive. Up went his cock again, only this time, it was not going to go back down in a hurry.

He noticed that the dance floor had suddenly filled up, and then he discovered why. The current dance track merged into a new one, one about it getting hot in here, and asking, why don't you take off all your clothes? And that is what the men started to do.

Baxter gave him an encouraging smile. He looked around. Every man in the building was starting to strip. He had no option but to do the same. Remembering what he had been told, Henderson started with his shoes and socks. He was well behind the other men by the time he was dropping his trousers. Like the other men, he left his boxers where they were. What he had not bargained for though, was his cock sticking out of their button-fly.

'Leave it,' said Baxter, as he went to tuck it in. She reached out and gave it a few strokes with a loose fist.

The music changed again. This time it was a sultry pop tune with horns playing a "stripper"-style accompaniment in the background. It was the cue for the women to put on a show; and for all those cocks to get even harder.

There were at least 15 women Henderson could have watched undress, but his eyes were always drawn back to the one closest to him. When she climbed in the car earlier that evening, he would have bet his house against the possibility of his boss stripping in front of him before the night was out. The temptation to rub his cock as her dress slipped to the dance floor was overwhelming, but he managed to resist it. This was a new game for him, but it was one he was enjoying immensely. He was desperate to play it out to its conclusion.

His eyes locked in on the black suspenders framing the top of her thighs, and the small triangle of silk fabric covering her pussy, just creasing into her slit. Henderson started to fantasise about sticking his cock into that slit.

Sheer delight swept through him as he surveyed the scene. His brain filtered out the men; all he could see was what seemed like a hundred women in gloriously sexy underwear, provocatively bending and wiggling, inspiring a thousand lustful thoughts in the minds of every man present. He was in heaven.

'They're heading for the basement.' Baxter stooped to sweep up her dress. She then took hold of his erection and towed him along behind her, leaving his clothes on the floor.

Once they were down below, Baxter continued on past

two rooms and on to the third one at the end. When Henderson stepped inside, Johnson and his hooker were nowhere to be seen. His eyes focused in on the large wooden cross close to the far wall. Leather cuffs attached to chains hung from the two upper ends. Two ankle restraints were resting on the small wooden platform at its base. To the left was a rack with an assortment of straps, whips and paddles on it. The hairs on the back of his neck stood on end. Is this heading where I think it's heading? he asked himself. Is she going to ask me to whip her?

The answer came when she guided him up onto the platform by his cock. When she let go of it, he stood there obediently. Uncertainty was filling his mind, but something inside told him to stay put.

Baxter opened up a large studded, leather collar and secured it around his neck. She then lifted his right wrist up toward the top of the cross. He did not resist. Moments later, both wrists were secured. His ankles followed soon after.

'Have you done this before?' Her voice sounded huskier than he knew it to be.

'No.'

'No, what?'

It took a moment for Henderson to realise what was expected. 'No, mistress.'

'Mistress Charlotte,' she asserted.

'No, Mistress Charlotte.'

'That's better.' She yanked down his boxers. His stiff cock caught in the fly as they went.

He saw the shadow on the wall. It was a silhouette of her curvaceous body, with a whip in its hand. He heard a gentle swish, and felt the flails slap against his buttocks.

'We will start slow and gentle.' The whip hit again. 'And then we will build it up. The pain will not be as bad as you fear. Before too long you will be begging me for more. What do you say?'

'Thank you, Mistress Charlotte?'

'That's right.' She struck him again. This time it stung.

Baxter kept to that level of punishment for a few minutes. He hissed sharply upon each thrash against his soft flesh. A red glow spread across his buttocks.

'Shall I leave some marks?'

'Yes,' he cried.

He was naked, and strapped to a cross in a cool dungeon. There was no door; anyone could walk in and witness his humiliation. Anyone could walk in and administer his punishment. He felt very vulnerable; he felt very aroused.

Whack! went the whip. He yelped for the first time. And he carried on yelping until the sixth, heavier hit. From then on in he managed to suppress his protests.

'I've wanted to do this to you from the day you joined CID.'

'You should have …'

'Shut up, pleb.' The next whack was harder.

'Yes, Mistress Charlotte.' His buttocks were burning with pain. They were also burning with pleasure.

'I knew you were a submissive from the moment I set eyes on you.'

'I don't usually …'

'What have I told you?'

He heard the swish, he felt the pain. Henderson took the rest of his punishment in silence.

As Baxter undid the final cuff, Henderson asked, 'Do I get to fuck you?'

'My, you are stupid. Of course you don't get to fuck your mistress.'

'Oh, I was only asking.' He became conscious of her staring between his legs.

'Have I not given your pathetic cock enough pleasure for one night?'

'Yes, thank you, Mistress Charlotte.'

Henderson dropped his head and looked at his rock-hard

cock. It was a cock that was absolutely desperate to find its way into a warm, moist cunt. Unfortunately, the most enticing cunt in the club had just been declared off-limits.

'Why don't we see if we can complete our night's work? I will go and find Johnson, he's sure to have a cock worthy of my attention. While I let him fuck me, I will see what I can get out of him - other than spunk that is. And you go and see if his hooker is willing to let you into her knickers without payment.'

The tension gripping his entire body was fading. The stinging pain in his butt was not. 'Am I allowed to fuck someone else?' he asked.

'If you must.' Baxter walked out of the dungeon, leaving Henderson to pull up his boxers and trail in her wake.

'What did you find out?' asked Henderson quietly, as they travelled towards town in the back of a cab.

'There was nothing to find out. Did you manage to fuck his daughter?'

'Sorry?'

'I assumed you had some idea when you said the retail park was somewhere to take your kids, not a hooker.'

'That is Johnson's daughter? And he took her to the Rattlesnake?'

'And why not? I didn't see him do anything to her he shouldn't. Did you manage to fuck her?'

'No, there was a long queue; I got sidetracked by an older woman.'

'Long black hair scraped back off her face, a stud through her cock-licking tongue?'

'Yes.'

'Ah, I guessed Mrs Langley would home in on you. She likes to fuck all new members. Did she stick a finger up your arse while you were doing her?' Baxter allowed her head to drop down onto the back of the seat. A knowing smile crossed her face.

Henderson was left speechless for a while. Eventually he asked, 'Am I right in thinking you have eliminated Johnson from our enquiries?'

'I was never sure why the DCI put him in the frame in the first place, but he was having none of it when I tried to tell him otherwise. Still, no doubt Devonshire has got the DCI out of bed by now.'

'I'm not following.'

'It's the boyfriend of our victim; that's why I sent DC Devonshire over to question him. So I'm guessing he will have put two and two together by now, and a number of squad cars will be converging on Swan's house as we speak.'

'Swan has been running the car scam?' Henderson sounded sceptical.

'That's what I am trying to tell you. I played back her interview tapes earlier, and watched her body language. You know, the stuff you don't pick up on at the time; a little twitch here, a little scratch there. She was protecting someone, and who is the only person she would protect, assuming it wasn't her mum who beat her up, that is?'

The bits and pieces of evidence started to come together in Henderson's mind. 'Bloody hell!' he exclaimed. He also started to realise he had been totally set up. His problem was that he was not sure whether that was a good thing, or a bad thing. It had certainly been an extremely wanton night, but would it jeopardise his career?

Baxter leant forward and slid open the glass screen. 'Malcolm, for an extra 60, could you drive some country lanes for a while?'

'You know the driver?'

'Of course, I phoned him, remember? In my position I need a taxi driver I can trust. Malcolm is a Saturday night regular at the Rattlesnake.'

Henderson shook his head in disbelief.

'Now, despite what Mistress Charlotte said back there, I

happen to think you have a wonderful cock. Get it out for me.'

Once again Henderson found himself doing as he was told. There was something about the woman sitting next to him that made men do exactly what she said. It was more than just her gorgeous tits and her peachy backside; it was her smell, the way she swayed, and the way she spoke. If a perfume manufacturer could put the whole package into a bottle, their competitors would go out of business overnight.

Her lips wrapped themselves around his limp shaft. She sucked, licked, and spat on it. It stiffened inside her warm, wet mouth. The sight of her head bobbing up and down in his lap was a wonderful sight indeed. When her hand went to his balls, he nearly spurted into her mouth.

She pulled away sharply. 'OK, let's get naked.'

Baxter's fingers went in search of the zip running down the back of her dress. This time she pulled it up over her head. Henderson was only one step behind her. By now they were on the brightly lit ring road. She was sitting in her underwear; he was sitting there without his shirt on. Cars were passing by in the outside lane of the dual carriageway.

The taxi peeled off at the next junction, leaving the amber lights behind. Henderson watched the driver's hand go up to a large rear-view mirror. His eyes penetrated the back of his cab.

Baxter pulled at the knee of Henderson's trousers. He tucked his fingers into their waistband, kicked off his shoes, and eased them down his legs.

'Take your boxers off and then strip me,' urged Baxter.

Just as Henderson was unclipping her bra, the internal light went on, stopping him in his tracks.

'Keep going, don't stop. Malcolm has watched me fuck before.'

Ping, the strap shot apart. Baxter slipped the bra down her arms. Henderson soaked up her wonderful tits. His hand went to them, squeezing them roughly. He then began to slap her nipples.

'Enough, take my panties off. You can abuse my tits later.'

All the time Henderson was slipping the flimsy excuse for a pair of panties down her thighs; his eyes were drilling into her pussy. Moments after, her panties flew through the air; she spread her legs and parted her lips for him.

'You're a crazy woman.'

'I just love sex. You will never know how it feels to have such power over men. Now, I want to sit on your face. I want your nose inside me. I want to suffocate you with my pussy.'

It was just all too much. Henderson yielded to the request. Baxter went up onto her knees on the bench seat. He lay on his back, put his feet up on the side window frame, and pushed his head between her thighs. Her sopping wet pussy came down onto his face; his nose slipped inside her slippery cunt. Baxter started to fuck his face. Up and down she went, squeezing his head tightly between her thighs as she did so. Henderson took sharp intakes of breath whenever he was able.

He started to wank furiously, his hips bucking as he pushed against the side of the cab with his feet. He looked like a man fucking an invisible woman above him.

'Come on baby, spunk all over your stomach.'

Baxter watched the creamy fluid spurt out of his cock. Her cunt convulsed, drenching his face with her juices. 'Fucking gorgeous,' she moaned, dropping her full weight down onto his face. She watched his cock slowly droop onto the lower part of his stomach, and ran her fingers over the sticky mess above its head.

'Next time, I will let you fuck me. I promise.'

'Good,' came the muffled sound from between her legs.

Mimi
by Jasmine Benedict

'Where is he, Miss Bates?' Detective Collinger leant forward and pressed his clean, well-mannered hands against the table. Planted wide, he splayed them, braced his average weight upon them and attempted to seem stronger than he was. Setting shirted shoulders, he appeared to be performing steps he'd memorised from some instruction booklet: *How to be a Man – The Foolproof Guide to Masculinity*, its step-by-steps unnatural in his hands.

Striving not to blink, he stared her squarely in the face, a few mere inches of illumined air between them. Clearly he was hoping to intimidate and therefore scare the truth from her, but not a chance in hell. Staring right back at him, all she felt was growing boredom, manifesting in a study of his eyes. They were grey; a placid, winter sea beneath a drizzly sky. Not dazzling, but intriguing all the same. Something in their likeness to a vast, slow-rolling ocean made her wonder if they too had hidden depths. Here and there, the dreary brine was streaked with darker aspects, and she felt they lent an enigmatic air. Yes, he seemed unsure and out of depth beneath the front he wore but, nonetheless, he had still made detective. Where it hid she wasn't sure, but somewhere in that lean, reluctant form of his, he must have had some balls.

Reaching forth from where she sat with dainty, silk-gloved fingers, the detective's quiet detainee dipped her gaze, watching while she trailed a feather touch along the full length of his necktie to its freely hanging point. Peering up through deftly lowered lashes once she had, she watched his young, expressive features with a smile, charmed by how they tensed with little flinches of unease as she defied his best "bad cop" act.

'Call me Mimi.'

Having made her offhand introduction, Mimi Bates reclined with effortless refinement in her chair, sliding down a little on the bare wood of her seat and hooking one lithe, stockinged leg across the other. As she moved, the sharply scalloped and ornately beaded hem-work of her dress was caused to shift, glistering and flitting as it slid against her upraised knee and settled to the fresh shape of her lap.

Mimi absolutely loved the way this garment moved; it was her favourite dancing dress without a doubt. Even now, the slithering, swaying weight of it at play about her thighs was quite enough to leave her roused. Hungry like a wolf-dog for the wild, she longed to be released back to the dance floor whence she came, dragged away by brutish johns whose raid had coincided with the playing of her very favourite song.

'I don't have to tell you just how serious this is ...' Detective Collinger attempted sounding fearsome. Tranquil as a dove, though, Mimi merely tipped her head aside and hummed that Charleston tune she loved so much. Yearning still to dance, she shimmied idly where she sat to the alluring skip and swing of mind-played music, rolling just a touch at her high fashion, slender hips while pale, slim arms crossed cavalierly on her knee.

'I see nothing serious in dancing,' Mimi stated, having hummed her way, unhurried, through a verse. Free from care, she tossed her head and beaded turban tassels cut a rug against her sleek-bobbed, auburn hair. 'Don't I just remind you of the Milky Way or some such sparkling thing?' she questioned with peacock glee, swinging, as she spoke, her airborne foot to set her slipper twinkling gaily where it dangled from her toes.

Quite unlike her captor, Mimi naturally possessed an easy aptitude for seeming what she wasn't. Daughter of an actress, she'd inherited – and honed by childhood mimicry – the mastery of façade. Heaving out a sigh that deemed things tiresome, she portrayed herself a creature prone to lapses of attention; just a scatty flapper, all her essence worn without, while not a thing of any substance dwelt within. That was what they wished to see, Chicago's proud police force; what they thought her with their narrow, mannish minds. Little did they know what chance they'd let slip through their hands when they'd assigned her to this rookie cop tonight.

Clearly having no clue how to handle her at all, Detective Collinger glared helplessly at Mimi, straightening rather promptly as she stroked his tie once more with half a mind to seize and cinch it round her fist. Pulling back, he almost seemed a party to her thinking, seeking safety in the distance of a stride, drifting further off though she'd desired to yank him forth and learn exactly what might make those sea eyes toss. Awkward while she watched, he ran one splayed hand down his torso, with the vague excuse of smoothing out his tie; veiling rather uselessly the thing it really was – a timid move to comfort self and gain control. Still, no matter why, the downward motion of his hand was welcomed cordially by Mimi's watchful gaze – silently invited to pursue the southbound sweep and take account of his physique along the way.

Starting at the centre of his chest, his hand descended, falling slowly while he drew a steady breath, leading Mimi's eyes to note, with favourable surprise, the unexpected signs of upper body strength. Smoothed in close beneath, his crisp, white shirt exposed the firm if narrow contours of a well-proportioned breast; prominent enough to bring to life in Mimi's mind a flash of dark, male nipple raked by glove-dulled nails … Smiling at the thought of it, she mused upon his figure, having seemed so ineffectual at first; now appearing bolstered by a layer of well-honed muscle, lending sinew to his tall yet slender frame. Sliding further still, his hand traversed a long, lean stomach, and she fancied it of similar construction; visualising smooth, trim flesh pulled tight to rippling muscles, while his fumbling fingers urged her eyeline lower. Rather maladroitly, those uneasy digits sought to tuck his tie beneath the waistband of his pants, stowing it away behind his belt, as if to safety, though to do so bred fresh dangers in itself. Utterly enamoured with him now, the flapper's gaze stayed captivated though his hands had done their task, contemplating keenly the way his tailored suit pants bunched and creased to form a starburst at the crotch …

'Miss Bates, don't play games!' Detective Collinger lunged forward, his bark abruptly interrupting Mimi's thoughts. Fierce this time, his hands came slamming down against the table and, had Mimi been less couth, she might have jumped. As it was, instead, she felt a thrill of startled pleasure stir within her at how violently he'd snapped; seeping like the potent, outlawed liquor she'd been drinking, or the wondrous, heady flush of wild romance. Fixing her irately now, his once calm ocean gaze was threatening to match his newfound voice; gruff and growling that had been, an angry, rumbling thunder clap, but doing less to frighten than excite. All at once the undertows she'd mused upon were turning; tides revolting as her ogling left him riled, flashing her a glimpse of something capable and fervent, though she knew his ire had sprung from deep unease.

'Games …' She breathed the word as might an atheist cite God; as though the thought of it alone were quite preposterous, glancing off aside to wax the air of one indifferent, though her vitals showed great interest indeed. Just as she'd desired, such brash impertinence provoked the flames of wounded pride to kindle in him higher, showing on the surface in a sudden, knee-jerk shove that sent the table shunting threateningly towards her.

'Games!' he snapped back angrily. 'Don't take me for a fool!' And, from his fractiousness, she knew that people had. Why else had his colleagues left him here interrogating her while they all picked out bigger cons to crack? Ever more, however, Mimi had the sneaking feeling that he might have been the smartest of them all. Clearly he was yet to be convinced of her naivety, and such mistrust at least deserved regard.

'OK ...' Mimi yielded, feeling bafflingly attracted to the straight, upstanding man of law before her. Tightening into fists, his mild hands clenched and she imagined them, all yank, amidst her hair ... 'Let's make a deal.'

Flashing sharp suspicion mixed with tremulous intrigue, Detective Collinger's sea eyes continued tossing. Broodingly, a storm of fierce conflict swept their depths and Mimi knew his mind was warring with her words. Gathering fearsome strength, the darker aspects clashed and merged until his gaze appeared a shadow of itself. Yes, she knew it well; that look of morbid fascination worn by men when faced with grand, dishonest chance.

'No ... No deals,' he settled after brief yet deep reflection, sounding resolute despite his squally eyes. Watching them a moment, Mimi ascertained that interest still remained, and arose to quit her chair.

'That's too bad ...,' she told him, stepping forth towards the table, making sure to never disengage his gaze. Catlike in her ways, she wished to watch his feelings spark there while she goaded him to meet her in the fray. 'I could tell you something that would put you leaps and bounds ahead of every other gumshoe in this place.' Temptingly she purred that – then employed a skilful pause, suspense constructed. 'If you make it worth my while ...'

Viewing him, unblinking, while her forthright words struck home, Mimi cast Detective Collinger a smile, making it quite clear that she was not about to yield to him, in spite of any offer she proffered. If he wished to bargain, it would all be on her terms; the way she executed every move in life. Judging by the damning scowl thrown back, he understood this, but was not prepared to pander as she liked.

'Miss Bates, you do know – if you're withholding information – that would constitute a felony itself.'

'And you'll prove it how?' asked Mimi coolly, smiling still and drawing nearer, elevated on her toes.

Once again, a moment's heavy silence fell upon them with the denseness of a theatre curtain's slump; silence in whose keeping Mimi tailored every move to speak regardless, making sure to keep him hooked. Placing down her own hands on the table top, she hitched then dipped, then hitched then dipped one languid, lissom hip, setting beadwork slinking once again against her skin, while she awaited his decision on her deal.

'So – if I agreed …' Detective Collinger responded rather quicker than she'd dared to quite expect, striving to disguise the way his eyes flicked down her body with a blink far too theatrical to tell. 'I suppose you'd want your name kept out of it?' he ventured and it tickled her how innocent he was. Tossing back her head, she chuckled gaily at his words, with just enough suggested jeer to piss him off.

'You're so quaint,' she told him, though he trembled with frustration. 'Who's to say the name I gave you's even mine?' Creeping fingers forth, she touched their silk-gloved tips to his and curtseyed forward till she could have kissed his lips …

Daring him to hold her gaze a meagre inch away now, Mimi watched Detective Collinger unfold; viewed so close, his every thought and feeling seemed apparent in the tempest that despoiled those ocean orbs. Part of him desired to flee, another part to punch her, but she didn't fear the happening of either; each was far too brief, too insignificant when measured in the shadows of the waves with highest peaks. Hunger was the mainstay of those most ferocious crests; the urge to throw her down and fuck her smugness from her. More than that, for his angry need to have her coupled, seamless, with a greed for what she offered. Frequently, she'd seen that look of avarice in the eyes of countless wannabes approaching Louis' office – Louis Marciano, that elusive liquor runner with whose whereabouts the cops were so concerned. Even, though, in Louis' chestnut gaze – her lover's gaze – that look had never seemed so striking; never as delicious as it was now on the once submissive waters of this bent detective's soul.

'Well, what do you want?' Detective Collinger spoke gruffly, and it seemed as though he feared she'd read his mind. Splintering through his voice, a note of chaos said he also feared himself as what she'd sparked in him caught light. Disinclined to answer, Mimi revelled in his ruin; in the downfall of the lawful man before her, letting just the faintest quirk of smiling sin betray her as she set about exhibiting her wants.

Moving with the slow, well-practised ease of one coherent in seduction, Mimi Bates procured a kiss; acting disinclined to grant the union of their lips, and feeling breathing quite escape him when she did. Though she'd lent him time, she'd known he wouldn't shy away; her tongue snaking forth to wet her lips had seen to that. Mesmerised, he'd watched it, swallowed thickly then, controlled by primal reflex, damped his own expectant pout. Ah, and now ... And now that soft, pink tongue she'd glimpsed so briefly had become a baffling force against her own; slick and hot, but tentative; entwined yet half abashed; now surging eagerly, now faltering, cowering back ... Mimi should have known that he would kiss enigmatically, as inwardly conflicted as he was. Need was battling duty; thirst for triumph battling decency; a mess of what he was and longed to have.

Musing while she kissed him, Mimi knew she had to stoke his darker aspects into blocking out the light; had to coax the rabid beast of want to take him over, if she really hoped to get her kicks tonight. Happily, she had it in her power to move such mountains; hedonism was the only law she knew. Often, she'd been told her lust for life could be contagious, and she planned to thus ignite him with her fire.

Set upon this tactic, Mimi brought one silken hand up, fisting firmly at the young detective's nape, urging him to rise with her, to straighten amidst their kissing, while she groped towards the table with her knee. Awkward as it proved, she scrambled up to mount the object, almost thwarted by the slide of stockinged skin, using all the fumbling jerk and jolt her efforts bred to make their kissing more chaotic and intense. If a near-tumble caused her mouth to break from his, she used the chance to nip severely at his lip, turning grunts and curses of profound exasperation into sacrilegious groans of hammed-up need.

By the time she'd squared herself, braced firmly on her knees, their clinch had deepened to a giddying degree; eagerly, the roused detective's arms had curled about her, and her heart skipped as he snatched her body near. Ushered forth in one sharp glide, she crashed up hard against him, choking, breathless, on an honest moan this time; loosening once the brief, taut flinch of shock had worn away, to let her willowy physique melt into his. Craving greater haste, her idle hand pushed down between them, yanking blindly at the buckle of his belt, causing him to falter, whimper feebly in her mouth and, though she suckled at his tongue, to tear away. Gasping breath, he eyed her like some wretched, cornered beast, both petrified and poised for battling to the death; violently his chest heaved and his fingers clawed her hips, one moment pushing, next imploring that she stay.

Fearing that the urge to shove her off might shortly triumph, Mimi set her mind on keeping him ensnared, moaning as her gloved hand breached his suit pants from above to seek and close upon his thick, half-rigid cock. Coaxingly, she petted him, caressed him in her silken palm, and watched the sweetest torture pleat his brow, feeling him grow harder, almost buckle at the knees, and give a throb that told of vainly battled need.

'Fuck me and I'll tell you where to find an even bigger fish than Louis.' Mimi spoke before he could, knowing he'd just make some stuttered argument that all of this was wrong and couldn't possibly go on. 'Fuck me ...,' she repeated, having not missed how his cock had twitched the first time she'd exhaled those sordid words. Dealing him a squeeze, she lent their import further weight this time. 'And I'll help you find Leroy Valentine.'

Whether it was caused by her precisely purred profanities, her wicked hand tormenting him, or both; whether by her vow to help him bring Chicago's biggest gangster down, the flapper's arrowed words hit home. For whatever reason – what amalgam of them all – Detective Collinger was swayed within an instant. Surging forth, his mouth reclaimed hers fiercely and she bowed back, only rescued by the swift work of his hands. Not so mild or bungling now, they knew what they were doing. One slipped rearwards to secure her at the small; fisting there, it crumpled ornate fabric, sought to gather it, and hauled it up till cold air nipped her rump. Hastening with desire, his other palm stole round and down to maul the contours of a pert yet yielding cheek, sending shivers through her as her pliant flesh was handled both with reverence and honest, primal need. Sinking, Mimi sought to work her silken legs from under her, to perch herself astride him at the brink, writhing as she sat upon the hand that toyed so studiously and arching lithely backwards toward a fall. Keeping mouths allied, she took him with her, hair in one hand while the other flexed and swept along his cock, working him to fast-approaching readiness and causing him to grunt some garbled curse against her tongue.

Folded atop her, the detective shrouded Mimi and she wound her graceful legs about his waist, urging that compact, athletic form profoundly near to meet the torture of a slow, meandering squirm. Once again he whimpered, groaned some oath whose sin she swallowed down, and thrust amidst the slither of her fist, seeking with his own impatient touch the very quick of her whilst fucking her exquisite, silken grip. Finding her a slick, hot mess of fevered, pulsing ardency, his thumb swept past her entrance from beneath, faltering as the slippery stroke provoked her hips to rear, before allowing half a touch to slip within.

Tangled up in rapture, Mimi cast her pretty head back, gasping breath as she released him from their kiss. Yanking on his hair, she urged his lips to spoil her throat instead and basked like cats in sunlight as they did. Wriggling at the hips, she forced his cautious touches deeper, bearing down until she had him knuckle deep, narrowing herself about a brace of half-crooked fingers and delighting with a purr of blissful glee. Much as she'd have liked to drag such sweet, slow torment out, though, Mimi knew too well that time was not on her side; interruption could come at any time and, judging by the way his cock was throbbing, so could he …

With this thought considered, Mimi freed that ticking bomb, emancipating the detective from his suit pants, wrestling him to liberty and feeling hot breath sear her neck where lust-struck kisses tripped, all pant and gasp.

'If you come before I do, the deal's off,' she informed him, and the threat of it alone seemed near too much. Whimpering in response, he gave a jerk, his whole core tightening, and exhaled the pent-up tension on a moan.

Seeming well aware that Mimi meant each word she purred, Detective Collinger grew suddenly mistrustful, taking swift possession of his own capricious manhood, lest she ventured to unfairly force its end. Hauling fingers from her, he replaced their pleasant probing with the pressure of his cock's distended head; pressing forth insistently, encountering brief resistance and distorting Mimi's sense as she was stretched. Mindlessly she gave a cry of sharp, euphoric agony, her pale arms thrown out, star-like, either side, arching up in earnest as she felt her gasping mouth be claimed and plundered midst the dark of lidded eyes.

Panicked by the sound she'd so obliviously made, Detective Collinger appeared a wreck of nerves, kissing her so fiercely that she felt her teeth abrade her inner lip as he fought to keep her quiet. As it was, his fretfulness proved sensible enough as he ensconced himself abruptly to the hilt, driving forth with one almighty thrust, the haste and force of which coaxed Mimi toward a thrilling, smothered scream. Reeling with the fierce, remorseless swell of rigid flesh so far imposed, she braced to take a frenzied pelt, clutching each smooth desk edge with the curl of slippery fingers as she waited for the onslaught to commence. Breathing hard, though, the detective only shifted to accommodate the movement of his hand, staying deeply buried, throbbing painfully but motionless, while trembling fingers dealt her clit a stroke.

That she hadn't banked on; so much softer, so much smoother than the pounding full assault she'd been expecting; writhing like a snake, she seemed consumed by slow-burn flames and could have sworn she felt their kindler breathe her name. Forceful and ferocious as they kissed, though, Mimi knew that she had made believe so delicate a thing, casting it aside as, with a skilfulness she'd failed to give him credit for, her captor did her in. Wriggle, rear and milk him as she might, she couldn't budge him; couldn't force him into fucking as desired. Helplessly instead, she had to take the slick, stroked ecstasy he gave her to ensure their deal went right.

Pushed toward a single-sided climax, Mimi thrust her slight feet hard against her lover's stubborn rump, seizing, as she felt one slipper slide, the chance to curl her stockinged toes to probe the snug, suit-clad divide. Gruff against her tongue, he growled some protest in response and Mimi knew he couldn't cage his need much longer; crushed up close, his chest heaved painful frenzy on her bosom as her body's nearing downfall coaxed his own. Scarcely half intended now, she tensed and pulsed about him, tearing groans in ragged cadence from his throat. Her hot, slick walls were choking his endurance and, at last, he seemed content he'd done enough.

Just when she'd grown certain that he might not ever take her, Mimi thrilled as the detective's hips drew off, coupled with a steeling of the muscles in his back that vouched the postponed blitz she'd forecast at last. Indeed, when it came, his onslaught certainly delivered, with his full weight thrown behind a raging thrust, driving in so deeply and so suddenly that Mimi near imploded, while the table took a shunt. Time was not afforded to recover from the volley, though; he stumbled with its jolt and powered on, prising out once more to plunge back in, all force and friction, twice, then thrice, then countless fierce occasions more. By the third time, Mimi lost all sense of comprehension and the world became a grand, chaotic blur. Still his strokes beset her, jerked and rough amidst their jarring throes, and still his breathless mouthing choked her own. All of this she felt, but without boundaries in between. His tongue, his touch, his driving cock, all merged as one; slick and hot and bruising in their own exquisite ways which, when combined, set every buzzing nerve ablaze. Cruelly overwhelmed, she neared the point of blacking out, her ears half deafened by the rush of coursing blood, leaving her to teeter on that seeming brink twixt life and death, the thrill of which secured her grand ascent.

Fired towards the skies, she blew apart as might a firework; vibrant pleasure bursting out in brilliant sparks, leaving her to twist and thrash and writhe through blinding throes that fast secured her lover's answering explosion. Unified, they keened out, but their kiss ensured they made no sound, her cries and his, as one, asphyxiated. Clinging to him wildly, Mimi arced as outer motion hung suspended, giving way to thick, deep jolts. Several moments passed in which she longed to simply stay there; to recover snarled and throbbing as they were. As her sense returned though, Mimi knew such whims were foolish; it was time to seal the deal and make escape.

Firmly as she could without appearing too ungrateful, Mimi pushed Detective Collinger away, straightening up herself, though trembling still and wracked with aching breath, to watch him seek to hold his own dead weight. It seemed far too much for him, and, before his softening cock had even left her, he was buckling at the knees, whimpering as he slithered free and stumbled blindly backward till his limp, exhausted body found a seat. Slumping there, he eyed her rather like she might have slain him; dazed and wide-eyed with his spent cock lolling free. Presently he recognised the latter, and his hands shook as he stowed himself to safety with a wince.

Witnessing this hasty show of modesty with interest, Mimi failed to share such corporeal qualms; perched upon the table edge with thighs still spread as widely as he'd left them, she was shamelessly exposed. Bared between, she knew he'd glimpse the opalescent sheen of sated flesh that proved he'd filled his bargain's part; letting him admire it was a bonus prize she opted to bestow him, to reward a job well done.

'East Elm Street.' She spoke up while his sea eyes drank their prize in. 'On the corner, looking out across the lake. There's a block of offices ...' His glistening brow grew furrowed as she said it and she knew exactly why. 'Yes, I know.' She nodded with a satiated chuckle. 'You've had tip-offs that you'd find him there before. But – your little raid uncovered nothing. Not surprising, 'cos, y'see, it's got a secret basement floor.'

Having offered forth such information, Mimi slithered from the table, lithe and languid as a lizard. Straightening out her dress, she bent to claim her fallen slipper and observed him as she donned it with her toes.

'In the elevator, press the ground floor button twice and then hit third,' she added, dallying towards him. Leaning down, she raised his chin and pressed a feather kiss against his swollen, speechless lips. 'Then come and thank me.'

Turning on her heel before he found the sense required for asking questions, Mimi swept herself away, slinking towards her freedom in a blaze of sparkling splendour, with a smile of satisfaction on her face. Such a pleasant evening, she considered, retrospectively; drink, dancing, sex with strangers and deceit ... She just couldn't wait until her fine detective friend found out she'd lied to him and sought her for revenge.

Speeding Ticket
by Shashauna P. Thomas

OK. I admit it. I definitely have a lead foot when it comes to driving. I can't help it. I've always had a need for speed. Ever since I got my learner's permit and felt the rush of being behind the wheel of a vehicle that can go from zero to 60 in 3.4 seconds flat, the only time the words "speed limit" entered my vocabulary was during the road test. Since then it has mysteriously disappeared and hasn't been seen since. Now this isn't to say I'm a reckless driver. I've never been in an accident. Although, I admit, there have been a couple of close calls. I may go fast, but I'm constantly aware of myself as well as the other drivers on the road. I like to think of myself as an aggressive defensive driver. One of my favourite things to do is get behind the wheel of my red 2009 Chevrolet Corvette ZR1 sports car, put the top down, find a long stretch of open road, and just drive wherever the urge takes me. Yeah, sure, I splurged on my car, but I considered that an investment. Everyone has their hobbies and their own therapeutic way of dealing with stress. My hobby is cars, and my therapy is the smooth hum of an engine, blurring scenery, leather interior, and a full tank of gas.

Even though I have a fairly expensive car, I'm by no means rich. Like everyone else in this country, I've suffered economic hardships. That's one of the main reasons I'd decided to make the big move from New York City to Albany. Besides the fact that driving in the city is hell, living in NY was getting way too expensive so I started looking outside the city for less expensive homes as well as someplace my job could transfer me. With the job market as tough as it is, it made more since to keep my job and just move to where transfers were available instead of starting the job search all over again. I'm one of many secretaries for the New York State Troopers. It doesn't sound like a glamorous job but it's steady honest work that pays the bills. Plus, working for law enforcement has its perks. One being that in the event I am caught speeding, with one flash of the proper ID, I'm most likely out of a ticket because of professional courtesy. At least, that's the usual case, but the first day I was to report to my new precinct was anything but usual.

As I said, I'd just moved upstate and was still settling into this nice two-storey house on the outskirts of Albany. Moving, unpacking, getting ready to start a new appointment and just trying to get use to the area was starting to get overwhelming. I had an overpowering urge to go for a ride and clear my head. I looked at the clock and realised I had three hours before I needed to report to work, plenty of time for a drive. I'd already laid out my work outfit and since I didn't want to wrinkle it I just decided to keep on the clothes I'd been wearing while I unpacked. It was a beautiful hot summer day, perfect weather to wear blue jean shorts, grey tank top, and black flip flops outside. My shoulder-length brown hair was pulled back in a ponytail. Grabbing my keys, and the new wallet my sister gave me as a birthday present, I headed out the door. I passed my everyday car, and went straight for my Corvette.

One of the reasons I loved my new home was its location. I could literally drive down the driveway and if I turned right I'd be in Albany in 30 minutes. If I turned left I'd have tons of highways and deserted roads; perfect places to go for a joyride when the mood struck. So I pulled out of my driveway, turned left, and within moments it was just me and the blacktop. I've got to hand it to upstate, they have some beautiful scenic views, lots of trees and plenty of lush colours during the summer. You have beautiful steep green hills mixed in with serene towns, farms, lakes, and rivers. As I drove, my mind ran through all the recent changes in my life and I wondered if I'd made the right decision by moving. Economically it made sense, but I'd rarely been this far upstate before; all my friends and family were either in NYC or down south, and I really didn't have a back-up plan if this transfer placement didn't pan out.

I've worked with the state police long enough to know each precinct has its own atmosphere. They reflect not only the personalities of the people who work there, but also the interactions between them, which often affected the overall dynamics. It always amazed me that no matter what office job you have, interoffice politics always comes into play. I found myself wondering what the people in this office were like? Were they as friendly as my last office? Was the office hectic or was it slow? What would my supervisor be like? My last supervisor was stringent, but fair. I've heard horror stories from other people who've transferred. One woman told me she had to repeatedly endure sexual advances from a superior until her second transfer request was put through. Some men just don't understand when a woman isn't interested, and think every woman swoons at a man in uniform. Personally, I believe they're half right. The uniforms are sexy; it's the men I can do without.

I've always thought of women as beautiful, attractive creatures, but there is definitely something to be said about a woman in uniform. People often associate the strength of the uniform with masculinity, but there is absolutely nothing manly about the uniform as it moulds to beautiful female curves. Just thinking about voluptuous breasts, a firm butt, and an athletic frame in that grey uniform had me squirming in my seat. I'd been so busy preparing for this move and getting all my ducks in a row I couldn't remember the last time I had sex. That's something I made a mental note to have corrected as soon as possible before sexual frustration drove me mad.

While driving, I happened to look down at the clock on the dash board. 'Ah, shit!' I had an hour before I was due at the precinct, and I still needed to go home, shower, and change. I hadn't realised I'd been driving that long and now as I slowed and turned around I also hadn't realised how far I'd gone. If I even wanted a prayer of a chance I needed to book it.

For some reason the roads were strangely empty for that time of morning. I knew I was going about 30 miles over the speed limit, but I hated the idea of being late on the first day. I didn't want to make a bad first impression. It was beginning to look like I was going to make it back in time as I was only two exits away from home. That is until I sped through an underpass and missed the state trooper parked on the other side. It was easy to miss tucked back amongst the foliage. I would've missed it completely if the bright sun hadn't reflected off the car. I began slowing down and started praying they either missed me or were going to let me slide as there was no one else on the road. The sudden flashing lights and sirens in my rear-view mirror told me I wasn't getting off that easily. 'Shit. This is the last thing I need right now,' I murmured as I pulled off on to the nearest turn-off. The gravel turn-off wasn't that far off the highway but it was hidden from view on both sides by overgrown bushes, making it slightly secluded.

I watched as the trooper pulled in behind me and waited for me to turn off the engine. As I stared at the clock on the dashboard and prayed this wouldn't take long I heard the trooper get out of the car and make their way over to mine. 'Licence and registration.' My head snapped up at the unexpectedly feminine voice only to find myself looking at the physical embodiment of my earlier fantasy. The uniform did nothing to hide the contours of her ample breasts, and

I'd bet my first pay cheque her ass was nice and round. 'Ma'am? Licence and registration.' She repeated. I stopped gawking at her and grabbed the registration out the glove box, and my wallet before I handed both to her. 'Ms Kathleen Swift, do you know how fast you were going?' Of all the times I needed to get out of a ticket this was the direst and yet everything I needed to prove I worked for the state police was at home. My special plates were on my other car, and I hadn't had the chance to transfer everything from my old wallet to the new.

'I really do apologise, officer. I know I was speeding but I'm kind of in a hurry.'

'You're a New Yorker. You're always in a hurry,' she murmured as she looked at my driver's licence. It still had my old address as I hadn't gotten around to changing it.

'Ex New Yorker. I've recently made the move upstate.'

'Well driving like a speed demon might fly in Manhattan, but it won't up here. I suggest you pay more attention to the speed limit and your speedometer.' Despite the slight censure in her voice, the radiant smile on her face showed she really wasn't pissed.

'This may be hard to believe, but I'm really a good driver. It just so happens you've caught me on a day I'm running extremely late. It's my first day at a new job.'

'A new job you might not make it to at all if you continued driving like that. Just because your car can go that fast doesn't mean it should, especially not around other cars.'

'What other cars? Look around, officer. We're all by our lonesome.' I couldn't help but put on my most charming smile. I knew I should just shut up, take the ticket, and get going, but I couldn't help wanting to spend some more time with the hot trooper. I should be wondering how late I was going to be and not how long her hair was under that hat.

'That may be true, Ms Swift, but that doesn't change the fact you've earned yourself a hefty speeding ticket along with a couple of points on your licence,' she said, reaching for her ticket book. I knew if there was any time to mention we worked for the same department it was now, but my raging hormones were much more concerned with the sexy woman before me than getting to work on time and a ticket I knew I could get taken care of later.

'Ah, but has it also earned me an unexpected interlude with a beautiful woman on the side of the road this hot sunny day.' The playfulness in my voice was a blatant invitation she'd have to be completely blind to miss.

'Are you propositioning me to get out of a ticket, Ms Swift?'

'No. I'm propositioning you because I find you attractive, and I was sitting here wondering if the feelings were mutual.' For a moment there her silence had me wondering if I'd stepped over the line. Then she unlocked my door and held it open.

'Why don't you step out the car, ma'am?'

I stepped out and she closed the door behind me. I didn't know what to expect, but I knew from the lecherous smirk on her face not to worry.

'Is there a problem, officer?' I asked with mock innocence.

'I was just thinking you might be hiding something and I should search your person. You know, just to be on the safe side.' She stepped closer, invading my personal space and pinning me between her and the side of my car.

'Well, by all means search me. I've got nothing to hide.'

Staring in my eyes, she placed one hand on my hip while the other trailed slowly up my abdomen. She leant her head into the nape of my neck and I felt her breathing brush warm air against my skin. After what seemed like an eternity her hand finally cupped my breast. She gently began to play with it as her other hand on my hip snaked around my back and began cupping my ass. The feel of her body inches from mine was driving me crazy, but when a warm breeze wafted the subtle floral scent of her perfume my restraint snapped. Within seconds, I'd whipped her hat off her head, tossing it inside my car. I spent the next two seconds admiring the beautiful brown hair she had pinned up in a bun before wrapping my arms around her neck as I slammed our lips together.

'Mmm, your lips taste like cherry,' she whispered against my lips.

'Cherry lip gloss,' I replied breathily before pulling her lips back on mine. As we kissed I felt both her hands at the hem of my top beginning to pull it up, exposing my bra. Then she pushed my bra up as well exposing my breasts to her wicked fingers. She gave a low growl into our kiss before she broke it to take one of my nipples into her mouth. The feel of her hands, her mouth, and the material of her uniform against my exposed skin had my juices flowing. My arms reached under hers as I began undoing her top. She helped me by undoing her belt then slapped it over the side of my car, never removing her mouth from my chest. Once I had her top completely undone I realised her breasts were even bigger than I'd initially thought; they were just held tight by a blue sports bra. God, I've always been a sucker for big-breasted women. I tugged up on the bra until her breasts slipped free. I began playing with her nipples.

'You have beautiful breasts,' she whispered as she moved on to my other nipple. Her hands moved down and began unbuttoning my shorts.

'Yours are amazing.' I barely managed to get the words out as she finally undid my shorts and shimmied one hand inside. We both groaned at the feel of my bare, moist lips against her fingers. Her hands were slightly calloused; she must enjoy doing things with her hands.

'No underwear, Ms Swift? Aren't you a naughty girl?' Her voice taunted me as her fingers, already covered in my juices, began pumping inside my aching channel. She applied just the right amount of pressure on my clit with the palm of her hand. With sure, deep thrusts her fingers repeatedly pumped in and out. My pelvis began rocking back and forth to the pace she set.

I've had sex in public before, but this was a whole new level for me. Even though the area was hidden from view, there wasn't anything stopping a car from pulling in from the highway. Just the thought of getting caught combined with the sensations coursing through my system had more of my juices seeping out, and my inner walls began to contract. Then she sped up her pace and bit my nipple, sending my climax slamming into me. My arms once again wrapped around her as I rode out my orgasm on her fingers. Once it began to ease I slumped back against my car. I watched as she slowly withdrew her fingers, raised her hand, and held it to my mouth. 'Lick them clean sugar,' she whispered into my ear. I sucked her fingers relishing the taste of my own juices on her hand.

'I hope you didn't think we were done,' I said as I began unbuckling her trousers. I kissed her as my own hand reached into her underwear. 'It's my turn to watch you come apart in my arms.' She moaned as I played with her clit. I'd just begun and her underwear was already soaked. Firm, circular movements of my fingers combined with the pressure I applied to her nipple with my mouth. Bracing herself with one hand on the car and her other hand on my hip, leaning into me, she moaned as I trailed kisses and licks up her neck. Her skin tasted so good, I could only imagine how good she would taste other places. With that thought, my hand lowered and I began pumping three fingers inside her pussy.

'Oh God … Yes! Just like that. Ohh …' She moaned as she rose to her tip toes, changing the angle of my fingers. All too soon I felt her pussy contracting, trying to suck my fingers in deeper. Oh, how I wished I had this lovely beauty at home, in my bed, with a couple of my toys that I'd yet to unpack. The thought had my own juices running down my legs. Increasing my pumping, I pushed her over her peak and helped her ride the waves of her release. Her screams of pleasure filled the air. I held her for a moment as she composed herself, placing comforting kisses on her neck. She leant back and gave me a short kiss before straightening up. She chuckled as she said, 'You're a naughty girl.'

'Oh you have no idea.' I grinned as we separated and began fixing our clothes.

'Well, seeing as you're new to these parts it would be mighty unwelcoming of me to give you a ticket. So I've decided to let you off with a warning this time,' she said, still sounding slightly winded.

'You know what happened between us had nothing to do with the ticket, right?' I had to know that she understood my actions came from arousal and not me using sex to get out of a ticket.

'I know. That's why I'm doing it,' she replied as she put her belt back on and I got back inside my car. 'Just promise me you'll slow it down and drive more safely next time. Don't let me catch you doing over 90 again.'

I smirked at her as I handed over her hat. 'I always drive safely, officer, but I do hope we catch up to each other again. Maybe next time we'll be able to spend more time getting to know each other.' I winked at her and turned on the car. She stepped back as I pulled out and followed the turn-off back onto the highway.

There were more cars on the road then there had been earlier, but luckily I got to my exit and back home without further incident. I rushed into the house and straight to the shower. I really didn't want to wash the smell or feel of the trooper off my skin, but I couldn't report to work sweaty and sticky on top of being late. I showered and dressed in record time, grabbed both my wallets and rushed out the door to my other car. Doing 10 miles over the speed limit instead of 30, I got to the precinct an hour and a half late.

'Yes, may I help you?' the older woman sitting at the front desk asked as I stepped in the building.

'Hi, I'm Kathleen Swift. I'm the new transfer from New York.' Her face lit up with recognition at the mention of my name.

'Oh yes, we've been expecting you.' She got up from behind her desk and motioned me to follow her.

'I'm so sorry I'm late. I was unexpectedly detained.'

'Oh, it's no problem, dear. You'll find we're pretty laid back here in the office. It's only recently picked up as we've been short staffed in the field. Even the chief had to pick up a couple of the patrol shifts.' She stopped in front of a small cubicle right by Chief Sanchez's office. 'This'll be your desk. You'll mainly be working for the chief, but when things are slow sometimes you'll help me and the other secretaries out with their paperwork, searching for files, answering phones, etc.' I nodded as it sounded similar to what I was used to in my old position. 'I'm glad you're here. Even though it's slow it's been a pain being stretched in different directions. You'll like working with the chief. She lives by the motto "work hard, play harder".' I nodded, thinking I liked the woman already. 'Plus Chief Sanchez has been so busy I doubt she even looked at the memo sent about you arriving today.'

'About who arriving today?' We both turned at the sound of a very familiar female voice. I watched as the sexy trooper from this morning walked over to us. Her smile was no less devastating then it had been earlier. I saw the moment she recognised me, and caught her slight hesitation, even though she hid it well.

'Well, speak of the devil and she shall appear.'

'Good morning to you too, Martha,' she said as she sashayed over too us.

'I was just settling in the new secretary. You know, the one on the memo you conveniently pushed aside for later.' She laughed and nodded gracefully. 'Chief Sanchez, I'd like you to meet the newest member of our team, Ms Kathleen Swift.' Then, turning to me, she continued, 'Ms Swift, this is Chief Rebecca Sanchez.' Introductions made, Martha hustled off back to her desk in the front to answer her ringing phones.

'It's a pleasure to finally meet you properly,' I said as I held my hand out. The same hand that was down her trousers a little over an hour ago.

'The feeling's mutual. And I look forward to our future discussion where you explain why you never mentioned working for the state troopers.' She shook my hand, but instead of releasing it she held it loosely in hers. My skin remembered hers and all the pleasure it brought. It tingled even now.

'Why don't we discuss that later tonight? Over dinner perhaps? At my place?' I replied.

Rebecca smiled, then stepped closer while pulling me forward.

'You're on, naughty girl,' she whispered in my ear and I shivered in anticipation. I had a feeling my transfer was going to work out even better than expected.

Internal Affairs
by Megan Hussey

'Exactly what do you mean by "manwhore"?'

Detective Pam McGee sat in a dingy office at the Clearview, Florida, police department; a law enforcement hub that governed the residents and activities of her small suburban hometown.

On a daily basis Pam faced a full array of garden variety wrongdoers; from pesky purse snatchers to bothersome muggers. And while most of these criminals came complete with shady, unwashed appearances ('Not to be shallow,' she sometimes shrugged, 'but I have yet to see a bodacious burglar'), her latest case focused on the most beautiful man she'd ever seen. Blast him.

As portrayed in a photo at the centre of her desk, one presented by her boss, Sergeant Bill Ramsey, Killian Kay boasted long golden hair and chiselled, flawless features. A set of penetrating aqua blue eyes completed this ethereal picture.

'Yeah, like his eyes are my favourite feature,' she mumbled, her own gaze scanning downward to behold Killian's tall, muscular body and pure bronzed skin.

'OK McGee, stop drooling all over the evidence.' Standing before her desk, Sgt Ramsey planted his hands on his hips and fixed her with an icy stare. 'Killian Kay is a wanted man.'

'And I can see why!' Pam nodded, adding in a dry tone, 'Seriously, Bill, is it a slow day at the old precinct? Is the drunk tank empty? Why are we wasting our time chasing after "manwhores", as you call them?'

Bill sighed.

'Pam, you know we've been trying to crack down on prostitution in this area, of both the male and female variety. We can't conduct a sex-biased investigation.' He shook his head, pointing to Killian's picture. 'This guy Kay is a male escort who has been offering sex services to local women. That, to put it simply, is against the law.'

'Well, thank you very much, Gloria Steinem in chaps.' The detective rolled her eyes. 'I've been pushing for equal pay and membership in the police fraternal society for years. Suddenly a manwhore comes on the scene, and you're pushing for equal treatment?'

Ignoring her sarcasm, Bill removed a file folder from a nearby briefcase and tossed it across her desk.

'Your assignment is to sting Killian Kay,' he announced.

'Do what to him?' Pam arched her eyebrows.

'You heard me.' Bill rolled his eyes. 'My secretary, posing as a friend of yours, made an appointment for you to meet Kay at the Royale Hotel downtown. All you have to do is talk to him a few minutes, then offer him money for sex. The minute he accepts, you arrest him.'

Pam nodded.

'And I take it that I don't actually get to have the sex?' She pursed her lips.

Bill shook his head, turning for the door.

'Get to work, McGee,' he barked over his shoulder.

The next evening found Pam in a low-lit hallway at the Royale Hotel, a Victorian-style getaway on the south side of Clearview.

She swept a tentative gaze down the length of her tall, athletic form; one usually adorned in steel blue uniforms and proper business dresses. Tonight, by contrast, she wore a ruby red cocktail dress and black high heels. Her long,

116

brown hair hung free down her back, and her plunging neckline was accentuated by a diamond necklace that shone in the light of a crystal chandelier.

'Geesh, my mom would be thrilled to see me dressing like some fancy lady tonight.' She grinned, but only briefly. 'Until, of course, she realised that I'm spiffing up for a date with a male prostitute.'

As if on cue the door before her opened, revealing a stunning blond gentleman dressed in a black silk dinner suit.

'You must be Pamela.' He graced her with a devastating, white-toothed smile.

'At this point I'm sure of nothing.' She bit her lip, adding silently, *He puts his picture to shame. Blast him.*

Killian Kay released a sultry chuckle that sent chills down her spine.

'Come on, my lady.' He crooked his finger in her direction. 'Let me make you feel welcome.'

Soon Pam sat on a floral settee, basking in an atmosphere that could best be described as a Victorian paradise. Above her hung a chandelier lined with glowing candles, and a domed ceiling adorned with a painting of cherubs in flight. Before her was a cushioned feather bed with a silken comforter and lacy pillows, overseen in grand fashion by a sheer lace canopy.

Beside her sat the man of her dreams. Killian's long, blond hair flowed in ringlets across his sturdy shoulders, framing a face that featured chiselled cheekbones and full, moist lips.

And there are those pesky eyes again. Pam smiled as he pinned her with his warm aquiline gaze; and she didn't resist moments later, when he took her hand in his.

'You don't have to be nervous, miss.' He kissed her hand in a gentle fashion. 'I'm here only to bring you pleasure.'

'I know. I'm just a little unsure about this. It's my first time -' Pam fumbled for the right words. 'With an escort, that is.'

Again Killian chuckled, moving closer to her on the settee.

'Oh I'm sure that other gentleman have sampled your charms, baby.' He leant toward her, filling her senses with his hot breath and citrus-tinged scent. 'I hope to be the best. You see, my lady -' He bowed before her, searing her with a look of narrow-eyed seduction. 'I live for the pleasure of women.'

'Good answer.' Immediately Pam reached into her purse, retrieving a cache that held a wadded pile of $100 bills. 'I have some money for you here.'

Taking the cache from her hands, Killian stood and crossed the room in slow, catlike strides.

Approaching a bedside table, he opened a convenient table drawer to deposit the money; and to withdraw an amber-hued vial of smooth, silky massage oil.

'Would you like a massage, my dear?' He gestured broadly toward the bed beside him. 'Perhaps that might help relax you.'

Pam paused a moment, contemplating the consequences of her next actions.

I really shouldn't do this. Even as these words crossed her lust-drunk mind, her feet lifted her aroused body from the settee and carried her toward the bed. *Oh but I'm going to, and I suspect it will feel damned good.*

Aloud she said, 'I'd love a massage, Killian.'

For a moment Pam and Killian just stared at one another; he romanced her with a charming smile that made her pussy gush.

Finally he took her in his arms and swept her off her feet.

'I can think of something you'd love even more,' he growled, pulling her body closer than close and covering her mouth with his.

Soon Pam lost herself in all things Killian. Wrapping her arms around his massive shoulders, she moaned as his luscious lips and long, thick tongue plundered her mouth.

Rubbing herself against him, she savoured the feel of his hard chest; and the harder erection that now strained the threads of his tight black pants.

She didn't resist as his agile hands stroked and kneaded her back, pausing to unzip and peel off her dress, along with her white satin undies.

'God, you're beautiful,' he breathed, tossing her body in a silken mass of sweet satin sheets.

'Well, look who's talking.' Pam looked up to find Killian still beside the bed, stripping off his own clothes with smooth, hot moves. Holding her gaze, he unbuttoned his jacket and sleek white shirt, revealing a muscular chest and chiselled abs. Then he slid his tight pants down his long legs, also showing off a bulging package encased in a ruby red Speedo.

'And now for that massage, my darling.' Pinning her with a wicked grin, Killian poured the massage oil across Pam's chest, rubbing her breasts until her nipples peaked in a show of raw desire. Then his fingers shifted downward, stroking her tummy as she sighed with delight.

'You sure do know your way around a woman's body.' She charmed him with a wicked smile. 'How long have you been in this, um, line of work?'

'About a year.' Killian touched her hips and thighs, applying some light tickling movements that made her clit throb with passion. 'I've always loved bringing pleasure to women, loosening their inhibitions and making them lose control.' His voice lowered to a sultry purr. 'And that's what I plan to do to you, babe. Right. About. Now.'

She squealed as he took hold of her clit, his palm kneading this throbbing nub as his fingers ventured downward.

'Feels so good,' she rasped out, her entire body lost in a wave of undulating ecstasy.

'It's about to feel better.' She barely heard Killian's voice as he dipped to kiss her lips; and to slide a single agile finger in the depths of her wet pussy. As his palm continued to create a delightful friction across the base of her clit, his finger probed her pouch in a subtle search for a woman's greatest pleasure.

Soon enough he hit the spot.

Pam doubled over on the bed and let loose with a heated scream, her body erupting in the vibrating waves of a genuine G-spot orgasm. Killian caught her in his arms, joining her on the bed and cradling her to him; soothing his lover as she quaked in his embrace.

'That was amazing.' She hugged him to her, drawing back to stare deep into his eyes. 'You're amazing.'

She frowned a moment later as he drew back, tilting his head in a show of curiosity.

'Amazing enough to avoid my imminent incarceration?' He arched a sardonic eyebrow.

Pam froze.

'How did you know?' She shook her head.

Giving her a reassuring squeeze, Killian laid Pam's body back on the bed and planted sweet baby kisses across her neck.

'A few years ago my kid brother got arrested for shoplifting,' he explained. 'You were the detective on the case.'

Pam closed her eyes, letting out a sharp breath as embarrassment overcame her.

'I'm sorry, Killian.' She cupped his face in tender hands and kissed his carved cheeks. 'I didn't want to do this.' She gestured helplessly. 'And now that we've gone this far, I couldn't arrest you anyway.'

'Nonsense!' She gaped as Killian flipped over on the bed, motioning for her to straddle him. 'I demand that you arrest me. Now, madame.' He waved toward the bedside table that held his professional props. 'I brought my own handcuffs and everything.'

Chuckling in spite of herself, Pam reached into the table

drawer and withdrew a mock policeman's hat, emblazoned with a fake gold star, along with a pair of cushioned cuffs, lined with red satin.

'Well, these are hardly standard issue.' She pursed her lips, bracing Killian's hands against the ivory headboard that bordered their Victorian bed. 'I think they'll do, though.'

Proving her point moments later, Pam positioned the hat atop Killian's head; admiring the way it set off his blue eyes and flowing gold hair. Then she cuffed her lover and locked her legs around his rock hard hips. He moaned with delight as she leant forward, stroking the strands of his silken hair as she licked the breadth of his chest; savouring every inch of his masculine perfection.

'I need you inside me, baby.' He growled, bucking his hips against hers as his abs rippled beneath her.

Eager to oblige him, Pam reached down and stripped away his ruby red Speedo, revealing a long, hard cock that seemed to salute her.

'And it's a good thing.' She planted a playful smack across the thigh of a chuckling Killian. 'You must show respect for an officer of the law.'

'I'll do whatever you say, officer.' Killian threw back his leonine head, gritting his teeth as beads of sweat formed on his brow. 'Just please, take me now.'

Letting loose with a playful whoop, Pam spread her legs and took her lover fully into her, savouring the feel of his throbbing shaft as it penetrated her pussy.

Collapsing on top of him, she assailed his lips with a hot kiss and braced her hands on his shoulders; taking him in a warm embrace as he continued to pump and probe her.

Their eyes flying open, they shared a look that bespoke pure passion as their bodies joined as one.

'Do you feel your power, officer?' Killian growled, dipping his head to lick her breasts.

'I feel you.' Throwing her head back, Pam tangled her fingers with Killian's as she rode him through the wave of a hot, blistering orgasm.

Moments later she uncuffed him, and their nude, sweaty bodies collapsed together in a mess of satin sheets.

'You're free now.' She giggled. 'I can't rightly punish a man for giving me the best sex of my life, now can I?'

She gasped as Killian swept her up in his arms, his cap tilting forward over his forehead as he pulled her closer to him.

'I'm not going anywhere, Pamela,' he whispered, staring into her eyes. 'I demand a long sentence, officer. With no hope of parole.'

Out of Body
by Giselle Renarde

When Officer Driscoll waved Shirley into the interrogation room, her stomach plunged into her shoes. She always felt ill at ease in spaces like this. The interrogation rooms were just like the cops, so angular and hard and unyielding. Cops could make just about anybody feel like a criminal simply by sitting them down at one of those scuffed metal tables. Culpability hung on the air – the stale air, which always smelled vaguely of coffee, donuts, and cigarettes all covered over by antibacterial cleansers.

As the officer's silence stretched into oblivion, Shirley's gaze flitted around the room. She looked everywhere but into the face of the burly man with the trimmed moustache and beard: up into the overheard fluorescents, down at the checkerboard tile, across to the windowless walls, and back at the expansive mirror behind her. She didn't have to be clairvoyant to know what that was all about ... but it helped.

'We don't usually consult psychics,' Officer Driscoll said, offering Shirley a seat at the table, 'but you've come highly recommended. Want me to grab you a coffee? Or a donut?'

'Thank you, but no,' she replied. Her stomach already felt as though it were full up with equal parts vinegar and battery acid. She couldn't help but glance over at the mirrored wall. 'We should probably just get started.'

'Right you are.' Driscoll nodded on as Shirley sat in the straight-backed chair. 'The parents are very concerned.

Thanks again for helping us out, by the way.'

Shirley took a deep breath, hoping it would soothe her stomach, but she just couldn't seem to take in enough air. She'd heard talk around town of the boy's disappearance. Everybody had, but they all seemed to think it was a case of ... Well, it didn't really matter what they thought. Police must have suspected foul play if they'd launched an investigation. It wasn't as though Luca was a missing child – the boy had to be a few years better than 18 by now.

Sitting across from her, Officer Driscoll opened a manila folder and shuffled through the dog-eared police reports. He attempted to pass his paperwork across the table, but Shirley waved away the information. 'Don't tell me,' she said. 'I like to start fresh. All I need is a personal belonging of the boy's to spark the insights.'

When the officer stepped out to fetch something, Shirley turned around to gaze at herself in the big mirror. The lights in the interrogation room were too bright to see through the two-way glass, but she knew the boy's parents were back there listening in. She would temper her responses accordingly.

'All I have is a picture of him,' Driscoll said as he swept back into the room. 'Will that be good enough? What do you think?'

With a nod, Shirley looked at the photo of a tall, dark-haired boy with the bronze skin of a young god. The flashes began immediately, one upon the next, like a deck of cards shuffling before her eyes. They came and went so fast she struggled to latch on to one. *A car and a man. Highway travel late at night. Stopping at a dank motel with burnt-out letters in the neon sign. Where?* Beyond the asphalt, there were fields for miles around. They could be anywhere.

Another flash, and she saw him clearly – the boy in the photograph, Luca, was completely naked against a whitewashed door. His hands were strung up over his head. Black leather cuffs encircled his thin wrists. The boy was somehow tethered to the top of the doorframe. His heart palpitated as he stood in wait. His cock surged. Shirley could see that gorgeous mass of flesh rising away from his lean thighs, and she could feel it psychically, bulging and distended, between her own. The tip was red, oh so red and engorged, aching with want as it pumped precome from his piss slit.

The master approached. His face was obscured by a leather hood like the ones Shirley had seen executioners wearing in historical films. She sensed Luca's trepidation as well as his unbridled excitement. The man wore a black leather thong that barely concealed a raging erection. He approached, holding a small riding crop in his fist. Shirley felt the vibrations of his speech, but the words themselves were muffled. More than anything, she felt what Luca felt – a racing heart, shortness of breath, the strain on his arms and pain in his wrists.

The man in the black mask raised the crop to Luca's chest, and for a moment all the boy could see was the sleek square of leather at its tip. Drawing back, Master struck him square in the side. It generated a nice little pang, but Luca wanted more. 'What do you call that?' he sneered. 'I barely felt it. Bet my old granny could hit me harder.'

Without a word, Master bent the crop back and struck his side in the same spot. This time the blow met his flesh so ruthlessly Luca leapt away from the crop. Of course, he had nowhere to go. He was strapped to the door. The man with surging muscles and a tanned body made some deep-voiced comment. Again it was inaudible to Shirley, but the resonance of that low voice pulsed through Luca's body. Master's tone was harsh and mocking, just the sort of discipline the boy required.

'No, not my nipples,' Lucas said. He was trying hard not to smile, but he couldn't keep his cock from leaping like an eager puppy dog. 'They're too sensitive. It'll kill me if you swat them.'

Closing in, the master stood so nearby the scent of travel sweat forced its way down Luca's nostrils. Master made another reverberating comment, which Shirley could not decipher, before tapping Luca's right nipple. At first, the sensation seemed pleasant. The pressure was mild and the speed rather slow. His force seemed to increase with every clout, until the leather walloped Luca's tender tit in double time and twice as hard. He squirmed in the face of such overwhelming pleasure, smiling even as he cried out in pain.

Under the black hood, Master's expression proved impossible to read. Only his sneering lips and enigmatic gaze remained visible. 'What are you looking at?' Master demanded. For the first time, his words rang clear, though they rumbled in Luca like an angry ghost. He looked away from the blue eyes flecked with gold and green. He looked at the 1970s-style bed with the threadbare coverlet. He looked at the outdated orange curtains, and the lamps on night tables that might have been picked from a trash heap. The place was a dive, and his erection grew harder the more he thought about the dirt and the grunge. He wanted this man to do everything to him that no one else had done before. Luca longed for the sweet sting of the whip and the adamant burn of a fat cock raging inside him.

'Fuck me!' Luca shrieked as Master gave his nipple one final thwack. 'Please, Master. I'm begging you, man. Fuck my asshole! Please do it!'

Though Luca begged and beseeched, Master's simple response was, 'No.' There was no arguing with the man in the mask. Luca was not entitled to ask for anything. He ought to be seen and battered, but not heard. So why did he bother with the entreaties when he knew that no meant no? Because Luca was also well aware that his begging would garner punishment, and it was Master's harsh chastisement that he craved.

With a quick flick of the wrist, Master whacked the top of Luca's erect shaft with the riding crop. It was such a delicious surprise that Luca didn't even react at first. He only watched that crop make contact with his hard dick, replaying that vision over and over again in his mind. And then a bolt of lightning rocketed through his body, from his cock right down to his toes. When he surged back against the door, his shoulders aching and his wrists strained inside those leather bondage cuffs, Master brought the crop down again. This time, that evil slip of black leather landed a little farther from the base of Luca's straining wood. *Twack*. Again, the tip of the crop moved up his shaft, striking hard and then stroking, like a cat that scratches you and then purrs to be petted. *Twack*. Again, a full blow landed further still from the firm base of his dick. The closer the crop head came to his sensitive tip, the more gratification he derived from the burn against his tender flesh.

Though he didn't say a word, Luca kept right on wishing his master would fuck his ass. Fuck it with anything. He didn't care what. It never mattered. He'd have preferred Master's cock, of course, but he understood that was asking too much. Anything would do, anything that could be thrust inside his ass, anything that could touch his hottest, softest, most intimate parts.

Like a mind reader, Master pressed his lips flush to Luca's ear. His breath was hot, humid, filling Luca's mind with heavy steam, and Shirley heard every word clearly when he said, 'My cock is too good for your filthy hole.' Luca's heart raced, and he tried to conceal a smile when Master shoved an insistent thumb through his lips. 'Suck this,' Master instructed. 'Get it good and wet. The best you deserve is my thumb in your ass.'

Luca did as he was told, swirling his tongue around Master's thumb, slathering it with lubricating saliva. When Master pulled out his thumb and reached down between Luca's back and the whitewashed door, Luca lurched forward to give him space. Their bodies were now so close Luca could feel the brush of hair on Master's thigh against his cockhead, and he thrust to get even closer, but to no avail.

Thrusting a splayed hand between Luca's butt cheeks, Master plunged his thumb right up inside the boy's asshole. With salivary lube, the assault didn't burn too much, but his ass ring still found the invasion quite a shock. Luca's tight muscles clenched and released the intruder in rapid succession, pulling him in, pushing him out, wanting it, refusing it. Without another word, Master took up the crop. As he thumb-fucked the boy, he smacked the underside of Luca's shaft with his leather disciplinarian. The blow landed harder than any that had preceded it, and the intensity of sensation urged Luca to leap away. He flew back against the door, driving that raging thumb deeper into his ass where it met an undeniable pleasure centre. As Master began to rub him there, Luca knew this act would invariably put him over the edge.

Strange pleasure rose through Luca's body. His naked thighs trembled. His balls churned the hot cream dying to escape its bodily prison. He was coming without permission. He'd pay for it later, but what did he care about that now? Master's riding crop landed hard against Luca's balls, and the great sting of it brought come surging out his cockhead like a jizz geyser. He cried out with pleasure, still apprehensive of Master's reaction, but too overwhelmed to keep it in. He spurted all over Master's hairy belly, watching the white cream landing hot and then dripping down that firm flesh until it reached Master's tight leather thong. What could be better?

A haze came over the scene, leaving Shirley gasping to breathe in the police station's stale air. Beads of sweat had accumulated at her brow, and she brushed one away with the back of her hand as it trickled down her forehead. She couldn't remember the last time she'd felt so hot and bothered, but she much preferred this phenomenon to its darker alternatives.

Officer Driscoll was asking her a series of questions now, asking if she was all right, if she needed a glass of water, but she closed her eyes and rejoined Luca's scene. The master was taking off his mask, finally giving Shirley a glimpse at his true identity – and it was none other than Terry, their buttoned-down travelling insurance agent! Shirley was clairvoyant, and even she'd never have guessed.

'How'd you like that?' Terry asked, giving Luca's bum a good smack before planting a loving kiss on his lips.

Luca laughed as Terry took him out of his wrist cuffs. 'How d'you think I liked it? I came all over the damn place.'

The insurance agent's blue eyes softened when he smiled. 'I love you, kid.'

'I love you more.' They kissed again, and a gush of warmth flooded Luca's chest. 'I always will.'

Chuckling to herself, Shirley turned away from Officer Driscoll to face the big mirror behind her. 'Your son is safe and in caring hands,' she assured the parents behind the glass. Luca was a grown man. It was up to him whether he'd come back home or stay on the road with his lover. Either way, his secret was safe with her.

What's All This, Then?
by Lucy Felthouse

Madison was bored. She still had a couple of hours left of her shift and it was dragging. There was absolutely nothing going on: no break-ins, muggings, domestic violence or even anyone being drunk and disorderly. For a Saturday night, it was unheard of. She almost wished that someone would commit a crime, just so she had something to do.

She decided to drive out of town. There was a road on the outskirts that was quiet in the evening. Youngsters tended to congregate there, drinking, smoking weed, and generally misbehaving. Perhaps she'd be able to bust a couple of kids for possession or something. She could but hope.

Madison drove the squad car through town and out towards her destination. Leaving the street lights of civilisation behind, she flicked on headlights' main beam. As she travelled further down the road she expected to hear the revving of engines. Silly racer boys with their souped-up cars and equally silly girls hanging off their arms often hung around here. The only sound was that of Madison's car engine and the tyres on the tarmac.

Frowning, Madison wondered if this shift was *ever* going to end. She planned to motor to the end of the road and head back to the station via another route. However, before she got much further, she saw a car parked in a lay by. She mentally rejoiced; this was bound to be someone up to no good. If it wasn't smoking drugs or drinking, then at the very least it'd be a couple of spotty teenagers canoodling. If so, she could put a flea in their ear and send them packing.

Pulling in behind the car, she killed her lights. If they hadn't noticed her already, they were clearly otherwise occupied. Madison didn't want to alert them to her presence and give them chance to stop what they were doing.

Hopping out of the car, she pulled on her hat and checked that everything she needed was attached to her belt. She doubted there'd be any trouble, but it was always better to be prepared. Silencing her radio, Madison approached the car; the last thing she needed was it suddenly crackling into life just as she was about to catch someone using illegal substances.

It was a clear night and the moon shone down brightly, illuminating the scene. Madison studied the car, surprised. It wasn't your typical boy racer-mobile. In fact, it was a very expensive car. Perhaps the driver had borrowed daddy's car. Either that or it was stolen. Bingo.

It wasn't until Madison was level with the boot of the car that she realised there was quite a lot of movement coming from the car. In an up-and-down fashion. The penny dropped. It was looking more likely that Madison was going to be making mention of the words "indecent exposure" as opposed to "illegal substances". Either way, the evening had suddenly become much more interesting.

Moving up towards the front of the car, Madison looked through the rear window. Even in the gloom, she could see exactly what was going on. Quickly, she realised that these two had gone way beyond the indecent exposure stage. They were full-on "at it". The couple's heads were on the opposite side of the car, so she couldn't catch a glimpse of their faces. All she could see were thrusting bum cheeks and splayed legs. However, it was obvious that these were no spotty teenagers. These were adults, and the car obviously belonged to them. Or one of them, at least.

Raising her hand to tap on the window, something stopped her. She continued to watch the rutting couple through the window. Madison had never had herself down as a voyeur, but something about this situation was affecting her. The man's tight buttocks were bouncing up and down, gripped and squeezed in the hands of the woman he was fucking. He had a broad back and muscular arms and legs. From this angle at least, he was definitely eye candy. The way they were going, she couldn't work out how the windows weren't steaming up. It was then she realised that all four windows were open a crack. They'd obviously done this before.

Moving closer, she could see more detail now. One of the woman's legs was around her lover's back, the other hooked over the driver's seat. This was one flexible lady. Madison's position meant that when the guy pulled back, she could see his meaty cock parting the swollen pussy lips of his partner, before thrusting back inside her.

Her own pussy fluttered. The thought of being fucked senseless by that cock - any cock, in fact - was getting her juices flowing. So were the noises emanating from within the car. Ecstatic grunts and moans spilled forth and Madison's senses went into overdrive. She imagined herself as the woman; being screwed senseless in the back of a car where anybody could catch them. The heat between her legs increased, and she felt her juices starting to seep into her underwear.

Madison was startled from her reverie as the movement in the car stopped. Freezing, she thought they'd seen her standing there and that all hell was about to break loose. Fortunately, they hadn't. The couple were simply changing position. Nevertheless, Madison ducked away from the window. The guy's sheer size and bulk had prevented the woman from being able to see over his shoulder before, but she wasn't about to take any risks.

After some less rhythmic jigging from the car, Madison heard a giggle, followed by the much deeper rumble of the man's laugh. Creeping back to the window and peering in, she saw that they were now in the doggy position. Luckily, they were still facing away from her. With two rear-views almost in her face, Madison could see everything there was to see. The woman's cunt was wide open and slick with juices. The man was rubbing his cock up and down her seam, coating his shaft with her wetness.

Madison's own pussy was getting very wet and her clit ached for attention. She wanted to be teased the way the man was teasing his lover, slipping his prick in between her folds and out again, without actually penetrating her. She thought he was exercising amazing restraint by not plunging back inside and continuing to fuck the woman's brains out.

Seconds later, she found out why. He had an ulterior motive. Slipping a hand between their bodies, the guy pushed his fingers inside her slippery hole, then removed them. He smeared the natural lubrication over her arsehole, before repeating the process. Positioning his cock head at her rear entrance, the man slowly penetrated her there.

Madison's eyes widened. He was fucking her up the arse! And judging from the noises she was making, she loved it. She watched, fascinated, as the woman's tight hole gobbled up her man's cock. Soon, he was buried inside her to the hilt, his balls crushed between their bodies. Pausing momentarily, presumably to let his lover's body get used to the invasion, the man then began to move with shallow thrusts in and out of her grasping hole.

Madison couldn't take it any more. The live sex show playing out in front of her was making her unbelievably horny and she was going to have to do something about it. Her pussy was burning with need, clit throbbing. Unzipping her mercifully large fly hole, she slipped a hand inside. Sneaking her fingers beneath the waistband of her knickers, she reached down and touched herself. Unsurprisingly, she was saturated.

Dipping her fingers between her pussy lips, Madison found that her clit was swollen and sensitive to the touch.

Slicking her juices over the aching bud, she started to stroke in tiny circles, all the while watching the action taking place inside the car. The guy was now fucking the woman's arse as roughly as he'd fucked her cunt. Surely, if they carried on like that, he was going to come?

Madison wondered whether he would come inside her bum, or would he pull out and spunk on her arse and back? She'd never been taken that way herself and tried to imagine what it would feel like; both having a cock up there and to have a man ejaculate inside her bottom. It obviously didn't hurt if done right; the woman's cries were of pleasure, not pain. Madison rubbed harder at her clit now, fingers sliding effortlessly over juice-slicked skin.

Back inside the car, Madison could see that one of the man's hands had snaked between the legs of his lover. The motion of his arm indicated that he was stroking her clit, just as Madison was stroking her own. Watching that, coupled with the sight of his powerful thrusts, though, she really wished it was her that he was pounding.

An intense and sublime tingling in Madison's abdomen signalled the approach of her orgasm. She quickly snatched her hand away. Although she desperately wanted to come, she knew her climax was likely to be so powerful that she'd find it difficult not to make a noise. She couldn't risk the couple hearing or seeing her. The potential repercussions were unthinkable.

Meanwhile, it seemed the couple were heading towards their own grand finale. The man's arm was pumping up and down as he busily frotted away at the woman's clit and his cock plundered her arse. Their grunts and cries were growing steadily louder. Madison put her fingertips back on her clit, working it slowly. If she kept herself teetering on the edge long enough, she figured a few well-timed strokes would make her come just as they did.

She didn't have to figure for long. Just as Madison reached the stage of having to grit her teeth to try and keep control, the woman reached her peak. A moment's quiet ensued, before her keening cry resulted in lots more frantic thrusting from her lover. Madison's time was now. Ending the agony on her tortured clit, she gave a series of swift, firm strokes and felt the blissful waves start to take over her body. Simultaneously, the man shouted out a string of expletives and an almost animal grunt as he reached his own peak.

Fortunately Madison's stifled cry, released into her sleeve, was lost. She dug her teeth into the stiff material of her jacket as the force of her climax almost brought her to her knees. Her soaking pussy grasped and twitched at nothing and Madison felt a delicious heat snake throughout her body. She rode out the climax, her legs shaking uncontrollably, barely holding her up.

Moments later, when she was capable of rational thought and movement once more, Madison shook herself. She really ought to figure out what she was going to do next. If the pair fell asleep, she was home free. She could get back in the car and be gone, and nobody would be any the wiser. If not, maybe she'd have to pretend she'd only just arrived and give them a bollocking. They wouldn't know the difference; the amount of noise they'd been making would have easily drowned out the sound of her approach.

Looking up, Madison's heart almost stopped. The couple were looking out of the window, straight at her. Under normal circumstances, this would have been a good time to act out the plan she'd just concocted in head. Trouble was, she still had her hand stuck down her pants. Not even the best liar in the world would be able to come up with a believable excuse for that.

Yanking her hand out, Madison did up her fly and wondered what the fuck she was going to do now. But before her brain could come up with something, the car door opened. The man, clad only in his jeans, stepped out and stood before her. His lover stayed in the car, still naked and grinning wildly.

'Well,' he said, looking down at her, a sardonic smirk on his face, 'what's all this, then?'

Blackmailer Transformed
by Serles

Lessie, wearing a white sheath dress, carried a plastic flute of wine to a small group surrounding Owen Wilson. She extended her white gloved hand and said, 'I'm Lessie Bunco, and I've been following your career.'

He turned, focusing his attention on her beautiful tanned face, black eyes, and hair. 'Are you also a supporter?'

'That's why I'm here. I know you were elected to the Barnwall School Board in 1990, served two terms in the state legislature in Illinois state legislature from 2004 until 2008, and last year were elected to the US House of Representatives, but I don't know you personally. That's why I'm here.'

'What else is there to know?'

The small group surrounding him had dispersed. 'Are you in love with your wife?' she asked, placing her hand on his arm.

He looked shocked and said, 'Yes, why do you ask?'

'Are you promiscuous?' she asked, running her hand along the top of her neck line which displayed ample cleavage.

'Certainly not,' he replied angrily.

'Too bad, it was nice meeting you,' she said, drawing her hand from her dress to her loins and turning away.

'Wait, why are you asking those kinds of questions?' he asked, taking her by the arm.

'If I have to explain, it doesn't matter.' Turning again,

she smiled innocently.'

He didn't let go of her arm.

'Do you mind?' He looked at his hand on her arm.

'How long are you going to stay?'

'I'm leaving. I found what I wanted to know,' she said, trying to pull away.

His grip tightened. 'Can you stay until the reception is over?'

'If you'll take me to a cosy place?' She ran her tongue over her ruby red lips

He hesitated, his eyes dancing in delight as he stared at her cleavage.

'Your room, for example. It's private and away from the eyes of the media.

'Is ten o'clock OK? I have a dinner to attend and some supporters to see.'

'What's your room number?'

'Ten sixty-nine, but be sure no one sees you at the door.'

'Do I look like a fool?' she asked, turning and sensuously walking away.

She arrived on the tenth floor a few minutes after the appointed time. Looking up and down the hall, she didn't see anyone as she knocked on the door. She was wearing the same outfit *sans* bra and panties. The door opened on the first rap.

'Come in, Lessie,' he said.

'You remembered my name,'

'I'm good with names, but especially those of beautiful women,' he said, taking her hand and leading her into the sitting room. 'Would you like some wine?'

'That would be nice.'

He went to the wet bar and poured two flutes. 'These fundraisers are hard work and there is seldom a break and not many females of your beauty. I like your dress, especially the neck line.'

'So I noticed,' she said, taking a sip of wine and running her hand inside the dress.

'Why don't you take it off for me?' he asked, downing his wine and unbuttoning his shirt.

'Wouldn't you like to help?' Turning her back to him, she took another sip of wine and felt the zipper on her dress being pulled to her waist.

His hands slid under her arms and tits, 'Nice, soft yet firm. I've wanted to touch them since I first saw you.'

She finished her wine and asked, 'Do you want to see them too? She turned to face him.

'Damn, they're larger than I thought. How big are they?'

'I'll tell you, if you show me yours,' she said, with a high-pitched laugh.

He unzipped his pants and fished out his erection.

She stepped out of the dress, kicked off her shoes, and walked to the bedroom.

'Damn, you're not wearing panties either,' he said, trailing after her.

They were both naked when they entered the bedroom.

She turned to face him. 'What do you have in mind?'

'If I have to explain then it doesn't matter,' he said, taking her in his arms, kissing her.

She returned his kiss with her lips, her tongue, and one hand on his average-size erection and the other on his ass. 'Is this why you got into politics?' she asked, when he dropped his head to her breasts. 'To have access to the ladies?'

As he shifted from one nipple to the other, he said, 'It docs make it easier.'

She smiled, hoping the camera picked up those words; she faked a sigh of pleasure and stroked his shaft.

'I hope you don't mind if this is a quickie?'

'It's your party,' she said.

He pushed her to the bed, crawling between her legs. 'Damn, you're beautiful. A perfect face, great tits, and a body to die for.'

She lifted her hips as the tip of his cock touched her entrance.

He slid into her quickly, fell to her body, stroked as fast as he could, and in less than a minute he arched his back and moaned as he climaxed.

Lessie writhed under his thrashing body, 'Oh, oh, that was wonderful,' she lied. Like most politicians he had more ego than stamina or endurance.

'I'm afraid I'm done for the night, but you're the best piece of ass I've ever had.'

'You're not bad yourself,' she said, rolling out of the bed. 'I've got to go to the bathroom.' She cleaned herself up and found him snoring when she returned. Dressing quickly, she stared into the camera. 'Take your clothes off. I need to come,' she said, before leaving the room.

Five days later the secretary of Lester Wilson came into his office. 'Mr Wilson, this large envelope came stamped personal and confidential. I thought you should open it.'

'Thank you, Margaret,' said a large framed man with a deep voice, and dark hair with traces of grey. He gazed at the envelope for a moment, wondering who had sent it, because he didn't do business with anyone in Chicago. The first page was blank, but the second was a photo of his son lying on top of a female, not his wife. Lester noticed the shape and tanned skin of the young lady. The remaining five pictures showed his son in a variety of sexual positions. The face of the female was blurred in all the pictures, but the quality of her body was unmistakable.

Damn and goddamn, he said to himself. My son's sexual misconduct has finally caught up with him. I wonder how much they want. On the back of the last picture, in news print he read, *Five Million. Will Be In Touch.* He picked up the phone and called his son. 'Owen, do you remember going to bed with a female with the great tan?'

'What … what are you talking about dad?'

'I have six pictures of you fucking a well tanned female, and I want to know who she is and when and where this took place.'

'I'm sorry dad; I never expected cameras and blackmail.'

'Answer the question, Owen.'

'It was about a week ago when I was in Chicago. She came on to me like gangbusters and I couldn't refuse.'

'I can see that. What's her name and where did it take place?'

'I stayed at the Chicago Hilton, Room 1069. Her name was Lessie.'

'How appropriate,' he said. 'That piece of ass is going to cost me five million dollars or you a political career. This is the last time I'm baling you out. Go home and be faithful to your life and job.'

'Yes, sir.'

Lester hung up and placed a call to Bob Canton, a private investigator he used on occasion.

'Bob, this is Lester. I have a job for you. Can you come by tomorrow?'

A late afternoon appointment was scheduled after Lester checked with Margaret to be sure he was free at that time. They shook hands when the private investigator got there and Lester slipped the pictures to him.

'I assume the male is your son and you want me to find the female?'

'You're correct as usual, Bob. They want five million.'

'What kind of leads do you have?'

'All I have is the Chicago Hilton about ten days ago. These pictures were taken some time Friday or Saturday. See if you can find this female with a great tan.'

She's got more than a great tan,' Bob said, standing and shaking Lester's hand. 'I'll have two men in Chicago tonight. They're both very good at finding this type of information. I'll have a report to you by Friday.

*   *   *

Lester spent a great deal of time studying the pictures. He surveyed the woman even more closely than his son. Her breasts must be at least a DD cup and probably a 34-inch rib cage, he thought. She had a heart-shaped ass, and the figure of a Stradivarius violin. Lester could see why his son would be attracted to a female who seemed to have a great tan, but it was more likely she was of mixed ethnicity or from the Middle East.

The next Monday, he sat with Bob Canton watching snippets of film of a well tanned and voluptuous black haired female. In several frames, she was with a handsome, pale-skinned man. 'Do you have their names?'

'They're registered as Mr and Mrs Joshua Daniel.'

'What else do you have?'

'Not much, but it appears they're scam artists. I should have more by the end of the week. I have a team working on it.'

'Good. Let me know as soon as possible.'

The call came at 4.30 Friday afternoon. 'Mr Wilson, there's a Ms Smith on the line. She won't tell me the nature of her call, but she insisted you'd be interested.'

'Thank you, Margaret. I was expecting a call, I'm sorry I didn't give you a heads up.'

The phone rang. He answered saying, 'Good afternoon Ms Smith, I've been waiting for your call.'

'This phone can't be traced and my voice is scrambled,' she said.

'I didn't plan to trace your phone, but of course, our conversation is being recorded.'

'Not a problem,' the mechanical voice said. 'Five million in small bills. How soon can you have the money?'

'The total isn't a problem but the small bills are. It'll probably take me several weeks to do that, but there are two other issues.'

'The originals is one, what's the other?'

142

'All the copies. How can you assure me that I'll get the originals and copies?'

'It's an age-old problem of trust,' the voice said. 'I'll rely on you not to call the police and you'll expect me to give you all the originals and copies.'

'I'm afraid there's not much trust on my side. After all, you're the one who has created this situation.'

'I believe it was your son.'

'Little lady, we're off the subject. I'm not going to give you any money without some assurance the tapes you have will never show up again.'

'The only assurance I can give you is my word.'

'On the basis of what's happened so far, your word isn't very good.'

'My only alternative is to reveal the pictures of your son to the media.'

Lester thought for a while. There might be a way to trick the con woman. 'OK, give me two weeks and I'll have the money.

'Good, I'll contact you two weeks from today and make exchange arrangements.' She hung up.

Lester sat in his room, rapidly reading a file Bob Canton had provided.

Looking up, he asked, 'Is it possible for you to pick her up?'

'You mean kidnapping?'

'Let's call it detaining her long enough for me to talk with her.'

'I'm not willing for my people to detain anyone without their permission.'

'Is it possible for you or your men to lead me to Mrs Daniel or Lessie Bunco?'

'We can do that.'

The next day, a white Ford SUV driving along Michigan

Avenue stopped just in front of a shapely female walking near the kerb. Two men jumped out and pulled her into the van, placed duct tape over her mouth, put a black bag over her head, secured her wrists, and drove to the Chicago Hilton hotel's parking garage. She struggled the entire time. The van stopped, she was hustled into an express elevator, taken to room 1069, and placed on a chair.

A deep, calm voice said, 'Ms Lessie Bunco, if you promise not to create a scene I'll have the bag and tape removed so we can talk. Nod your head if you agree to my request.'

She nodded her head and the two men removed the bag and tape. Sitting directly across from her was a man probably in his late forties or early fifties, attractive, with greying hair, wearing a black charcoal suit with a blue shirt and a power red tie. His arms rested on the arms of a sofa.

'You can leave now,' he told the men.

'Who are you and why have you brought me here?' she asked, her voice intense.

'I think you know who I am and why you're here. Do you recognise this room?

'You're Owen's father, you've kidnapped me to insure getting all the videos and pictures, and I have no idea what or where this room is.'

'This is the room where you fucked my son, after you seduced him.'

'Hotel rooms all look alike.'

'I can see why Owen was smitten by you.'

'What did you say?'

'I said you're beautiful.'

'You brought me here to tell me that?'

'No, I came to make love to you.'

'What?' she asked, looking shocked.

'I fell in love with your pictures.'

'You couldn't see my face.'

'I didn't have to.'

'It's not going to happen.'

'Why not? Isn't it worth five million dollars?' he asked, pointing at a stack of brief cases.

'That's the money?'

'That's the money. It's yours with two conditions.'

'What are they?'

'Joshua brings the camera and any copies here, and you make love with me.'

'That's all?'

'That's all.'

She looked befuddled. 'What's the trick?'

'No trickery, no conspiracy, no scheme. I just want you to fuck me as well as you did Owen.'

'How well did I fuck him? Did he tell you?'

'He said you were wonderful and made him feel like a man. I want to feel that way. That's my offer. Are you willing to go to bed with an old man, to make me feel special?'

She looked at him and at the briefcases. 'Let me see what's in the briefcases.'

'Do you want to inspect them all?'

'No, I want to see the third one from the left.'

Opening it, he showed her the money.

She looked at stacks of $20 and $50 bills. 'Take a stack from the bottom and thumb it for me.'

He flipped the bills like a deck of cards in front of her face. 'Satisfied?' he asked.

'Looks good to me and so do you. You're much better looking than your son. Untie me so we can get started.'

Lessie surveyed him as he took the case back to the wall. She noted he had a nice body; wide shouldered, slender, muscular and tall.

He removed the plastic restraints, took her in his arms, kissed her softly, smelled her perfume, and heard her heart beat. He whispered in her ear, 'I've been dreaming of this moment since I saw the first picture.'

He's a perfect gentleman. This may not be so bad, she thought, not responding to his kiss.

Kissing her ear, her neck, her collar bone, he took her in his arms, pulling her close to feel her full breasts against his chest. With his hands on her ass, he pulled her softness into his hardness.

'I can tell you're ready,' she said, grabbing his ass and grinding her loins into him. She kissed him, feeling his smooth lips on hers, smelling his expensive cologne, and tasting his Crest toothpaste. The kiss lasted a long time and she didn't resist when his tongue probed at her teeth and entered her mouth. It was as though electricity surged from her mouth to her breasts and clit; she was excited.

He moved his hands to her bra strap. With the dexterity of a card sharp, he unfastened the four hooks and eyelets through her blouse.

You're good,' she said, standing back, pulling her blouse to her waist, allowing the bra straps to slide off her shoulders, and removing the cups from beneath her breasts.

'They're magnificent. May I?' he asked, reaching for her.

'For two and a half million each,' she said, smiling and holding them for him, wanting him to touch them.

'A bargain at any price,' he said, running his hands along the side of each one.

She was pleasantly surprised because he didn't attack her as most guys did, including Joshua. The smoothness of his hands caused her to shiver when he bent forward and tenderly kissed each tingling nipple.

'Do you mind if I take off your skirt?' he asked in his deep, resonating voice.

'Help yourself,' she said nonchalantly, and raised her ass to allow the garment to be removed. 'Take the thong too.'

Lester placed his thumbs between her waist and thong and pulled it slowly to the floor. When he rose, he stopped and kissed her cleanly shaved pubic region.

'That tickles,' she said, surprised at the manner in which

146

he behaved.

Stepping back, he said, 'You're one of a kind. Would you turn around slowly?'

She performed a pirouette, slowing at each profile and shaking her firm, upright breasts, and wondered why she felt the need to display her assets so sinuously.

He took her in his arms, kissing her with his tongue swarming hers.

Again, she was shocked by the effect and she became more eager.

The kiss lasted a long time. His hands slid down her back to her ass, which he fondled. Then, without a word, he picked her up, carried her to the bedroom and laid her on the bed. He undressed.

Resting on an elbow, she watched him meticulously remove his clothes and drape them over a chair. When he removed his shirt, she was struck by the thatch of brown and grey hair coving his chest, and found the rest of his body to be the same. The removal of his shorts revealed a long, hard, curved cock. 'Very nice,' she said, rolling on her back, spreading her arms and legs in welcome.

He stood looking at her. 'I fell in love with your body and with you,' he said, quietly and seriously.

'I can believe the first but not the second statement. You're just a dirty old man who wants to get his rocks off.'

'We'll see,' he said, pouring a strongly scented lotion over her upper body. He knelt behind her head and, with the hands of a masseuse, massaged her face, her neck, her chest, and her stomach. Returning to her breasts, his hands circled them several times before concentrating his touch on her nipples, while he kissed her face, eyes, ears, neck, throat, and finally lips. His tongue gently explored her mouth.

Lessie wasn't used to this type of treatment even from Joshua, and despite her mental resistance her body responded to his tongue in her mouth, and the pleasant pressure on her breasts and nipples; she was awakened to

147

her desire.

Leaning forward, he took a nipple into his mouth and continued to fondle the other with his hand. He held her areola loosely while running his tongue up and down, from side to side, and in circles. After a minute he shifted breasts.

Pleasure built within her. First his kisses, then the warmth and scent of the massage oil stimulated her, but her arousal increased rapidly as he sucked first on one and then the other nipple. His head went back and forth between breasts and her determination not to react to him faded and she writhed under the invigorating onslaught.

While sucking on one breast, he slowly moved his hand to circle her belly button, and then to caress the area around her pussy. Brushing his hand back and forth across her pussy lips caused her to sigh. His finger slipped up and down her slit several times before inching into her. His finger expertly curled along the upper inside of her pussy and massaged the area as hard as he could.

Her resistance to his actions melted away as he stroked her G-spot. She arched her back and moaned long and hard. 'Damn it, you're not supposed to be this good.'

He removed his finger, sought and found her clit. Softy and slowly, his finger circled her love button, before fondling it in all directions.

His touch triggered an involuntary flood of pleasure from her clit, to her core, and to her brain. She moaned and groaned, she arched her back, she wiggled under him, and reached for his cock just above her head. She pulled him into her mouth, sucking.

He fell to her body, thrust his head between her legs, and his mouth replaced his finger on her clit and enthusiastically licked, bit, and sucked the most sensitive place in her body.

She spit him out. 'Your cock I want it in me. Give it to me,' she cried.

He didn't respond; instead, he continued his assault on her clit.

She went ballistic under him. Moving in all directions at the same time, she screamed, 'Stop, stop, stop, it's too much. I can't stand it.'

He switched positions while putting on a condom. Kneeling between her legs he slipped his thick cock into her pussy.

Joined, they groaned together.

She humped him. Over and over again she pushed herself up and down his shaft, pulled back and did it again and again until she screamed, 'Fuck me!'

He systematically stroked her while using his thumb to knead her clit until she climaxed in another frenzy of movement.

She felt so good it hurt. He continued stroking her until she was in an almost constant state of bliss. Finally, she felt him swell and harden. With one last thrust, warm fluid jettisoned into her and caused her to erupt. At last, they lay cuddled in each other's arms, enjoying the ecstasy of sexual pleasure.

Lessie snuggled up to Lester and fondled his crotch as they flew to St Louis, Illinois in his private plane.

Five briefcases of cash and one containing a digital video camera, several DVDs, CDs, and photographs were stored in the plane's hold.

'Are you going to miss Josh?' he asked, kissing her on the cheek.

'Not as long as I have you. He's part of my past. You're my future.'

'Are you going to miss the lifestyle?'

'No, I never liked it.

'Do you think you'll like being married?'

'With you, yes.'

'Good, because our blood will be drawn at the terminal. We'll pick up the licence tomorrow, and we'll be married in three days. The three days we have to wait will be the beginning of our Hawaiian honeymoon, which won't conclude until the end of the month.'

'I love you,' she said, standing and slithering out of her clothes. 'Are you a member of the Mile High Club?'

The Puzzle of Natalie X
by Cèsar Sanchez Zapata

The name Scab suited the dodgy bugger. Moreover, he fit to a T the description the aging strip club owner had slipped me the night before. Sometime after midnight, when the joint was just revving up its gears, I arrived outside the massage parlour he was known to frequent. The roads were surprisingly quiet for those parts, save for the pack of chavs hanging at the bus stop, drinking cheap cider and passing around a spliff. A uniformed constable strolled along the park across the way, expanding and collapsing his ASP baton, stealing furtive glances at the crew from the corner of his eyes.

Truncheon or not, still five against one; the bloke wasn't mental.

True to form, Scab was wearing a maroon leather jacket and black denims; he had stringy orange hair mopped sloppily on his head, and a tattoo on his neck of an eagle with its talons bared. He was precisely where the old girl said I'd find him, on a dark alleyway off Drake Street in Rochdale.

I didn't count on collaring him with his trousers down, though. And his stalk hilt-deep in a young redhead with skin so white it was nearly translucent.

He had her pinned against the wall, boosting his prick inside her like a battering ram, his mouth clamped on her big, hard teats. For her part, the girl showed every sign of being utterly enthralled with the pounding; she bucked back

151

maniacally, gasping up a storm comparable to a freight train, and had her eyes screwed tightly shut. She couldn't be a day older than 19; still she had the business down to an art. Made me wonder how long she'd been turning tricks.

I sneaked up on them easy as pie. The way they were getting on like a house on fire, I doubt even an earthquake could've slowed them down.

'Hallo, hallo. Beg your pardon, chaps.'

He whipped about, low and fast, the sign of a man born of the streets, going for the razor he kept tucked neatly in his inside pocket. I swung my open hand down against his wrist, then seized him by the neck tight enough to get his attention. Funny thing, me thinking about Peters at that exact moment. If he'd been alive, he'd have loved me getting my hands dirty. That was always his specialty, after all; he derived some perverse pleasure from knocking a punk on his dome, enjoyed it thoroughly.

'Shut your mouth and listen,' I growled. 'If you make me reach for my badge, things will go much worse for you. If you make me reach for my pistol, all your problems cease to be. Understand?'

He nodded urgently, already turning blue. I thrust him back against the concrete building. He doubled over, sputtering, choking. The girl, however, remained calm and collected, not so much as a flinch. She hadn't even made an effort to cover herself up. Her breasts were still rippling with each breath, covered in a sheen of his sweat. In another time and place, by George; she looked ripe for a good ride, that one.

'Did you miss the part where I was a cop?'

She grinned, lazily, properly pleased with herself. 'But I've done nothing wrong, officer. Well, a quick, consensual shag in public. Naughty, naughty me.' She curled her red, luscious lips on the tip of her finger. 'Perhaps I can pay my fine now – if that suits you.'

'What is it, then, eh? What are you on – Vicodin,

codeine, maybe some nose powder? Surely, I won't find any on your person when I search you. No, I'm certain you have a prescription for all that, yeah?'

A stitch of hesitation flashed quickly across her expression. She glanced at Scab, then back at me, her entire demeanour reprogrammed in an instant. I kept my face hard, eyes set, and lips pulled taut. Without further ado, she packed her tits back in the baby blue vest top, and twisted the skirt over her tail end.

'Right. Go on, get lost. It's your lucky day.'

She scampered off, heels clacking on the pavement, her arse tickling as she disappeared round the corner of the liquor shop.

Scab flattened his back against the wall, steadying his breathing. His pants were bunched around his Rushers and his short, thick knob hung flaccid on his leg. He was all sken-eyed, seemed positively scared out of his wits. Hard to believe he'd once been a member of the East Tyrone Brigade, the paramilitary group waging hell from Northern Ireland during "the Troubles". Those blokes were hardened animals, ready and willing to die for their cause; this nutter was a bloody muppet.

'Lift your knickers, daisy. I've no use for that mouse diddy.'

He raised his trousers. Then he fished out a cigarette, but his hands were shaking so bad he had trouble lighting it. When finally he did, I'd got my mad up proper, and was breathing down his neck.

'Hear me good. By reputation, you're about as bright as a beach ball, so I'll talk slow. I'm not gonna shake you down if you tell me what I need to know. Don't speak yet. Nod if you comprehend what I'm saying.' He did. 'That's a good monkey. I'm told you run a stable of kerb crawlers on Deeplish and Milkstone. Keep your alans on, that's not why I'm here. You're a small-timer, mate - four, maybe five cutties on your payroll. But you do some scouting work, too, isn't that right? The big houses call on you whenever they're seeking out new blood; you've an eye for fresh talent, they say. As a result, you know their operation. Intimately.'

'Is the GMP planning a raid on the Big Three?' He scoffed, shaking his head. 'Them girls are the furthest thing from stupid, lad; they've covered their arses. Sitting pretty on dirt dossiers for every chief constable in England. Photographs, recordings, security tapes – the works.'

I shuffled closer, balling my fists. He cowered; his hands shot up in defence.

'Mind yerself is all. You'd have to be a right looper messing with those birds.'

'That's not my play,' I said. I handed him a ripped sheet of paper with a single name scrawled on the front. He laughed as he read it, smarmy little twit. He shot his eyes up at me, then, grinning like a wild dog off his leach.

'What d'you want with her, then, Inspector? Bring her in for questioning? Official police *business*?'

The look I gave him about made him wet his keks.

'Let me a make a call,' he said.

A tiny bell rang in the corridor just before the golden elevator doors slid open, and out stepped the woman who called herself Natalie X. To describe her as exquisite would be admitting there were no words in the Queen's English to truly express her beauty. She was as ravishing a creature as ever walked the Earth. Percolated, actually, on four-inch stiletto heels. Sylphlike and yet built as an hourglass. A posh, classy bird with a body that could make a man bite his tongue clean off. I almost forgot she was the most expensive escort in all of Manchester.

Inside the dark suite, I stood in a corner and watched her approach through the open doorway. She was younger than I'd imagined, yet she moved with an air of confidence far beyond her years. She moved, well, like sex incarnate. Like a woman who'd found a fortune between the curves of her

154

thighs, as a consequence of which, her every muscle stirred with lascivious intent, with the sole purpose of seduction and lust.

There'd always been business in knobbing, I suppose. No shortage of customers. These days, it was a thriving industry enterprise. The right people, with the right brains, could make a fortune in that racket. From what I understood, this woman was worth more money than I'd see in my entire lifetime; not all of it made on her back, but all before the age of 26. For some people, though, money isn't enough reason to keep a good thing going. Scab said she was poised to retire.

She paused in the doorway, sheathed in penumbras. I could see her face very clearly from where I was, though, and it never faltered; she showed not an ounce of insecurity. Right from the start I knew she was cold as steel.

I flipped the light switch, and slipped from my nook. Her eyes squinted a bit, readjusting, then she glanced around until she spotted me.

'Forgive the theatrics,' I said. 'Hope it hasn't turned you off any.'

'You wanted to inspect the goods?'

'I enjoy making an entrance.'

'As do I,' she said, her voice all silk and lace.

I moved to her, as she slipped off her coat. My fingertips grazed her shoulder blades and the soft flesh of her neck. My nose drew in the soft fragrance of her perfume.

'Would you care for some Champagne, Natalie?'

She licked her lips, seductively. 'I love a man who can treat in style.'

I paid close attention to her body gliding throughout the suite, her marvellous legs and that shapely arse confined by her dress. I rushed the glass of bubbly to her and we peered at one another over the fizz. Her eyes packed more sex than most women's entire bodies can sustain. Her thin fingers wrapped around my wrist, leading me down to the couch

155

beside her.

'You know my name,' she said. 'That's a trifle unfair given I don't know yours.'

'Peters,' I answered. 'Mr Peters.' She showed not a jot of recognition, not a wince of familiarity. Of course, Peters wouldn't have used his real name. He was smarter than that, at least. Or perhaps she was simply one hell of an actress.

She lifted her glass once more. 'It's always a thrill to have a client ask for you by name. Except I don't believe we've ever met, have we?'

'No,' I said, all at once, feeling hot and frisky. Her body gave off so much warmth, and her eyes, those damn, wicked eyes. 'You were very highly recommended.'

'Oh. Then I mustn't disappoint.'

She suddenly jolted off the couch and to her knees between my legs. Her hands moved quickly up my thighs, converging centrically. She had my belt off and trousers down in a heartbeat, and was scooping my prick out with her lips. She buried her head in my lap, swallowing my cock into her mouth. Enveloping my root in what was quite frankly a sauna with its dial turned to hell, moist and hot as an inferno.

She went about her work, skilfully, with malice aforethought. Once I could take not another flip of her tongue, I ordered her to her feet.

Since my first time with a pro when I was still a teenager, I'd never shaken the notion that all whores were frigid, that their desensitized hearts iced them over. Not her, not Natalie X; she attacked me as much as I did her. She tilted her face closer to mine and, never taking her hand off my pecker, she kissed me, barely touching my lips but touching them in a way that was profoundly tender. I don't remember if I pulled away to gauge for a reaction, or if it was her, surprised by her own nerve. Neither of us spoke, that's the point; we were both shaken up. I kissed her the second time, sure as hell, and bit the nape of her neck, her earlobes, her shoulders. My one hand overflowed with her soft, flowing hair, while the other held her arse firmly and pulled her tighter. I could feel the hot lips of her cunt against my erection. She shifted higher a bit, so my prick caught under the hem of her skirt, bundling it around my shaft as she settled back. Now the tip of my cock was flush upon the damp material covering her pussy. She moaned into my mouth, scalding breaths slithering into my throat, as she reeled her hips fervently against me. With a single finger, coating it in her own juices, she pulled the panties aside.

I kissed her so viciously there wasn't a chance her lips wouldn't bruise. I tugged the straps of her dress down off her arms, huddling her tits up and lathering one with scattered kisses, then the other. Our panting and moaning echoed off the walls of the room, creating that symphony of sounds which is sweetest to the ears. I kept kneading her breasts with my hands, and tugging the length of my prick on her creamy twat.

When she most wanted it, yet least expected, just when she'd given up on the possibility of holding out long enough to have me inside her, I plunged it into her cunt, all the way in, and she cried out with pleasure. A single stroke, a brutal thrust, and she was coming. Who can figure how we went about it, but next thing I knew, we'd rid ourselves completely of our clothes. I picked her up and, with my stalk still throbbing within her, I ambled around the room, stopping here and there, fucking her to that point of mutual explosion, then licking off the fuse before we could burst.

I carried her into the next room where we tumbled on the bed. Then we were off to the races, arses shaking frenetically, pelvises smashing and grinding. She was screaming my ear off at the end, digging her nails into my buttocks as the rest of her went stiff and rigid. I was hilt deep when I finally came off; I'd never be able to pull it in time, so I tried nuzzling in even deeper between her legs. I gave her all I had, every last drop.

She was whimpering seconds after, yet when I tried to dismount, she urged me not to take it out. Bit longer. She said she liked the way it vibrated, trembled inside as it was wilting. I stayed as long as she wanted, then I rolled on my back.

I don't know how long I had my eyes closed. When finally I opened them, though, I was alone on the bed. With that cold, empty feeling I get curdling in my stomach whenever things have gone to shit.

'What are you casting about for, inspector?'

She was standing above me.

With my pistol aimed at my chest.

I startled awake, tearing the sheets from my legs. She squared her knees, locked her elbows, good balance, solid posture. She'd fired a gun before, no two ways about it.

'Don't look so shocked,' she said. 'It's an occupational hazard. I can smell a cop a mile away. You all exude a certain stench.'

'Brilliant. A whore I can track from ten miles. Even one as sophisticated as you. Even one who handles management and bookings for all the high-end escorts in the city.' I cleared my throat, trying my best to stay calm with a standard issue pointed at me. 'A property tycoon's daughter, however, is a little harder to spot.'

Her eyes grew wide, hit like a ton of bricks.

'Lass, I do this for a living.' I sat up against the headboard, crossing my arms. 'I didn't see it earlier, because the light out there is so dim. But you have different coloured eyes. One's blue and the other hazel. A condition called *Heterochromia Iridium*, if I'm not mistaken. *Very* rare, indeed. Inherited from a parent.'

She shifted her feet sluggishly, took a stumble back. Her calm veneer was dissipating rapidly. I'd knocked her out of focus; she was on the defensive now, and that's typically when mistakes are made. I swung my legs over the side of the bed and stood.

'Only one man I know has the same condition, and that got me thinking. Why would a woman in the prime of her life, successful and rich, suddenly terminate an operation as lucrative as this? Criminality notwithstanding.'

'A *thousand* reasons.'

'Perhaps. But none as convincing as love, Ms Carter. *Brigitte* Carter, I presume?'

She didn't respond, but her silence was all the answer I needed, and by then, I was close enough to take the gun if I had to. Close enough to reach out and touch her. Grab her and pull her against me. Her breasts were lush and her nipples rosy and pert. I could still taste her on my tongue, and feel her quim tugging on my cock.

'It was never about money for you,' I said. 'Your father has enough to buy up all of Blackpool. You were bored. You wanted your kicks. Be an entrepreneur. See how far you could take it. And now you're getting married. To the son of a Manchester city councillor, no less. The news is plastered all over the papers, though never with a picture of the blushing bride-to-be. You made sure of that.'

My prick had steadily been on the rise, and now was standing fully at attention in the space between us. The bright red crown pulsed an inch from her pussy. I don't think she could keep herself from looking down. A fire smouldered in her eyes, her luscious mouth parted.

'What'll you do next?' she asked.

'You're the one with the weapon.'

She shook her head. 'That makes two of us.'

She threw the gun on the bed and leapt up at me. I countered her momentum and had her wedged against the bathroom door, her legs curled high on my torso. There wasn't any time for foreplay, as hot as we both were. And there was no kidding ourselves that it'd last as long either. I hammered her to kingdom come, a blind, careening fuck of that sort that only works in dreams because nobody real can possibly stand that much savagery without feeling like a beast, and moments after her eyes lurched to the back of her head and her breasts melted like butter, I came for a second time.

She got down while I was still recovering. I felt her move around behind me, and my instincts took over. I swung my body left, dodging low. My wrist caught with a clatter, a searing pain ran up my arm. It took just another moment for my head to get it. I was chained, handcuffed to the door handle. She was pointing the gun at me again.

'Is this some bloody fetish trip you're on?'

'I know why you're here,' she said, voice slightly shaking. 'Detective Peters ... He was your friend.'

My teeth clenched automatically. 'He was my partner.'

'No! He was a blackmailer and a crook! He was a *murderer*!'

Just like that, it clicked; the whole damn thing that had eluded me for days during my investigation of Peters' death. 'Blackmail, of course! He found you out, realised who you were. You couldn't have your soon-to-be father-in-law involved in this mess, not with the old chap shouting at the top of his lungs for social reform and a crackdown on brothel prostitution. Peters would have known that. He couldn't have afforded the girls otherwise; he had leverage. The two of you worked out an arrangement. He keeps quiet, you supply his fix.'

A renegade tear rolled down Brigitte's cheek.

'Tell me what happened.'

'It won't matter –'

'It will.'

Her hands trembled and the gun wobbled in her grip. 'You're a liar! You're a degenerate just like he was!'

I raised my hands higher, cutting straight into the air. The lass was fired up; if I didn't play things cool, I could kiss my arse goodbye. I lowered my voice, steadied the tone even and easy.

'I'm not, Brigitte. I'm nothing like Peters. But he *was* my partner. I have to know why he's dead. You can understand that, can't you?'

She looked away a moment, but only a moment, then she was back, straightening her shoulders and aiming the barrel clean at my temple. 'The girl I sent him called me in the middle of the night. He was drunk, being extra aggressive. She begged me to come over. I arrived just in time to see the shit hit the fan. He was strangling her – right there! On the bed; he was going to kill her! I jumped on his back and he flipped me over into the dresser. I think I passed out, I'm not sure. Gemma, that was the girl's name, she must've managed to get away and grab his weapon from off the nightstand.'

'She killed him in self-defence.'

'No, no. He killed *her*! He overpowered her. He beat her with the butt of his pistol until there was nothing left to beat. He beat her so bad her parents wouldn't have recognized her – if she'd had any to claim her body. Then that bastard, he turned on me. He hadn't had enough. You should've seen the smile on his mug, the sneer! His prick had got hard from the beating and he was holding it out to me – like a trophy!

'He smacked me across the cheek; I brought my knee up straight into his groin. The gun dropped out of his hands, just there, by the door. We both scampered for it; I nearly had it. He seized my ankles and tugged me back. I was so afraid, terrified. I kicked him with all my force, hit him on the head. I grabbed the gun, he launched himself at me …'

'And – you shot him.'

She was crying as the memories flooded back, her breasts shaking beautifully with each of her sobs, but then suddenly her eyes and jaw tightened and she lifted her chin, proudly. 'I'd do it again. In a heartbeat. That scum didn't deserve to live. He wasn't worthy of that badge.'

I didn't say a word. I'd known Peters all these years. I knew what kind of a man he was. He was a fine detective, but a lousy human being. I defended him when others

161

voiced derision. I enabled his behaviour by turning a blind eye. I lied at any inquest conducted by the Independent Police Complaints Commission. I was as much to blame for his death as I was for the young woman he'd killed.

It was at that exact second, not a second sooner, I realised I'd never considered Peters a friend. He was my partner, assigned by order; I'd always operated under the assumption that I owed him some stretch of loyalty. But when he died, I wasn't torn with grief, or motivated by rage. Even when I heard the call over the radio, walked on the scene and found him, bloodied and shot through the chest – there was no grief or sorrow. I sought his killer because that was my duty, piecing together puzzles is what I did. I figured he'd have done the same for me.

Brigitte grabbed her dress from the floor outside the bedroom and pulled it over her head. She fit it snugly on her gorgeous body, fit like a glove. I watched her in awe, with lust conquering each and every one of my senses. She slipped her feet into the stiletto heels and turned to leave, then had an afterthought.

'You seem to be a good cop,' she said. 'You were doing your job when you came here. Even when you fucked me, I think. For me, it's always been a job, this racket. Once in a while, though, the armour fissures a bit; something pierces the hard exterior, know what I mean? On those rare instances, it becomes a pleasure.' She bent down at the waist, setting my gun on the ground by her feet. 'Tonight was a pleasure, inspector.'

'I bet you say that to all the boys.'

She smiled wanly, and started back-tracking to the door. 'I'm getting married tomorrow. To a man I've come to love deeply. You'll be back on your shifts, and I'll be permanently off mine. You have two options here,' she said. 'I've no doubt you'll do the right thing.'

Then the puzzle that was Natalie X was gone.

For ever.

Damsel in Distress
by Troy Seate

The street looked like a movie set. Tumbleweeds had found homes in front of a gas station, the Sheriff's Office, and two other buildings that stood on opposite sides of the wind-swept, two-lane blacktop.

'The only way in hell Sara would stop here is if she was running on fumes or had to pee, or both,' Sam muttered, stepping out of his car. He wondered if the wind always blew like this. The decaying automobiles and a few scattered trailer houses strewn across the landscape were the only windbreaks in this sad and lonely place. Plus those four pitiful brick buildings on either side of the highway.

Sam shielded his face from the swirling sand and debris and walked into the Sheriff's Office. An officer with a crew cut and a thick neck looked up at him from behind a desk.

'I'm looking for Sheriff Layton,' Sam said.

The officer twisted his neck a half-turn. 'Sheriff!' he shouted out the side of his mouth. His head swivelled back and trained on Sam who tried to act nonchalant in the dismal two-desk office.

A tall, well-built man entered from a rear door. 'What's the problem?' he asked. His gunmetal grey eyes seemed to burn a hole through Sam.

Sam fished a typed letter from his pocket. He handed it to the man who studied the note and nodded sagely.

'Well?' Sam said.

'Well what?'

'You sent this letter about my wife.'

'Guess I did.'

Sam's mouth formed a begrudging, crooked smile. *He's going to play games with me. Drain it for all it's worth.* 'Look, sheriff, let's work this out so Sara and I can be on our way. If I could see her, I'd appreciate it.'

Layton smiled. 'Okay, Sam Bingham from Scottsdale. You can see her but first, I have a few questions.'

'Your letter said my wife was being detained for obstruction of justice. I tried to reach you by phone, but all I got was a recording.'

'Sara said you'd come.'

'Of course.' Sam was losing patience. 'Why didn't you let her call or pay a fine? Three days is a long time for a woman to be missing. I contacted the Highway Patrol two days ago.'

'Sorry for your inconvenience,' Layton said apologetically. 'Way out here phone service tends to be a crapshoot. I'll straighten it out with the Patrol.' He laid the letter on the thick-necked officer's desk. Sam noticed the deputy, or whatever he was, had been looking at a *Hustler* magazine. 'Now, about those questions.'

'What questions?'

'Would you like to have a seat, Mr Bingham?' Layton said.

'I'd like to see my wife.'

'Sure you would. But first, why would you let her drive across the desert alone? Lots of things can happen to a woman travelling alone.'

Sam sighed and shrugged his shoulders. 'She had a business appointment. I'm sure she told you that.'

'Yes, I guess she did mention that.'

'You haven't told me why she's being detained.'

'Do you believe in taking advantage of unexpected opportunities?' Layton asked.

Sam looked at the sheriff, then at the other man and

shuddered. Their expressions reflected anticipated humour awaiting a punch line.

'I think I'll make a phone call.' Sam took his cell phone from the clip on his belt and started to dial.

Layton slid next to Sam before he could react. He grabbed Sam's phone and tossed it to the seated officer who plucked it easily from the air. The officer grinned at his accomplishment and shoved the cell phone inside his desk.

Fear gripped Sam like a blow to the chest. He could smell the dried sweat in the creases of Layton's uniform and his onion-laden breath on his cheek.

'Now, wait a minute ...' Sam stuttered while horrible images assailed him. What if two prisoners had broken out and killed the real sheriff and deputy? What if two lunatics had escaped from an asylum, tortured and killed Sara? What if?

'Answer my question and we'll get this business over with,' Layton said, taking a step back. 'Do you or don't you believe in unexpected opportunity?'

What have they done to her? Sam's fear curdled his stomach, making him feel ill. 'I don't know. Maybe.'

'That's a pretty piss-poor response,' Layton breathed, 'but I guess it'll do.' He patted Sam on the shoulder. 'Since you cared enough about your wife to come for her, it'd be a shame to keep you apart any longer.'

Layton turned away and started toward the rear door. Sam momentarily considered reaching for the pistol in Layton's holster, but the man behind the desk had shown he was quicker than he looked.

If anything has happened to Sara or happens to me, the Highway Patrol knows about this place,' Sam said with a touch of bravado.

'Oh, really?' Layton said, turning and raising his eyebrows. 'That's not surprising seeing as how the patrolman for this part of the state is my cousin. He and I and Deputy Dawg here have a lot in common.' Layton continued toward the door while talking to Sam. 'Don't go getting yourself all worked up. We're just funnin' you. Gets pretty boring way out here in the sticks. Lots of people come through but not many single women. It's dangerous on these long stretches through the middle of nowhere, but we've taken good care of Sara.'

Sam looked past Layton and the deputy at the door in back where the cells must be.

'You can see her, but last time I checked, she was having a *siesta*, so wake her slowly. She's been pretty jumpy.'

'How about my phone?'

'Greg, let Mr Bingham have his phone and his wife's personals when we come out.'

Layton opened the backdoor. 'You coming?' he asked Sam.

Sam followed the sheriff to the connecting threshold. It was dark in the other room. He could only make out the bars on a few cells.

'Can you turn on a light?' Sam asked.

'Sara might not be quite ready for the bright lights.' Layton walked to a cell and put the key in the lock. The cell door groaned open.

'Then bring her in here,' Sam demanded.

'Who's running this place?' Layton said jovially. 'She's probably asleep. I'll stand with the door to the office open so you'll feel safe while you talk to her.'

'I'm not going in there. I can't see past the bars.'

'All right, ya big baby,' Layton teased and stepped into the darkened chamber. 'Mrs Bingham, your husband's here,' Layton said softly. 'Mrs Bingham? Time to rise and shine.'

A dim, dusty glow from the office shone through the bars. As Sam's eyes adjusted, he could only see a small bed covered with a rough blanket. 'Where is she?'

Suddenly, Sam's shoulder blades were jolted as he was forced forward from behind. Before he could get his momentum stopped, the deputy had shoved him into the unlocked cubicle. Layton quickly sidestepped Sam and rushed out of the small space, locking the cell door behind him.

'What the hell?' Sam rushed the bars. 'What are you pulling here?'

The silhouetted figures of the sheriff and the deputy stood on the other side of the locked cell. 'Yeah, Sara's been waiting for almost three days now,' Layton said cheerfully, his features masked in the dark haze within the chamber. 'She's been very cooperative.'

The deputy reached back and flipped a switch. The room lit up with the force of a thousand watts from overhead fluorescent tubes. Sam looked around the cells. There was but one other occupant. A woman in the next cell. She was standing with her back against the bars, on the opposite side of the cell, facing him. He first noticed the familiar almond shaped eyes and the unsightly strip of duct tape that covered her mouth. Then the fact that she was naked.

'Sara,' Sam said. At first, he thought she had her arms outstretched in some kind of crucifixion pose, but he soon realised her wrists had been lashed to the bars. He ran to the row of bars that separated their two cells. 'Sara. What have they done?'

A high-pitched giggle erupted from the deputy. 'Don't worry, Bingham. You'll get her back, eventually.' Layton and the deputy opened Sara's cell and stepped in. Layton held the woman's head and pulled the tape from her mouth as gently as possible.

'Sam!' Sara cried.

He gripped the bars, barely believing the scene of his naked wife between the two uniformed men.

'We get such a kick seeing the reactions when men reunite with their sweeties. How different all of you act.' Layton looked at Sam curiously. 'I guess the cat's got your tongue. Don't worry about Sara. We haven't hurt her. We've just been playing some parlour games, waiting for her beloved hubby to show. Greg and I have kept her nice and wet, but we've given her plenty of time off.' The two uniformed men studied Sam's face, their eyes dancing with mirth. 'We have to rest up between fucks. Sometimes for an hour or two, maybe, before we fuck her again.' Layton began to laugh. It was a small laugh at first, then it rumbled into a roar that echoed through the room of cells. It was the sound of a man enjoying a victory, a man no longer concerned about disturbing anyone's rest.

Layton unzipped his trousers and let them drop to the floor. Sam could see the sheriff had an erection inside his boxer shorts. Sara said nothing. Sam knew there was nothing she could say. What was going to happen would happen regardless of words.

'She's being awfully quiet now,' Layton said, 'but we've gotten a lot of grunts and groans out of her for three days and nights. The sheriff pulled down his boxers. His erection was sizeable. 'We just tied her up here for your benefit,' he continued. 'Mostly we've been fucking her on the cot or on one of our desks. This time, you can watch from the safety of your cell.'

Sam did watch as the sheriff slipped on a condom, stood in front of Sara and positioned her legs around his waist. The deputy held her ankles together so she would remain in place. Layton dropped her onto his cock. Sam couldn't see much except for the back side of the sheriff's drawn-up balls and his muscled butt cheeks tightening each time he thrust his cock inside Sara. The thick-necked deputy stood next to the participants. He was alternately squeezing Sara's tits and grinning at Sam, hoping for a reaction.

Sara's eyes were closed and she seemed to be gritting her teeth while the sheriff pumped away. Soon, it was Layton who groaned. His ass quivered as he dumped his load into the condom inside Sara's pussy.

Layton pulled away and let Sara's feet drop back to the cell floor. He patted her cheek. 'There,' he said. 'What was that Sara? About the 20th time? Who would have thought you could take so much cock in such a short period of time. I bet hubby over there had no idea.' He looked at Sam. A crafty smirk carved his mouth into a distasteful thing. 'You've got one sweet piece of ass here, Bingham. Lon and I truly appreciate your good taste in tits and pussy.' He pulled the condom off and tied a knot in it. His dick still dripped a last dollop of semen onto his rumpled boxers. 'Go get him, Lon,' Layton said to the deputy while he pulled up his clothes and tucked his dick and his shirttail back inside his pants.

Deputy Lon unlocked Sam's cage. 'Don't want no trouble from you,' he said as mean as he could muster. He took hold of Sam's arm and led him into his wife's cell. 'Guess what you get to do?' the deputy told him and started to giggle.

'That's right, Bingham,' Layton pronounced. 'We want to see *you* fuck your wife. Like I said, it gets kinda slow out here.' Layton and Lon backed away from the couple. The sheriff rested the heel of his hand on the butt of his pistol, menacingly.

'What's going to happen to us?' Sam asked.

'You do what we ask. Fuck your wife, and we'll let the two of you go.'

'I don't think I believe you, considering what you've done.'

Layton raised his hands. 'What have we done? We detained your wife until you came to pay her fine. She's not marked or bruised. There won't be any semen in her but yours. You want to know the truth, Mr Bingham? I think she's enjoyed the last three days even though she won't say so.' The sheriff's hand returned to his gun. 'If you want to get out of here, let's get this donkey show started.'

Sam dropped his jeans and briefs as ordered. 'I'm sorry about all of this, sweetheart. I guess I have to do what they say.' His penis did not show any interest.

'Untie Sara's hands, Lon.' Layton ordered. 'Sara, you get to fuck your husband now. He obviously needs a crank or two. You two can kiss and all that shit, if that's what it takes.'

Sara looked into her husband's eyes and something passed between them. She kissed him sweetly and reached down for his dangling cock. She massaged it until it came to attention.

Layton stepped up to look at Sam's dick. 'Damn, boy. That's pretty impressive, but I think I've got about an inch on you. That means I've been up inside your old lady farther than you ever have.' He belted out another raucous spate of laughter. 'Well, stick it in her, fuck-head.'

Sam lifted Sara so she could throw her legs around him the way she had been forced to do with the sheriff. He tried to make it quick for her while the law enforcement officers gaped. Finally, his cock spat its creamy fluid inside her. He lifted her so that she could stand.

'I think me and my deputy have been pleasing you better than what I saw in that little display, Sara. Maybe you'd like to stay with us and let hotshot here go on back to Scottsdale by himself.'

Sara finally spoke. 'Please let us go now. I've done everything you've asked. Please.'

The two uniformed men looked at each other. 'Pull up your pants, Bingham. Lon, fetch Mrs Bingham's things.'

The deputy soon returned with Sara's clothes. Her high-heeled business shoes and purse rested on top of the pile.

'I guess I don't have to make the speech about keeping this between you,' Layton said to the Binghams while they dressed. 'She's not injured. Your word against ours. No harm done, really. Wouldn't you agree, Mrs Bingham?'

'Just let us go. I promise we won't say anything.'

'That sounds just fine. Still need money for the speeding ticket, though. Can't be detaining people just for the hell of it, can we? Now get your yuppie butts on out of here.'

Layton looked at them as if nothing out to the ordinary had happened then said to Sam, 'Bet you won't let her cross the desert alone next time.'

When Layton was through with the Bingham's, Lon pulled Sara's car in front of the sheriff's office next to Sam's. 'You all try and be careful driving back,' Lon giggled. 'Watch your speed. The Highway Patrol's not as understanding as me and the sheriff.'

The Binghams drove their respective vehicles about a mile down the road beyond sight of the buildings, the decaying automobiles and the scattered trailers. They pulled off the road and climbed out of their cars. Sara sidled up to Sam. 'It's good to see you, Sam-Bam.'

They embraced for a long time. 'It's good to feel you, Sara the Terror.' Then a small giggle rose in Sara's throat. It became a chortle and finally a hearty laugh. Sam pulled her away and looked into his wife's almond eyes. He smiled back. 'I was really worried when that cocksucker of a sheriff threw me in that cell. I almost creamed in my jeans until I realised it was just a sex deal.'

'Can you believe it?' Sara exclaimed. 'Who would have ever thought my fantasy to get gang-banged by a couple of strangers would have come true like this, on my way to a meeting? I tried really hard to act like I despised it. The more I whined and cried, the better they fucked me.'

Sara looked at the low sun and brushed her long hair back from her face. 'They weren't very creative, though. Once I had to scream, "Please don't make me suck your dicks," before they got the idea. It was like Brer Rabbit begging not to be thrown into the briar patch. I think they were afraid I might retaliate by biting them off. Nothing but their cocks in my holes, although I'm sure they were convinced they were humiliating me. If they only knew that we haven't run across anything yet that we consider humiliating.' Sara laughed again at some recollection. 'You know why Lon didn't lay the wood to me while you were there?'

'Can't imagine,' Sam said.

'He has a little stubby dick he can barely get out from under his belly. Probably embarrassed to whip it out in front of you. I think the most fun I had was when they had me on the sheriff's desk and Lon got his couple of inches to stay in for a few strokes. I groaned for him and you know what he said? He said, "Suffer, bitch."'

Sam joined in on Sara's good humour. 'We should make a photo with our BDSM gang. Have somebody's prick shoved in your mouth and another one in your ass. Send it to them and write, *Wish you were here.*'

'They would probably think our debauchery was due to what they did to me,' Sara answered. 'I say, fuck 'em.'

'What about your meeting? Are you going to be in trouble?'

'I'll blow a couple of guys when I get back, and they'll understand that shit happens.'

'Let's get out of here. I want you to tell me more about Stubby and his pencil dick over a good dinner.'

Belly Dance
by Landon Dixon

He cut a mighty impressive figure galloping across the green lawn on his chestnut steed, decked out in a white Stetson and buckskin jacket, a pearl-handled Peacemaker slapping his thigh. Until I realised the elderly cowpoke was only ten yards away, and not getting one whit bigger.

Colonel Tilson T. Pickett trotted on to the patio aboard his miniature horse, slid off and grasped my hand, all five foot nothing of him. 'Dick Polk?'

'Yes, sir,' I replied, the quarter-pint pony sniffing my crotch.

The Colonel ambled over to a pitcher of iced tea sweating bullets atop a picnic table, reached up and took a swig straight from the source. 'Want you to find out who knocked up the missus,' he drawled.

'Vi Voom?'

He swung around, glinting at my navel. 'That's the filly.'

I gazed over the man's five gallon hat at his rambling Hollywood Hills ranch house, scowling. 'How 'bout I find the thief who stole her virginity, while I'm at it?' There were more oddballs in this town than in the Elephant Man's drawers. And they always seemed to call on me.

'Already got someone workin' on that one,' the Colonel snorted.

I nodded.

'She's pretty near four months along, I figure,' he reckoned.

'Maybe you're the hombre salted her eggs?'

His beady blue eyes went wistful as a sunset range of sage, his white cowcatcher trembling at the corners. 'Mister,' he gulped, 'my lil' pardner's been limper than Hoover's economic recovery plan these past six months. Nope, Vi's been gettin' her voom from some other coyote these days. And I want you to find the varmint.'

The Colonel had lassoed his millions churning out oaters in the silent era, when Hollywood was just a dusty corral of a town. He'd sold his movie studio just before the Crash, spent the next year buying up farmland dirt-cheap in the Salinas and San Joaquin Valleys. Now he owned more spreads than a madam, handled more vegetables than a coma ward.

He'd kept his hand, and other parts, in the flicker biz when he'd married struggling B-actress and gas jockey sweater girl, Vi Voom (aka Esther Rottweidler). They'd been hitched in '31, their marriage holding together for one-and-a-half years and counting now – an eternity by Tinsel Town standards.

I slipped past the guard at the back gate of Ace Studios with a ten-spot handshake, parked my flivver along the "Avenue of Stars". Vi Voom had profited handsomely from the giddy-up her husband's wealth and connections provided, because Ace was almost big time. Her dressing room was the last door at the end of the road, and it had the largest knocker.

The Colonel had told me he'd gotten the "good news" about his wife from Meyer B. Wallenstein, Ace Studios' tyrannical head and rumoured cross-dresser. Vi had spilled her guts when Wallenstein angrily confronted her about a perceptible belly bump she'd added to her act without his OK.

The Colonel didn't want Vi knowing he knew, so I eschewed her front door for the rear window. I waded into the gardenias and dahlias and pressed my pan to the pane. And my hat went airborne like in a Chaplin short.

'Jeepers peepers!' I croaked, staring directly into the stripped bare, super-voluptuous figure of Vi Voom. The doll was joyously bouncing up and down on some lucky stiff's thighs, in the cowgirl position, the biggest pair of jumblies I'd ever seen outside of a carnival cooch show bounding around on her chest in unmistakable glee.

The star of *Montana Mountain Woman* was even more va-va-voom in person. Her perspiration-slick hooters were creamy white enough to pour into a kitten's lap dish, her lust-distended nipples cherry red enough to guarantee her a lifetime membership in the Leon Trotsky fan club. The babe's cannonballs were catapulting up and down with a fearsome intensity, in rhythm to her rapturous ride, her long mane of wavy red hair flying right along, her eyes burning bright green as every flat-chested dame's envy whenever she popped them open.

I thumbed back my hat and made love to the glass, the gal's gyrating headlights scorching my glims through the gauze and lace window-dressing. She and her laid-low lover were grinding the legs off a black leather couch. I couldn't get a make on the man-trampoline, because his head was buried under the raised armrest closest to me, his body probably mopping the floor. All I could see was a pair of hands gripping Vi's waist; a waist, I noted briefly, that had some definite oomph to it – like there was a bun not doughed by the Colonel baking inside.

'Fuck, yes!' Vi shrieked through the clapboard and candy glass, riding roughshod over her lover's saddlehorn. She arched her back and neck and ran red-tipped fingers through her streaming ginger hair, her breastplates flopping up and down and all around like the Big One was only seconds away.

I snapped half the muscles in my neck keeping track of her billowing chest-pillows, my orbs pinballing right along with her jutters. She grabbed her dewy melons and tried to squeeze them. But even Primo Carnera hands wouldn't have been able to fully contain all that tumbling tit-flesh. I jerked my rod out of its buttoned-down holster and stroked like a studio sycophant, knowing the end was near.

'Fuck, baby! I'm coming!' Vi screamed with an abandon usually reserved for contract negotiations. Her body shook like a Long Beach tremor, boobs galumping their orgiastic delight.

I fisted as hard and fast as any Sharkey-Schmeling tilt, both my heads primed to explode.

Vi let out one final piercing bleat of ecstasy and then collapsed on top of her pinioned lover. They rolled over and spilled on to the floor in an avalanche of breast-meat. My trigger-hand froze on my shooter.

The bottom now on top was a woman! A lean-limbed, short-haired blonde with a thousand watt tan and a dime store face. She had a rig for pussyifying strapped to her peachy bottom, the rig holding the dong that had plunged Vi screaming over the slippery edge.

The two dames hugged each other, slapped their tongues together, Vi's bazooms burying the other doll's tipple-tits. I grunted, cocked my hammer again. There was no conceivable way the Colonel's wife had gotten her glow on this way. But that wasn't going to stop me from watching the passion play to its sticky conclusion.

His name was Haskell A. Long, but everyone called him "Hop". Because he was top bellhop at the Chateau Montrose, and because he sopped up beer like a bar rag, brewed it like a kegmeister. He was a long, skinny drink of brackish LA River water with oil-slick hair and a beak you could've used to pry open a grape Nehi.

'I don't got time for no two-bit gumshoes,' he snarled.

I grabbed myself a handful of brass-buttoned monkey suit and chest hair, slammed the guy into a potted plant. His pillbox cap came loose. 'I want to know if Vi Voom's been raising any ruckus out back – and with whom?'

Outside of the studio lot – and the spacious backseat of any Duisenberg roadster – the best place for the stars and starlets to horizontally align themselves, far from the telescopic glare of the press and their spouses, was the fern and flora-enshrouded back cottages of the Chateau Montrose. The beds were spacious and sturdy enough to accommodate warring gang-bangs, and the linen was steam-cleaned at least every other day. And anything else your heart desired, including room service, was just a Hop A. Long away.

'With "whom"?' Hop sneered. 'Pretty big word for a dick, ain't it?'

'Here's another one, sudsy: pro-hi-bi-tion.'

The guy's brow furrowed like Missouri farmland.

I gave him another shake, hard enough to jar his tongue loose this time. He let go with the spittle, confirming Vi's vivacity in the sack, naming practically the entire starting roster at Central Casting as her co-stars. The double-scoop doll obviously wasn't letting her husband's inflationary problems get her down any.

'Art Rentura, Tub Saunders, Dutch Fujita ...'

We were up to the T's, with no end in sight. 'OK, OK,' I groaned, figuring on the Colonel easily qualifying for my special bulk discount rate. Because I'd be racking up the hours from here to Encino chasing down joyriders. 'Just write me out a list.'

'I ain't got that much ink,' Hop protested.

I stuck him in behind the desk in his cubbyhole office/medicinal ale dispensary, and he made with the scribbling.

'And this is only a month's worth,' he cackled, shaking writer's cramp out of his wrist and handing me a phone book worth of names. 'That broad goes through –'

'Huh?' I interrupted. 'What'd you mean, "only a month's

worth"?'

He scrubbed the base of his beak with a nicotine finger, lifted a leg and eased out some barley in its gaseous state. 'I mean, Tit-tanic's only been starring at the cabins for maybe a month or so.'

I tossed the cast of thousands back at him. 'Then you can light the Olympic Torch with this kindling, because it's as useless to me as a liver is to you.'

If Vi was already four months into the baby-baking process, and Hop's dirty laundry list was only one month old, then, much like my last year's tax return, something didn't add up. I still couldn't pipe any chin music Vi's way, so I figured I'd question the one other person who might be able to supply me with some straight answers; the one person every actress confides in the most, and trusts the least – her agent.

Sid Wither's office was at the sun-baked, traffic-clogged corner of Figueroa and Sunset. A white-thatched gnome of a man with black-rimmed specs housing lenses lifted straight off the Mount Wilson telescope, Sid had represented everyone from Sparky the Wonder Lizard to Tyrone Power in his less than illustrious career. Stars ascending, and stars descending. Vi Voom still hadn't gotten too big for him.

'Don't even ask me, Dick,' he pouted, pulling a black cigar that should've been labelled "Nautilus' out of his wrinkled puss. 'The agent-client relationship is –is … sacred, like … a Tinker to Chance to Evers double-play.' Sid was a Cubs fan.

'Meyer B. Wallenstein told me she's in the family way,' I stated bluntly.

'What!? He did!?'

'Sure he did. Now let's talk testicles, Sid. Whose flesh pony has Vi been saddling the past four months or so?'

He slammed a spotted hand down on his blotter, his face turning a dangerous shade of yellow. 'That loudmouth *dummkopf* Wallenstein! I'll murder the bum!' He popped out of his chair, stumped to the door.

'It's a long walk to Ace Studios, Sid.'

'I – I got a call to make!' he blustered, waving his stogie around like the sword of justice. 'Private!'

He shuffled off stage right, muttering a good line about how he was going to give Wallenstein a piece of his mind. We both knew he couldn't afford it. So, while Sid was off phoning some studio hack for directions on handling a nosy dick with a snootful of dynamite, I popped the lock on his wooden filing cabinets with a hairpin and extracted a folder marked "Voom". I quickly sifted through the forty-page contract with Ace Studios, my eyeballs rolling to a stop when they hit Article 51, Clause 5 (b) (iii).

The case broke like a pregnant dame's water.

'Suck my tits! Suck them!' she screamed.

'OK, OK! Keep your panties on – for now,' I grunted.

I had my hands full, trying to grasp Vi Voom's naked juggernauts in Cottage 104 of the Chateau Montrose backlot. There was breast-flesh spilling out all over the place. My mitts have been known to overflow frying pans, but in this situation they weren't nearly big enough, my fingers long enough, to span the glowing globes that Vi had to offer.

She was bare from the bulged waist up, her head thrown back and her hands throttling my shoulders as I hefted her mammaries as best I could. The sweat on my hairy palms finally helped glue my meathooks to her smooth, heated knockers, give me some traction. I dipped my coconut down and licked an upthrust jutter.

'Fuck, yes! That's the way!' Vi hollered.

I swirled my wet tongue all around the puffy, pebbled base of one of her peaks, then the other, squeezing the doll's dirigibles, pulling muscles in my shoulders and arms, and groin. I sealed my lips around a rubbery poker and sucked on it.

'Suck my tits!' Vi bellowed again.

I nursed on her other nipple. Then bounced my conk back and forth, licking, sucking, biting. Her eyes wept tears and my face sweat, my arms quivering like Erich Von Stroheim's barber, as I grappled with the gal's overstuffed meatloaves. They were every bit as tender and tasty as they looked – soft, silk-textured udders with succulent dimples.

She squirmed around in my arms, and hands. I wrestled her down onto the bed.

'Fuck me!' she howled.

I let her boobs sprawl loose long enough to tear open my trousers. She shimmied out of her skirt, jugs trembling delightfully. I cocked back my hammer.

And she suddenly stopped me.

'Got a rubber?' she asked matter-of-factly, despite the frenzy in her emerald eyes.

'Uh, no, I don't,' I lied, testing the doll's limit, the theory I had.

I'd been able to get this far with the lusty-busty by merely claiming to be a fan and fellow actor ("man holding sanitational urn" in her last sand and sandal epic, *Desert Dunes*) and buying her a drink in the bar. But now she was blocking homeplate.

She shoved me back, rummaged around in her purse.

I was good to go deep in seconds. Even had a choice of colours.

I rammed her like the *Lusitania*. We both groaned. I gripped the pointed tops of her heaving buoys and pumped with all the steam I could muster.

'Harder! Faster!' she demanded, wet as coastal Oregon, gripping as a Hammett detective yarn.

I frantically pistoned away inside her, riding her wallowing, sweat-slick breasts with my hands, sucking up a mouthful of nipple whenever I could. The bed creaked, my back broke, and Vi wailed sweet, hot, profane ecstasy into my face. I ladled all the shuddering tit I could up to my mouth and sunk my teeth in, pumping like a Signal Hill oil well, bucking with my own orgasm.

The clinging calm after the sexual storm was for ever shattered when I casually remarked, 'You know, Vi, you're not pregnant. You're just fat.'

That gunshot-like crack was her indignant hand striking my impertinent kisser.

See, you can be a lot of things in Hollywood – gold-digger, muff-diver, serial adulteress – but one thing you can't *ever* be if you're a screen siren, is fat.

Vi Voom was a big-boobed betty with the big appetites to match. Which is why she had a clause in her Ace Studios contract that forbade her from tipping the Toledos at over 130 pounds, on penalty of termination. The only exemption being if she was "with child".

So when Meyer B. Wallenstein had confronted her about her tummy roll, Vi had played the baby card. And been messing around like a casting couch repairwoman ever since to make the claim credible. Plus, it was good exercise.

The Colonel took the news with a horse laugh and a tip of the Stetson to his wife's ingenuity. He wanted a passel of young 'uns, sure, but he damn well wanted his own brand on 'em.

Who Pays?
by JR Roberts

My boyfriend, Darren, and I are heading out of town on the
M5 South. It's September and there is a spell of late warm
weather, and we don't want to waste it staying in town. We
are totally out of cash so we decide to just drive down to the
coast in his battered old car and mess about at the beach. I
laze in the passenger seat of the car enjoying the sun's rays,
magnified by the window, as they pass through my thin
white cotton shirt and warm my skin. My eyes are closed
and I'm totally relaxed. Darren has some strange
instrumental music playing which sends me further into a
dazed state.

I sense him taking quick looks at me and don't open my
eyes as I ask, 'You OK?'

'Yeah, just admiring the view.'

I smile. We are still in the phase where our conversations
to each other are never far from a sexual suggestion. The
relationship will probably end when this early shagathon
time cools off; he's not long-term material. He's much more
sexually experienced than I am and in the couple of months
we have been together he's opened my eyes to a whole new
world of delights. He's rough and ready; not the type you
take home to meet the parents. Sex is like that too; he likes
to be rough, fast and hard, and he's always ready.

'Keep your eyes closed.'

'Why, what are you doing?'

I tense slightly and become fully awake but keep my eyes

closed. I feel his left hand brush my chest as he fumbles to undo my shirt.

'Darren, no, someone might see.'

'Shh.'

It takes him a minute with his left hand to undo the buttons to my waist while he holds the wheel with his right. Then I'm aware of him pulling the shirt open so my naked breasts are on show and I instinctively wriggle down in the seat to hide myself from other motorists. His fingers now stroke my breasts, flicking at a nipple with a fingertip until it responds and hardens, sending pleasant sensations through my body. I feel the tell-tale tingling between my legs and I know I'm responding. I'm afraid someone might see but, at the same time, hugely excited at being exposed.

I feel him fumble with the button of my jeans.

My eyes fly open and I grab his hand. 'No, Darren, that's too much!'

'Lie still or you'll put me off my driving.'

'That's a joke, isn't it? Your mind's not on it now.'

'Shh, undo it. I can't do it with one hand.'

I sit back and close my eyes again. This is dangerous but I still want to let him do it.

'Good girl.'

He pulls down the zip. 'Now ease them down a bit.' As I do, he's forcing his hand down the gap that's created between the jeans and my crotch and I feel his fingers press against the tight material of my underwear. There is a squelchy feeling.

'You love it, don't you, you sexy minx?'

How can I deny it when he's got the evidence right there at his fingertips?

He bypasses the tiny garment, roughly pushing it down enough to get access to my pussy. His two middle fingers hook into me in this strange fingering position and I hear the giveaway sodden sound as he pushes the fingers in as far as he can. This unusual position means his palm is in contact with my clit and I instinctively hold his wrist and push it hard against me and I hear him chuckle.

He takes the hint and rubs it firmly up and down. I gasp and strain to open my legs wider but can't, due to the confines of the jeans. Can I really be thinking of trying to have an orgasm in a moving car on the motorway?

Darren suddenly pulls his hand out and hisses, 'Get dressed.'

Oh no; I see a police patrol car ahead indicating for us to pull over onto the hard shoulder and I scrabble frantically to get my jeans up and button my shirt.

Before I've finished a police officer has stepped out of the car and is walking towards us. He indicates for me to lower the window and leans down with his hand resting on the roof to look in. 'And what are you two up to, then?'

My face has flushed scarlet and I take a hurried glance at Darren. He's got that boyish, innocent look on his face but he's not fooling anyone.

'I've been a few cars behind for the last mile or so and your driving has been erratic, sir. Would you both like to step out, please?'

More like erotic, I'm thinking! I gingerly step out of the car and Darren comes round from the other side. I glance at him and he gestures with his eyes towards my chest and, as I look down, I see I've missed a button on my shirt and the smooth valley of skin between my breasts is framed by the gap. I pull the shirt down to close the gap but too late; Mr Plod's seen it too. He raises an eyebrow and gives me a quizzical look and I blush to my hair roots. It's cooler outside the car and I'm aware of my stiffening nipples, knowing the rosy peaks will be showing through the thin cotton material of my shirt. Pulling it down tightly to close the gaping front is making it worse and I squirm uncomfortably under the gaze of the two men.

The officer is much older than Darren, maybe forties; he's thick set, broad-shouldered, whereas Darren has the thin, wiry frame of youth. Darren looks quirkily sexy when he's naked; a slim body, almost hairless chest, narrow hips and a long, rather slim cock that curves upwards when it's erect, as it often is when we are together.

The officer ends the silent moment as he begins to write on a form he has attached to a clipboard.

He's speaking to Darren. 'Name? Address? Can I see your licence, sir?'

He now goes on to explain the offence he is charging Darren with and we groan as he explains it is a £60 on the spot fine.

He looks up from his writing. 'Got a problem with that, sir?'

'Yeah. Ain't got no money, mate.'

'I'm not your mate. What about your girlfriend, I'm sure she can help you out?'

'Nah, she ain't got none either.'

'You've got a problem, then. Haven't you, sir?'

He stands and eyes us with his arms crossed over his chest, making me feel very inferior. He's about six two, hair cut very short, military style, dark but greying, an angular face. All the gadgets the police carry attached to their belts and waistcoats make him look very imposing. There is awkward silence again.

His gaze rests on me and he looks directly at my breasts. 'As I said, maybe your girlfriend could help you out as it appears she was part of the problem.'

What the hell is he suggesting? I want to cross my arms over my chest too.

I stare at Darren and he looks confused, not sure if he has understood what has been implied here. He looks at the officer. Man to man, they totally understand where this is going, and I shudder as I see Darren's features crease into a wicked smile and he gives the tiniest nod.

'Come on, babe?'

I'm still damp from my fingering in the car and my pussy

gives an involuntary jerk and I realise the thought excites me. I nod at Darren. No words are spoken but it's agreed, I'll pay the fine.

The officer speaks first 'Let's get you off this dangerous carriageway, sir. Miss, up the embankment, please.'

I think it's more dangerous up there!

I look up at the embankment; it's steep but certainly climbable. Much of it is covered in bramble bushes and small trees.

'Go on, you first.' The officer gestures to Darren to start walking. I expect him to take my hand to reassure me as much as to help me, but he doesn't and strides on and up with his long legs. I scramble after him in my little gold sandals; they're totally unsuitable for hill walking but I struggle on, trying to catch up with him. My foot turns in a hole hidden by the grass and I'm thrown forward, but just before I end up on my knees, a firm hand catches my arm and prevents me falling. I didn't realise he was so close behind me and look round, startled, expecting him to be angry at my clumsiness. His face is straight, unsmiling, but there is no anger and I'm very surprised when he asks me if I'm OK. I nod without speaking. He's about to fuck me and drive away, wham bam thank you ma'am; why is he asking me if I'm OK?

'On you go, then.' His voice is quiet and husky, and as I look at his serious face I imagine for a second I see it soften, and my pussy gives another of those involuntary jerks. Is he going to change his mind and let me off? And I realise I hope he's not.

I'm breathless as we round the bushes and are hidden from the carriageway below. The exertion of the climb, mounting excitement, and nervousness makes me tremble.

What is he expecting; a threesome, the two of them on me? Is he going to watch Darren and me or have me to himself? I hope it's the latter. No one speaks as he unzips and removes his padded waistcoat; the radio crackles as he lays it on the grass. I can see the dark hair of his chest through the white cotton of his shirt, the same way he can see the pink peaks of my nipples through mine.

'Let's see what you were trying to hide, then, young lady.'

I look over at Darren and he has a leering grin on his face. He loves this, and he adjusts himself through his jeans; his cock will be straining to break free.

'Don't look at him, look at me,' the officer snaps.

I turn back to look at his face; there is aggression in his voice but it's aimed at Darren, not me. I lock eyes with him and see smouldering lust there. Darren is forgotten; it's just him and me.

My heart quickens and I take a couple of ragged deep breaths to steady myself as I begin to unbutton my shirt from the top down. I want him to see, want to show him.

I see a nerve tighten in his cheek, the only indication of the tension in him. I provocatively run my fingertips down from my collar bone, between the narrow opening of my unbuttoned shirt front, between my breasts, over my belly, making a muscle there contract at the tickling touch, all the way to the waistband of my hipster jeans.

Still holding my gaze, he says, 'Let me see.'

He is close enough for me to hear but Darren can't, and in my peripheral vision I see him move forward. 'Get 'em out, babe.'

The officer's response is immediate. He turns on Darren. 'Step back, sir, you are playing no part in this. You committed the crime, the reward is mine.'

Darren steps back as he realises it is him who is paying by being made to watch while the law takes his girlfriend. I see anger on his face and he mutters some swear words.

'Keep your mouth shut, son, or you will find yourself in a lot more trouble.'

Darren shifts from one foot to another, his fists clench and his face tightens with anger, but he doesn't speak again.

The officer turns back to me and we lock eyes again. His voice is steady and he commands, 'Show me now.'

I slowly slip the shirt from my shoulders, provocatively allowing it to slide down my arms, and catch it with my hands. Now his eyes leave mine and travel down to my breasts. Although his face remains expressionless, his body's response is visible by the stiffening within his trousers, causing the front of them to tighten. Half naked, I stand tall before him as he feasts his eyes on my flesh and I feel excited and powerful, knowing the sight of my body is causing the arousal in him. He steps towards me and I tense as I think he will touch me but he doesn't; he takes the shirt from me and holds it in one hand.

'Now the jeans.'

Again I take a couple of deep breaths to steady myself and begin to undo and unzip my jeans. My fingers feel weak and won't work properly; not from fear but anticipation and excitement like I've never felt before. I pull them open and expose the bright triangle of my G-string and wriggle slightly as I ease both garments down over my bottom to mid-thigh before straightening up again. It was Darren who asked me to remove all my pubic hair and now I'm glad I did as I stand totally exposed, my arousal evident too as a silvery drop leaks down my thigh.

Darren moves towards me again, catching my attention, and I glance at him. He speaks to the police officer. 'Come on, mate, we can both have her. She's up for it.'

In two strides the officer has reached Darren, grabbed him and twisted his arm behind his back, holding him motionless. His voice is low and menacing. 'I told you I'm not your mate and I told you to stay back, sir. As you obviously are not of the mentality to understand I can see I will have to make sure you do as you are told.'

With his free hand he unclips the handcuffs from his belt and snaps them on to Darren's wrist. Roughly pushing him ahead, he angles him around the bushes towards a small tree and smartly handcuffs him to it.

I hear Darren shout, 'You can't fucking do this.'

The officer walks back around the bush, leaving him there to rant and swear to himself.

He takes me by the arm, his grip gentle this time, and leads me totally out of sight and earshot of Darren. He doesn't want us to be disturbed again and neither do I.

This time he doesn't move away. I turn to face him. He is very close and I look up at his face. His breathing has quickened and his lips are slightly parted. I can't wait any more. I want his kisses and his touch. I stretch up with my own lips parted and his restraint melts away. He kisses me hard, capturing my mouth with his, his tongue forcing its way into my mouth. His hands are on my body, stroking my skin, running down my back to grip my buttocks, squeezing and pulling me hard against him. I can feel the stiffness through his clothes as he grinds his hips against my belly, rubbing his erection between us. Moans are being forced from me into his mouth as the ferocity of his movements squeezes the breath from me and takes my arousal to a still higher level. I'm aware of just how strong he is, used to manhandling criminals, and me, a tiny woman, is powerless in his hands like a rag doll. I willingly submit and let him dominate me.

He releases me and I stand gasping, trying desperately to keep my balance. Quickly he undoes his trouser fly and pushes down the black boxers inside to hook out his huge, swollen penis. I stare at it with eyes wide, mesmerised. It is totally in keeping with his physique; thick, menacing, and very powerful. A shudder of excitement runs through me as I realise where it is going.

He must have seen my reaction and taken it as fear. He speaks gently. 'I won't hurt you.'

The mixture of power and gentleness is an overwhelming combination and I sway.

He reaches out and catches my waist, turning me with my

back to him, and I feel the hot hard member nestle against the small of my back. His hands rise to my breasts. Such large, strong hands are so gentle. His featherlike strokes are delicious and when his fingertips draw circles around my aching, taut nipples it is sweet agony. Is he doing this for himself or me?

Suddenly he stops, takes hold of my arms and folds them across my ribs, holding them in place with his own. He has me imprisoned against his chest and I am aware just how hard my heart is hammering, my breathing coming in short gasps, restricted now by the pressure of him holding me tight. Silent and motionless we stand. Oh no, is he going to stop?

He bends his head and softly kisses my neck and I move my head to the side to offer him more flesh, the only movement possible in this position.

His mouth brushes my ear and he whispers, 'Do you want me to stop?'

I don't know what to say, confused and light-headed with passion. I don't answer.

'I will stop if you don't want me to carry on. I'm not punishing you.'

I whimper, 'Please don't stop.' To stop now would be the punishment.

His grip loosens as he releases my arms. His hands move down to my hips. 'Bend forward.'

As I do, I feel his penis slip down between my bum cheeks and the shaft brushes my swollen lips for the first time. Holding me in place with one hand, he uses the other to lower his cock and I feel the smooth, wet head press against the hot, slick, aching entrance to my body. It nudges at me, trying to find entry; I'm swollen and tight but there won't be any resistance. I'm more than ready; the cool air in the shade of the bushes highlights the wet trails down my thighs and I know my juices have run from me.

He's struggling with the angle, as I'm too low. 'Stand on

my feet.'

'But I'll fall.'

'No, I'll hold you.'

He puts a steadying arm around my waist and partially lifts me as I step up onto his shiny black boots. Unaided, it would be impossible to stay in this position but he holds me firmly and allows me to lean forward enough so he can reach between us and firmly push himself into me. Thankfully, he has me held tight as my legs buckle at the sensation of my swollen pussy muscles being forced to loosen to let him in. It jerks one, two, three times as it stretches, allowing his fat cock to bury itself inside me. I'm groaning and moaning. This is beyond anything I've ever experienced before.

Again I'm reminded of a rag doll, bent in half, floppy and useless. With a hand gripping each hip he begins to move me forward and back. He leans me forward to the very end of his cock and I fear it may slip out as I'm so sodden, but in this position I don't have any control over his movements; he has all the control. Deliciously slowly, he pulls me back until he is ball-deep embedded in me, filling me to the limit. I'd like to see his face but in this position I can only look down and see my tiny feet with bright painted nails in gold strappy sandals, balanced on his big, black boots. The sharp contrast between male and female.

His movements increase in speed and strength and each time he pulls me back my bum hits his hips, sending a jolt of sensation through my body, tightening my muscles around him, grabbing him as he is fully in and clutching at him as pulls free of them.

Only the surrounding skin is stimulating my clit and it cries out for more friction. Is it right for me to help myself? Of course it is, and I bring up my hand to help. I jump as I touch it with dry fingers; it is so sensitive and quickly I moisten my fingers and touch it carefully again. It's sweet heaven and I begin to rub. He must see what I'm doing.

Maybe he's pleased? Or is he only interested in his own gratification?

My orgasm builds quickly and I feel the twitching of muscles inside as I reach the point of no return and hover on the brink. His cock slams into me one more time and the jolt sends me spinning over the edge. Contractions clench in waves, gripping him inside me. Helpless and out of control, I succumb to it and fall forward as the sensations course through me. There is a huge rush of blood to my head and consciousness almost slips away for a moment. His rhythm slows and his body stiffens; he is going to come too. The growl through his gritted teeth turns to a roar as his orgasm is upon him. Short, sharp jerks tell me he's pumping me full of come and he holds me tight against him until he has forced every drop out. I'd like to see his face but I can't.

If he'd just used me he could fling me off him now. He doesn't, his powerful hands lift me forward to step onto terra firma again, time to come back down to earth. As I pull up my underwear and jeans I turn and see him re-dressing himself. His face is expressionless again; well, what did I expect?

He hands me my shirt and pulls on his waistcoat.

I feel a little confused and sad; I'd like him to take me in his arms and hold me lovingly and tell me how wonderful it was, but that's not going to happen. It was just a fuck to pay a fine, wasn't it?

We face each other in silence and he speaks first. 'Come on, let me take you down first, miss.' He's reverted to the professional police officer.

He takes my arm firmly and we begin the descent to the two waiting vehicles below. He opens the passenger door to Darren's beat-up car and silently I slip into the seat. He slams the door and I watch him climb back up the embankment to retrieve my boyfriend.

In a couple of minutes they emerge from the bushes and make their way down. As they stand beside the car I hear him speak to Darren. 'Get in the car, sir, I'll get your ticket.'

I can see the anger on Darren's face and sense it by the stiffness of his movements as he gets into the car and grips the wheel as we wait for the officer to return from his vehicle with the form he's filled out. We sit in tense silence.

The officer walks back, folding the form, and hands it to me through the open window. He holds on to it for a second as I take it and I look up and our eyes meet. Is he telling me something?

He bends, looking through at Darren. 'Drive carefully, sir, and you two have a nice day.' It sounds so funny but I dare not laugh as Darren is obviously so angry.

He tries to start the car and it takes two attempts before it splutters into life, mocking him further. He mutters, 'Useless piece of crap.'

As we pull into the traffic and speed away, leaving a cloud of exhaust fumes behind us, I see the officer in the wing mirror, standing with his arms folded across his chest watching us. For the first time, I'm sure I see him smiling.

Darren lets go with a tirade of pent-up abuse. 'Who the fuck does he think he is? I'll have that fucking bastard.' He often makes idle threats.

I'm thinking it would have been nice for him to ask if I was all right, was I hurt? But no, he carries on with his livid ramblings.

I think, but don't dare say, yeah, yeah, yeah, shut up now, and shut off to him.

I still have the form in my hand and unfold it. It's filled out in small, neat handwriting and right across the middle is written in capital letters, "PAID IN FULL". I smile and refold it, noticing there is a Post-it note stuck to the back.

It reads, 'Dump the bad boy, you need a good man,' and underneath is a mobile number.

I stifle a big smile behind my hand and slip it into my jeans pocket as I reach over and turn up the CD player to drown out my soon-to-be ex-boyfriend's whining voice.

Return of the Black Lily
by Elizabeth Coldwell

Jocelyn's sweet lips were busy between my legs, lapping at my clit. When she glanced up from time to time, anxious to make sure she was satisfying her mistress, I gave her head a reassuring pat, letting her know I was enjoying everything she was doing to me. Still, as I took another liqueur chocolate from the box at my side, biting through its crisp outer shell to the syrupy, brandied filling, I could barely stifle a sigh. Who knew retirement would prove so dull?

Oh, I had all the time I wanted to indulge my every whim, along with more than enough wealth to make my life very comfortable indeed. And with beautiful, submissive Jocelyn as my lover and slave, I should have been the happiest woman on earth. But I missed the thrills of my previous life, the one that had placed me in this most enviable position.

Under the alias of The Black Lily, I'd been a highly successful jewel thief. The police had pursued me, but I'd never been caught, even though I'd taken all manner of risks, creeping into bedrooms in the dead of night in search of booty. For my weakness wasn't just money, it was beautiful women – and I'd met plenty of those in the course of my adventures, though none as delicious as Jocelyn, who I'd met while she was modelling an item I was attempting to steal.

My problem, I decided, as Jocelyn's tongue lashed against my clit and sent me tumbling into orgasm, was that life no longer held an element of risk. I had to do something dangerous before I expired of boredom.

But first, I had the small matter of a weekend in the country to negotiate.

The invitation came as a complete surprise. I hadn't seen Catriona for years. We'd been best friends at boarding school, but our paths had diverged when she met and married a wealthy industrialist. They'd been living in Switzerland, until the marriage came to an abrupt end when Catriona caught him fucking the au pair in the marital bed. It was by no means the first affair Rex had conducted, but it was the first one she hadn't known about. As she told me later, it was the simple lack of etiquette that appalled her. In the divorce settlement, she'd been awarded his old family home, Mottram Hall – he'd kept his properties in Zurich and New York, and his private island in the Maldives. Catriona was keen for me to see her new residence – and to bitch about Rex, I was sure – and invited me along to a house party she was throwing. The prospect of spending a weekend marooned in the wilds of Suffolk, up to my knees in mud and surrounded by the sort of chinless wonders I'd spent much of my career depriving of their valuables, filled me with dread. But I was sure I could anaesthetise myself to the worst of the horrors to come with the aid of enough gin. And I'd have Jocelyn to amuse me in the evenings. Or so I thought.

The day before we were due to travel to Catriona's, Jocelyn came down with the flu. It gave me the perfect excuse to phone Catriona and tell her I was awfully sorry, but I wouldn't be able to make it, but dear, sweet Jocelyn insisted I go. She would be fine in my absence, she assured me, sniffling prettily into a man-sized tissue. Deep down, she knew how much I'd been looking to get out of my visit; refusing to let me stay and nurse her was simply her way of earning a thrashing when she was well enough to take it.

The devious little vixen.

Thoughts of striping Jocelyn's perfect backside with my favourite riding crop sustained me on the train journey out to Stowmarket. From there, I took a taxi to Mottram Hall, oblivious to the driver's attempts to engage me in conversation.

All too soon, the car pulled up on the Hall's gravel forecourt. Extensive renovations had been carried out before Catriona moved in, and despite myself I was curious to see inside. Unexpectedly, I was experiencing the rush I'd always got when preparing to case a joint. I shook my head, dismissing the urge. Catriona was my friend, and I'd made it a rule never to steal from my friends. All thieves have a code of honour, and I'd stuck to mine throughout my career.

'Darling, you look marvellous!' Catriona emerged from the drawing room to sweep me into a huge hug.

'So do you.' This was no idle compliment. When we'd been at school, Catriona had yet to shake off the shackles of acne and puppy fat. Entering her thirties, she was a woman in full bloom, with an enviably curvaceous figure and lustrous flame-red hair cut in a sleek shoulder-length bob. Yet her husband had cheated on her repeatedly. Some men just didn't appreciate a good woman when they had one – and neglected wives were always grateful for attention and skilful loving, a need I'd been more than happy to satisfy on many occasions over the years.

'Why don't you come through and meet everyone? I've told them all about you.'

That I doubted. I could count the people who were aware of my double life on the fingers of one French-manicured hand, though I still took a good look at of Catriona's guests as we were introduced, just to make sure I hadn't robbed them at some point in the past. I didn't recognise any of them, but it's hard to be sure when they've had their nightdress pushed up over their head and you've been intimately acquainting yourself with their tight, sweet pussy.

'Dinner will be served at eight,' Catriona informed us. 'In the meantime, let me refresh everyone's glasses and I'll give you a tour of the house.'

Aperitif in hand, I followed my friend and her other guests as she showed us the dining room, the bedrooms and her own addition to the house – a specially constructed conservatory with indoor swimming pool. I regretted Jocelyn's inability to attend the festivities; she would have looked magnificent doing slow lengths of that pool – especially as I would have ordered her to do so naked.

Finally back in the drawing room, I noticed something I'd missed when I'd first entered. A cabinet was mounted on the wall, containing a selection of what I instantly recognised to be genuine Chinese jade figurines, several centuries old.

'These are beautiful,' I said, stepping close to get a better look.

'Oh, collecting them was one of Rex's hobbies. That's only a fraction of his collection, but those particular items were his pride and joy.' Catriona smirked, taking a generous swallow of her dirty martini. 'That's why I made sure they came to me in the settlement.'

One piece caught my eye above all the others. Whitish-grey in colour, ornately carved and accurately shaped, it couldn't be anything but a phallus. My fingers itched to close round its fat girth.

'This one is beautiful. Tell me more about it.'

'I thought you'd like that. It's late Ming dynasty, dating from the 17th century. I've no idea whether it was modelled after anyone, but if it was – well, he was a very big boy.'

Catriona seemed to have drained her glass in remarkably quick time. She was clearly debating whether to mix herself another martini when a uniformed waiter popped his head round the door to announce dinner was served.

We enjoyed a surprisingly lively meal, though that was as much to do with Catriona as anyone else's contribution to the conversation. The wine flowed – much of it into her glass – as she entertained us with a series of anecdotes about her ex-husband's lack of bedroom prowess.

'Those little sluts were welcome to him,' she muttered between mouthfuls of sole Veronique. 'I had more fun with my vibrators than I ever did with him.'

Poor Catriona. I sympathised with her. Like me, she had all the material trappings of life, but she didn't appear to have anyone to share them with. How long had it been since she'd last got laid?

Even as I reflected on how lucky I was to have found Jocelyn, part of my mind kept wandering back to the antique jade dildo. The last beautiful thing I'd had such an overwhelming yearning to possess was Jocelyn, and I'd made her mine without too much difficulty. Though I tried to concentrate on what was being said around the dinner table, I couldn't stop myself mentally working out how easy it would be to make off with the phallus. The cabinet was locked, but there wasn't a lock I couldn't pick, given enough time. All I had to do was …

'Don't you agree with me, darling?'

I hadn't realised Catriona was addressing me till she repeated my name. 'Don't tell me we're all boring you?'

'Not at all,' I assured her hastily. 'I – I was simply wondering where you'd found your chef. This chocolate terrine is delicious.' To reinforce my words, I scooped up another forkful of the creamy, cocoa-rich confection.

'Oh, Henri is an absolute diamond. I wouldn't be without him.' Catriona pushed her empty dessert plate aside. 'Coffee and brandy in the drawing room, I think.'

We sat for an hour or so, the conversation finally turning away from Catriona's litany of complaints against Rex to the current state of the stock exchange and the possibility of the weather being suitable for a long walk the following morning. When I tried, and failed, to stifle a yawn, people glanced at their watches, registered the lateness of the hour, and began to retire to bed.

Much as I wanted to call Jocelyn before I slipped beneath the covers, I knew she'd be asleep, dosed up on paracetamol. Despite all the rich food and alcohol I'd consumed over the course of the evening, sleep eluded me. This was the first night in months when Jocelyn hadn't slept at the end of my bed, curled up beneath a thin coverlet, and it felt wrong to glance down and fail to see her slumbering form.

More than that, the jade dildo continued to issue its siren call, and I was helpless to resist it. What I was about to do was a flagrant abuse of Catriona's hospitality. Yet I made no attempt to stop myself as I wrapped my silk robe round my naked body and silently crept out of the room. I wanted excitement, a return to the risks I'd taken in my Black Lily days, and what could be riskier – and more thrilling – than stealing something from beneath the nose of my oldest friend?

The landing and staircase were shrouded in darkness. I didn't switch on a light, relying on my strong night vision and the occasional shaft of moonlight peeping through a break in the clouds. Loud snoring came from behind one of the bedroom doors as I passed. The room next to it was Catriona's; I paused by it for a moment, but heard nothing.

Silently, I let myself into the drawing room. A moment's inspection told me the lock on the cabinet housing Catriona's jade collection was painfully insubstantial for the job. My trusty set of picks were back at home, but a straightened-out hairpin did the trick in their place. Just a little wriggling back and forth and the lock clicked open.

When my fingers touched the smooth surface of the phallus, a shudder of sheer pleasure ran through me. If I'd been wearing panties, my juices would have flooded them. Stealing had always been an aphrodisiac as far as I was concerned, and I pictured myself pushing the dildo up into my cunt. Just because I wasn't into men didn't mean I didn't enjoy the occasional spot of penetration, and I knew the thick length of jade would fill me very nicely indeed. Absent-mindedly, I stroked it up and down, wondering who it had been carved for, and whether she'd used it on herself, or some willing courtesan, as sweet and submissive as my own darling Jocelyn …

'Just what do you think you're doing?'

Turning, still gripping the dildo, I saw Catriona standing in the doorway. Caught red-handed, for once in my sweet-talking life, words escaped me. Finally, I managed to stammer, 'Well, I couldn't sleep and –'

'Monica was right. She said you were a thief, but I refused to believe her. You think you know all there is to know about someone …'

'Darling, Monica's lying. Or she's confusing me with someone else.' Monica was the sweet-faced brunette who'd been sitting opposite me at dinner. I hadn't paid her too much attention, caught up in the spectacle Catriona was making of herself, but she must have been studying me throughout the meal.

'There's no confusion. She told me not long after she and David moved into their place in Virginia Water that she woke one night to find a woman in her room, dressed all in black, rifling through her jewellery box. This woman overpowered her, fastened her wrists to the bed posts with her own stockings, then stripped down her leggings, settled her pussy over Monica's face and made Monica lick her till she came.'

'How scary,' I said, never relinquishing my hold on the dildo. 'I do hope poor Monica wasn't too traumatised by the event.'

'Not at all.' Catriona moved so close to me I could smell the expensive face cream she'd applied before retiring to bed. 'She said it was the most exciting thing that'd ever happened to her. When the burglar finally released her and escaped back out of the window, she didn't even think to call the police. She just pulled up her nightie and brought herself off time and again, remembering the way the woman had dominated her. And she'd only lost a pair of ruby earrings she didn't even like that much.'

'That's some story. But what does it have to do with me?'

'Apparently, Monica never got a proper look at the woman's face. But she'll never forget the tattoo on her thigh. It was a very distinctive design, she said. A black lily.'

As Catriona spoke, she glanced down at my leg. I followed her gaze and saw the front of my robe was slightly open, giving her a perfect view of the tattoo etched at the top of my inner thigh. The flower that had earned me my nickname.

'You see why it's not too much of a stretch of the imagination to hear a tale like Monica's, then see you with my prize jade phallus in your hand and think I'm about to become your next victim – Lily.'

'Oh darling, you couldn't possibly …'

'Yes, I could.' Catriona's eyes glittered. For all she'd drunk tonight, she sounded clear-headed, almost menacing in her calmness. 'I invite you into my home, wine and dine you, and this is how you choose to repay me?'

'So now you know who I really am, you're going to turn me over to the police, I suppose?'

She shook her head. 'I should, but I have a more suitable punishment for you in mind. I vowed that after what Rex did to me, I'd never let anyone screw me over again. I'd give them a taste of their own medicine, whatever that might happen to be. And in your case, I know exactly what it will involve.'

Catriona grabbed for my wrist. Though she was an inch or so shorter than me, she was surprisingly strong. Or maybe I'd grown soft in my retirement. We struggled. She pushed me backwards, so I went tumbling over the arm of her antique love seat. The dildo dropped from my fingers as I fought to stand upright. Catriona pounced, forcing me down.

'Years of judo training, darling,' she hissed in my ear, as she scrabbled at the belt of my robe. Untying it, she pulled it out of the loops holding it in place and used it to tie my hands together behind my back. 'Of course, I only took an interest for so long because I was having an affair with my judo instructor, but it's nice to know the skills have finally come in useful.'

'You were having an affair?'

'Oh yes, and Rex knew all about it. He didn't care I was fucking Gunther, because I turned a blind eye to all his affairs in return. It all worked very well, till that little slut of an au pair came along.'

I writhed beneath Catriona as she vented her rage, unused to being in the position of the victim rather than the aggressor. I'd never been made to submit before, and for all that I protested and raged to be freed, my nipples were like diamond chips against the sofa cushions and my pussy was fluid with juice. Something about being tied up turned me on; I'd simply never realised it until now.

Catriona's hand traced a slow trail up the inside of my thigh, coming to rest on my tattoo. 'This is some piece of work, but then so are you. I'd never have believed it of you if Monica hadn't been so insistent. Just like a pretty little magpie, aren't you?'

I recognised the tone of voice, crooning and almost hypnotic. I'd used it on Jocelyn so many times, as I warmed her up for a whipping. Was that what Catriona intended to do to me? Panicking at the thought, I redoubled my efforts to free myself, not sure I could handle pain as well as the humiliation of having been caught in the act. But her knot-tying skills were the equal of her judo moves, and I was held fast. All I succeeded in doing was rucking up the silky robe, baring more of my tits and arse to her.

'You have such a gorgeous body too. You really look

after yourself, don't you, Lily? I bet men are always telling you that.'

'I don't care what men have to say about me,' I retorted.

'So the rest of the story is true. You only fuck women. How intriguing.' Catriona's fingers skimmed dangerously close to my pussy lips. I fought the urge to beg her to slip them up into my wetness. 'Have you never wondered what it's like to have a big, hard cock inside you?'

'I don't need cock. I have toys for that.'

'And so do I ...'

Something pressed at the entrance to my pussy. Something big and hard, with a slight chill to it. Realising immediately what Catriona was about to fuck me with, I moaned, my pussy letting out a gush of cream.

'You wanted this, Lily. Well, you've got it ...'

Catriona eased the jade phallus between my sex lips, my tight channel spreading to take in its almost freakish girth. I'd used dildos of this size before, both on myself and Jocelyn, but the fact I was being penetrated with something so old, so valuable, added a whole new dimension to the sensation.

'If only you could see the way you look right now,' Catriona said. Her dominant façade had dropped, and she seemed genuinely impressed by the ease with which my cunt was swallowing up the ancient sex toy. 'Bound and packed full of fat jade cock.'

Glancing over my shoulder, I saw she'd taken the opportunity to slip out of her own night attire, realising I wasn't going to try to make a run for it. Her breasts, though considerably larger than my own, stood up in gravity-defying fashion; I suspected they'd been something else Rex had treated her to in the course of their marriage. The hair on her mound was the same arresting shade of red as that on her head.

'Fire crotch,' I murmured, wondering if she tasted as good as she looked.

'What did you call me?' She seemed to have realised she was supposed to be in charge of this situation. Reasserting her control, she withdrew the phallus almost all the way, before shoving it back up into me. Reaching under me with her free hand, she rubbed at my clit while she fucked me with the dildo. Now I knew how Jocelyn felt whenever I ploughed into her with my strap-on; soft and pliable and melting around the big fake cock.

Catriona was channelling all the baggage she'd brought from her failed marriage into my punishment, pounding my cunt so fiercely I knew I'd be sore in the morning. But I welcomed the sweet pain. Together with the wicked treatment her fingers were dishing out to my clit, it was too much for me to resist. Toes curling, head thrown back, I howled out my orgasm so loudly I was convinced I'd wake all Catriona's guests.

At last, she pulled the dildo from my hole, which seemed to release it with more than a measure of reluctance. I'd hoped she was going to untie my wrists. Instead, she came round to stand in front of my face, her fiery pussy only inches from my lips.

'Thank me for fucking you so nicely,' she ordered.

As I stuck out my tongue and started to lap at her cunt, I thought of the story I'd have to tell Jocelyn on my return home. How it appeared I'd finally met my match, and how I'd loved every moment of the treatment I'd received at my old friend's hands. But I also knew that when I left on Sunday evening, the jade dildo would be hidden away in my overnight bag. Catriona wouldn't expect me try and take it, not after everything that had just happened, but when I want something, I always get it. And when Catriona discovered it had gone, despite all her efforts to prevent me stealing it – well, I'd cross that bridge when I came to it. The Black Lily was back in business, and being bad had never felt so good.

The Fire Triangle
By Mia Lovejoy

I used to believe that the line between right and wrong was black and white. But as I stepped across the boundary line of yellow caution tape to investigate the fire at Blackbird Pond, my work boot on the scorched landscape left a charcoal grey imprint. Morality is relative, I'd discovered. And feelings don't always make sense. Sometimes you just have to let go into the Mystery.

The first day I met Claire, I went to work feeling bad about myself. Another disaster in the bedroom; for about a year I'd had trouble getting it up. *'Just get some fucking Viagra already,'* my wife had screamed in frustration. Her words stung as if she'd slapped me physically rather than verbally. As I left the house in a heated rush, I purposely slammed the garage door – just to drive her nuts – causing the framed wedding photo on the wall to become askew. I turned the key to my V-8 engine, silently berating Limp Willy for not kicking into gear on command the way my loyal Ford always did.

I didn't want things to be this way between my wife and me. Wasn't so long ago I'd get hard as nails from just a peek at Holly's pretty pussy or a sniff of her snatch. I'd have sex on the brain 24/7 and my big bad boner was a steady source of pleasure for both of us throughout nearly 18 years of marriage. But everything had changed with my 40th birthday, when the demons of old age and mortality started fucking with my head. After several humiliating incidents of impotence, I began to avoid sex to save my pride. Of course, ignoring the problem created a whole new set of problems, but I couldn't ask for help. It's an unspoken assumption among fire guys: *counselling is for pussies.*

'Hey, Vern ...' My boss, Iron Gut Gil, greeted me. 'Are you ready for this year's baby-faced boys?' With his "Burn in Hell" mug he gestured toward the new recruits awaiting training in the conference room. Acidic coffee sloshed over the rim, scalding the scantily clad she-devils adorning the mug. 'Except one of them ain't a boy. Check her out.' From his office, we could see them but they couldn't see us.

She was not a beauty in the traditional sense; she had too many freckles and her facial features were kind of horsey. And that wild and kinky hair ...My God! It was flame orange, like an Arizona sunset. But when she crossed the room to pick up an orientation packet, I was spellbound: She was beauty in motion. Her stride was unabashedly confident; her long legs propelled her forward in a graceful bounce that made her pert tits jiggle. The Beatles song *Something in the Way She Moves* played in my head. 'Unbelievable!' The word was followed by an awkward pause as Gil sized up my reaction and grinned. 'Where's she from?' I quickly recovered a professional tone.

'Transferred from the Douglas District. Has rehire rights. The DM wouldn't say why she wanted to leave, but looks to me like she's no stranger to scandal.'

'She married?'

'Nah ...no husband, no kids. Drives a beat-up Subaru plastered with liberal bumper stickers. One of them says *My Other Car is a Broom* so hopefully you can figure that one out, Einstein.'

'She lives in *Bisbee*, I suppose?' My derogatory tone conformed to Gil's disdain for the tiny town tucked in the Mule Mountains that was home to a wide variety of misfits – hippy artists, druggies, and yes, even self-proclaimed witches.

'Of course. Betcha ten to one she's a lesbian too.'

'Like you wouldn't get off on watching some girl on girl action, Gil!' I didn't want to disrespect her, but fire guys expect you to talk like that.

I began training the new recruits on the fundamentals. 'The three legs of the Fire Triangle are oxygen, fuel, and heat.' I drew a triangle on the whiteboard and labelled its component parts. 'You need all three for a hot burn. To suppress a fire, you must take away at least one leg of the triad.' Even though it was a rote training spiel, I still get nervous speaking in front of groups. To cope, I find someone in the audience who is attentive and encouraging – someone who maintains eye contact – and then latch on for dear life. Claire was intensely attentive. Between us we had all the chemistry needed for the Fire Triangle that was raging between my legs: the fuel of her smouldering hazel eyes and her unflinching stare; the heat I felt quickly creeping through my crotch; my nervous I-need-more-oxygen pant. I am a married man, I reminded myself; to fan these flames could be devastating. So in the name of fire suppression, I looked away.

'A *lightning-caused fire* can be a good thing; nature's way of cleaning house. Nowadays we monitor and let them burn if they don't threaten life or property.'

'Who writes the prescriptions on this district?' Claire asked. That she knew enough to ask that question meant she was familiar with agency policy at a higher level than was required by her seasonal position of FPT – Fire Prevention Technician. Managers can put a fire "in prescription", thereby using nature's healing properties to restore proper balance to the landscape; it's like a naturopathic doctor working with nature rather than against it.

'I do.' This time I held her unblinking stare, lest her eyes roam to the bulge in my pants where Unfaithful Willy stirred to life at the sound of her velvet voice.

'I'm very interested in prescribed burns. Could I shadow you on one?'

'Um, sure. That's outside the scope of your duties, but if you're eager to learn, I could teach you … Claire.' When I said her name aloud, I liked the way my tongue caressed the back of my teeth, sending pleasant shivers up my spine. 'Back to the topic.' I hoped I sounded more in control than I felt. 'In a *controlled burn*, the Forest Service sets the fire with drip torches and controls its path with firebreaks and back burns. The goal is to reduce the build-up of flammable fuels that could lead to a firestorm.'

'Cool! I wanna start fires,' exploded a guy in the back of the room; his two buddies laughed. Habitually suspicious, I noted his physical description – square jaw, huge muscles, good looks – before I asked for his name.

'Richard Long,' he replied.

'We call him Dick,' his friend with the buzz cut hair chimed in. Dick Long … Were his parents drunk when they named him? I wondered.

'That's Big Dick to you,' he corrected Buzz. More male laughter; Claire rolled her eyes.

I explained to the newbies that destructive, uncontrolled burns usually start in areas of high public use, like campgrounds and roadside pull-outs. Just as I launched into my spiel about investigating arson fires, Claire exited the room abruptly, letting the heavy door to the patio slam shut. Through the floor to ceiling window everyone could see her rummage through her purse, pull out rolling papers and a baggie of brownish-green leafy material. It appeared she was just about to roll a fat one, but first she took off her uniform shirt and hung it over a nearby tree branch, presumably to protect it from the incriminating odour. She was braless in a tightly fitted undershirt that said *Outrageous Older Woman*, though she didn't look over 33; her cleavage was creamy and youthful, her erect nipples clearly visible through the taut fabric. Tongue-tied, I stuttered and stumbled a bit more about the psychology of arsonists. Finally I just gave up and stood there staring – my mouth open in disbelief, my cock in a stiff salute – as she lit her big doobie. I have no choice but to arrest her, I thought. Everyone is watching this flagrant violation of the law. I patted the handcuffs secured to my belt and headed for the door just as I caught the first whiff of her exhale circulating through the air vents; it was a clove cigarette, not marijuana. Thank God I hadn't intervened! I felt stupid enough as it was.

'No fair … Can I go out for a smoke too?' Big Dick was already taking out his Marlboros. He gestured for Buzz Cut and Buck Tooth to join him.

Buck said, 'I'm staying here. That chick scares me.'

'Afraid she'll do you with some hocus pocus?' Dick's hands gracefully mimed casting a spell and ended in an exaggerated tug on his bulge. 'Maybe a love spell,' he said, gyrating his pelvis.

This was it: I had officially lost all control of the training session. I was sliding down a slippery slope in every area of my life: I couldn't satisfy my wife; I couldn't keep a younger female interested; I couldn't hold the attention of new recruits, who would inevitably replace me in the not-so-distant future. Should I accept that it's all downhill after 40, like my dad did? Might as well tattoo a double L to my forehead – Limp Loser. So then and there, I just let go. I focused hypnotically on the pentagram necklace dangling from a leather cord between Claire's perfect breasts, marking the exact spot where I longed to bury my face and cry.

That night, I awoke in the wee hours from a sexual dream with a boner as hard as a posthole digger. In my dream I was Supercock, doing Claire and my wife at the same time, while both squealed with pleasure like greedy little piggies. In my half-awake state I thought about shoving my hard

211

dick between my wife's soft ass cheeks – let her feel who didn't need Viagra after all – but I didn't dare wake her. If I fucked her with more passion than I had in a year, I feared she'd somehow see through my veil of smoke and mirrors to the source of my magic remedy: the red-hot love-triangle porno fantasy that played in the dark theatre of my filthy mind. So instead I pulled back the sheet, took my swollen sausage into my calloused palm and worked up a friction that burned hot as a grease fire. In less than a minute I blew like a stick of dynamite, my spunk exploding all the way up to my neck. I mopped up the mess, secretly thrilled to realise I still had it in me.

The next morning, Claire was waiting for me at my computer, eager for her first lesson. After 18 years of working for the government, I was accustomed to a bureaucratic time table. She had an *act now* urgency which scared and thrilled me. I suggested we arrange a meeting in a week or two, but she wouldn't be put off. So I sent the boys to patrol alone.

I spent the morning in close proximity to her enchanting body. I explained the formulas and principles of the prescription process. She devoured the information and asked for more. The heady scent of her patchouli clouded my thinking; I gave out the access code to the burn plans protected in the F-drive database. As we shared the mouse, the heat of her hand drove Willy wild with want. He leapt and raged like a caged monkey beneath my uniform pants, so I gave him a good beating in the bathroom on my lunch break.

Weeks passed without seeing much of Claire. In that time, there had been a suspicious fire in a proposed management burn site for which I was unable to determine a cause. There was no tell-tale evidence of an incendiary device; no recent lightning activity. Sure, this fire would be beneficial to the land. But that didn't alleviate my uneasy feeling. Could Claire have started this mysterious fire on her own, too impatient to wait for the wheels of bureaucracy to turn?

I put my worries on the back burner as I dealt with a flash fire of personnel relations: my FPTs could no longer work together. Claire claimed Big Dick had exposed his erect cock to her in the bushes; Buck Teeth gave fire and brimstone sermons proclaiming all non-Christians would burn in hell for eternity; and Buzz said he 'wouldn't work with a dyke'. The end result: Claire threatened to file grievances for sexual harassment and religious discrimination unless she was allowed to patrol alone. Anxious to avoid a conflagration, I agreed to her demands. She also asked to take June 21st off as a religious holiday, saying something about a Litha or Midsummer celebration. But I was short-staffed and had to say no.

The next day, while patrolling alone, Claire radioed in the Bottlebrush fire which, coincidentally, was also in a proposed burn area. Atypical of arson fires, it did not threaten people or property. But as the only Level Three Law Enforcement Officer on the District, my suspicions were highly aroused and I would have to investigate.

I researched the Wiccan religion on Sunday morning while my wife attended mass. Among my findings: it's not satanic; there are no animal sacrifices. They don't believe in heaven or hell, sin or confession, the evils of sex and nudity. Among the core tenets: the Divine is both male and female; the Divine is present in Nature; Nature should be honoured and respected. I was surprised to find that it wasn't so different from my own beliefs. I had just started reading about the Law of Threefold Return (which I hoped would be as titillating as it sounded) when my wife returned from church, suggesting a picnic in the Mule Mountains.

After a hardy lunch and a bottle of wine, we lounged on a sunny rock. Holly confessed to buying some Viagra from an internet site, but she didn't want me to feel obligated to take it. She would store it in the medicine cabinet as a back-up, just in case I ever wanted it. Instead of reacting angrily or clamming up, I apologised for the times I'd let her down. I assured her she was still very sexy to me – that my erectile problems weren't connected to her desirability. I told her she was my One True Love, and I meant it. 'I guess there's some things about getting older I still need to work out,' I confided. 'Just trust my process, baby. It'll be OK.' Gil would have given me a rash of shit for this counsellor-speak, which was not my typical style of conflict resolution. I can't explain why, but I had an intuition that Claire was somehow influencing this New and Improved Me, magically guiding me to say these healing words my wife desperately needed to hear. Holly and I didn't have sex, but the dead wood had been pruned that afternoon, making way for new growth.

I went to work early on Monday, June 21st. I noticed a big wooden wheel in the bed of Claire's patrol truck that hadn't been there on Friday. She said she'd picked it up over the weekend while cleaning a dispersed campsite. I couldn't imagine how she lifted it alone, but I didn't press her for details. I told her I'd be working in the office. Soon after she left, I raced to my rig to follow her.

The first four hours passed rather uneventfully as she patrolled, picked up trash, broke up fire rings and made prevention contacts with the recreating public. Twice she stopped to roll and smoke her odd cigarettes, using the tree branch ritual to protect her uniform shirt from odour. I focused my high-powered binoculars on her tight tank top – which pictured a wheel that looked alarmingly similar to the one in the back of her truck – and the words *Pagan Wheel of the Seasons*. She flicked some stray ashes from her bosom with those orange-painted fingernails. Willy stirred to life but I refused to give him any attention (though after hours of playing peeping tom, I desperately wanted to).

She ambled along the road toward Blackbird Pond, an

area temporarily closed to the public. I followed, riding over mounds of honey-gold hills on this first day of summer, my ass gently bouncing on the coiled springs of the plush bench seat. My threesome dream came back to me in Technicolor, and my dick got hard as a shovel. Damn, but I could get used to this perpetual hard-on, like I was 20 instead of 41! I was delirious with desire by the possibility of being caught, even though *she* was the one suspected of wrongdoings. *Wrongdoings* – the word sounded petty; inconsequential. Arson is a serious federal offence, I reminded myself. Sober up, fool! People do hard jail time for this!

Claire unlocked the gate to the restricted area – a site I had put in prescription for a future burn – and parked atop a grassy hill of dried cheatgrass. I watched through binoculars, hidden in a cluster of oaks. She stashed her uniform shirt in the cab and heaved the wagon wheel over the open tailgate, her lovely back muscles flexing through the spaghetti-strapped tank. She dumped her heavy backpack, and then moved the truck into a cluster of trees dangerously close to where I was parked. I ducked down and stayed as quiet as my pounding heart would allow.

'Dispatch …FPT Three is out of service for lunch.' The radio transmission squelched so close to my ear I almost crapped my pants. After regaining control, I dared to peek. I watched entranced: Claire's naked Pagan body, skipping, singing, and dancing, until she reached the hilltop once more. I left my truck and scrambled to a rock outcropping to get a closer look.

Claire's muscles rippled in the sunlight as she lifted the wheel into rolling position. Her graceful arms reached upward as she proclaimed to the heavens, 'May we find balance between land and sky … darkness and light … fire and water. On this Midsummer Day, when the sun is at its strongest, I am compelled toward direct action to heal this damaged landscape. May this Pagan ritual of subordinating the sun wheel to water also please the Divine and prevent drought.' She took a container of white gas from her backpack and doused the wheel. When she picked up the fireplace lighter, I could hold myself back no longer: I ran into the full exposure of the noonday sun.

'Don't do it, Claire!'

She actually laughed. 'Why not?' We were within arm's reach now; I was panting, trying to catch my breath. She moved so close I could have kissed her. 'There's so much in this world that needs to be healed,' she said softly. 'I choose to be an instrument of the Divine.' Her eyes travelled down to my Divine hard-on, then back up to my eyes, daring me with that penetrating stare.

'I'm not as brave as you,' I confessed. 'I can't just take things into my own hands like that.'

'It's your choice, Vern. You have the power to change. If you want something bad enough, you *just do it*.' She turned to ignite the gas-soaked wood, which burst into flame instantly. Then she faced me again, her naked form backlit by firelight. I knew I should call Dispatch. But I couldn't move; I was spellbound. With one hand, Claire played with her lovely breasts, pulling and squeezing the nipples; with the other, she parted the hair of her burning bush, giving me an eyeful of her aroused sex. I watched her middle finger dance in spiralling circles over her erect clit while the other four feverishly worked her pretty pussy lips until they swelled like a flower in full bloom. Her sexy scent commingled with the smell of smoke. Her orange-painted fingernails were a blur of colour as she worked herself into a frenzy; quickly, expertly. As she climaxed, she threw her head back in unselfconscious ecstasy, crying out her sweet release to the sky.

By now the dry grass surrounding the wheel had caught fire. A breeze forced the flames downhill. 'Make a choice,' Claire said. 'Will you turn me in? Or will you join me?'

It seemed clear to me I'd made my choice – my pants now down to my knees incriminatingly, my sword so straight up and stiff I could impale myself upon it – a gallant knight nobly defending his spirited enchantress. I grabbed a stick and gave the wheel a hearty shove, becoming an accomplice in Claire's illegal Litha celebration. We clasped hands and watched the fiery wheel roll down the hillside – igniting the dead cheatgrass in a blaze of glory – before plunging into the dark muck of Blackbird Pond. I felt free, like a huge burden had been lifted. Suddenly, I ached to share this feeling with Holly. Instead, I kissed Claire.

Our passion ignited like a drip torch to a dry landscape. The flesh of her belly pressed tight against mine, we kissed with abandon, my divining rod wildly seeking her hot, wet hole. But she stopped me – took my face in her hands and stared into my eyes – as we panted for oxygen.

Then she released me. 'Well I'll be damned!' I grinned. 'You're *not* a lesbian.'

'I share my body with whoever I want. Women and men. I love both.' She stared appreciably at my manhood and my pride swelled. 'But I sense you and your wife are more traditional than that, and I want my actions to heal, not hurt.' Her body backed away from mine. 'Take it home. Use this passion to fan the flames with your wife.' I groaned. Though Willy was angry and frustrated, Vern was grateful; relieved.

And so from the ashes of destruction, I was reborn, like a phoenix. With new clarity, I took in my surroundings. 'We need to get the fuck out of here,' I told her. 'Fast!'

That night, Holly and I went at it all night long, like we were newlyweds again. She was utterly thrilled by Eveready Willy with his freshly-charged batteries. As the morning light crept in I stared at Holly's profile against the pillow, her hair wild and free, her lovely face flushed with the dawn's rosy hue. She had the unmistakable look of a thoroughly satisfied woman.

While getting ready for work, I caught my wife in the bathroom counting the Viagra pills. When she realised none were missing, she beamed with the smile of a giddy girl. My love for her swelled instantly and I took her right there, bent over the porcelain sink, her ample tits slapping our rhythm against the mirrored medicine chest.

When I entered the office, Gil eyed me carefully as he spoke. 'How 'bout we call in the L.E.O. from Bisbee to investigate the Blackbird fire?' He picked up the phone.

'No,' I replied too quickly. 'I need to handle this on my own, Gil. Please.' So much was unspoken, yet it seemed we understood one another perfectly. He nodded and put down the phone.

I'd sworn, by oath, to protect. But what exactly did that mean? Of course I'd save my own skin in order to protect my wife. But who, if not I, would protect Claire from burning at the stake of prejudice? I thought long and hard. I even contemplated planting evidence: a Marlboro cigarette butt that had been between Dick's lips. Some would say I abused my power, but I believe my actions, like Claire's, were for the greater good. I concluded my investigative report of the Blackbird fire, typing the final words that put my obsession to rest. *CAUSE: UNKNOWN.*

By the next spring the hillside had been restored to a healthier state, the cheatgrass replaced by native species. Aided by my glowing recommendation, Holly moved on to a training program for fire managers in Missoula, Montana. And my wife and I … We're more in love than ever, our home fires burning hotter than a witch's tit.